None of the Ram's vital parts had been hit by autofire

"If you think you can drive this thing without killing us, get over here."

The French DGSE agent immediately jumped into his lap and took the wheel. The smell of her perfume and closeness of her warm body was a slight distraction to the warrior, but he put it from his mind.

Once Bolan was sure Fauna had control, he slid out and over to the passenger seat. He quickly checked the action of the Belgium-made FNC.

Bolan leaned out the window and snap-aimed to align his sight post along the back of the Fiat. He flicked the selector to full-auto and triggered a long burst. Several rounds hammered through the terrorist's chest.

Bolan readjusted his aim and tried to take out the tires, but the Ram truck suddenly skewered to one side. If they couldn't keep up the pace and take a prisoner, then the triggers would be lost. And who knew what mayhem would be unleashed on the West.

underestimated him when setting up an ambush once. We

MACK BOLAN ®

The Executioner

DON PENDLETON'S
THE EXECUTIONER®
FEAR RALLY

A GOLD EAGLE BOOK FROM
WORLDWIDE®

TORONTO • NEW YORK • LONDON
AMSTERDAM • PARIS • SYDNEY • HAMBURG
STOCKHOLM • ATHENS • TOKYO • MILAN
MADRID • WARSAW • BUDAPEST • AUCKLAND

First edition March 2002
ISBN 0-373-64280-6

Special thanks and acknowledgment to
Jon Guenther for his contribution to this work.

FEAR RALLY

Printed in U.S.A.

A régime which invented a biological foreign policy was obviously acting against its own best interests. But at least it obeyed its own particular logic.

> —Albert Camus, 1913–1960
> From *The Rebel,* "State
> Terrorism and Irrational Terror"

There is no logic in creating or using biological weapons. But when terrorists attempt it, the solution lies in swift and decisive retaliation. That is the only logic they understand.

> —Mack Bolan

To all members
of the World Health Organization (est. 1948)—
who tirelessly strive to conserve life,
alleviate suffering and promote health

Prologue

Coast of Algiers

A foul, brooding silence had settled upon the darkened and deserted western docks. The only sounds to break that silence were the water that lapped against the side of the rusty freighter moored near the pier and the scraping of the crates as they were moved onto dollies and off-loaded.

Colonel Mamduh Nokhtari watched intently from a vantage point on the roof of a dilapidated building near the equally run-down wharf. He could feel the anger well inside of him as he spied on the men of the freighter. A small crew of Algerian military troops stood guard, weapons slung across their backs, while the freight workers unloaded the allegedly secret cargo. But it was hardly a secret. Nokhtari knew exactly what was inside those crates.

The U.S. arms shipment was nothing more than another subversive attempt by his enemies to repel the recent alliance between his men and the Da'awa wal Djihad. Yes, his new ally would be most interested when he told him of their discovery. These weapons would further their cause. The Algerian soldiers would be in for a very unwelcome surprise.

Nokhtari gestured ever so slightly to his fellow GIA— Armed Islamic Group—rebels positioned in the shadows of the buildings surrounding the pier. One minute remained before they struck. The trucks were in position in the garage attached to the building where he maintained his vigil. Once the men below were neutralized, it would take only a short time to load the crates and be gone. The Algerian military could never respond fast enough to stop Nokhtari and his men. They would disappear before any sort of reasonable force could be amassed.

The freighter was another issue. Markings adorned the vessel, but the lines didn't fit any known type presently in operation. In actuality, Nokhtari's intelligence people were certain the freighter was an old Russian-made Koni-class frigate disguised as a Saudi Arabian commercial ship. This disgusted the Algerian guerrilla. It was obvious, even from that distance, that the men on the freighter weren't Saudis. They were Americans, and Nokhtari wasn't the least bit surprised that the enemies of Islam would try to pass themselves off as their Arab friends.

Nonetheless, that was fine with him. It would make their deaths that much sweeter. Nokhtari could taste the revenge in his mouth. It was time to act.

Nokhtari was about to rise when he heard a vehicle approach. He slid forward and looked over the low parapet. A British-made Land Rover 1 Tonne command vehicle roared up to the wharf. Two military men, one driver and one officer, emerged from the front. A man in civilian clothing exited the rear escorted by four Algerian army troops. Nokhtari strained his eyes to make out the new arrivals, but it was too dark. He didn't want to risk breaking radio silence, but he needed to make sure the civilian newcomer was kept alive. He would have to make that his personal mission—the man could have information important to his cause.

Nokhtari brought the shortwave radio mike close to his lips and whispered, "Avoid new arrivals, particularly the civilian."

A short burst of static came from each group, and Nokhtari clicked off with a nod, satisfied that all of his men understood their instructions. He gripped the stock of his Galil assault rifle in anticipation. This sudden appearance wouldn't alter their plans in any way. They had worked the strike out to the last detail, and nothing could compromise that now. *Nothing.*

Nokhtari turned to one of his men and nodded. The Algerian guerrilla, dressed in black commando-style garb, stepped forward and slung the single-rope ladder over the side. He quickly secured it to a stanchion welded into the roof, then lithely vaulted over the side.

Nokhtari immediately followed his pointman, descending the knotted rope hand under hand until landing on the concrete below with catlike grace. He took up a covering position on the opposite side of the pointman and waited until the remaining four men from his team came down the rope, as well. Once they were all present, Nokhtari gave a quick nod and made a slashing gesture across his throat. The terrorists spread out as the other teams began to emerge from their hiding places around the docks.

Mere moments elapsed before the first shots were fired.

Nokhtari rushed for the men still cloistered around the Land Rover as the Algerian troops along the pier began to drop under the heavy field of fire laid out by his men. The GIA terrorist leader moved in under the cover of two of his escorts. One of the Algerian soldiers guarding the tall man dressed in civilian clothing tried to bring his weapon to bear but he was too late. Nokhtari triggered his AR on the run, 5.56 mm rounds drilling through the soldier's chest and flipping him onto his back.

The remaining trio of guards tried to fan out, firing their weapons at Nokhtari and his men. The guerrilla leader dropped to his stomach, a jarring pain shooting up his elbows to his shoulders. One of his men fell under the quick, controlled bursts of the Algerian soldiers. He had to admit that they were very good—probably members of the army's elite forces. Nonetheless, Nokhtari and his remaining men had the element of surprise on their side.

They felled the three soldiers with a barrage of return fire, their Galils barking in the night as flame spit from the muzzles, 5.56 mm and 7.62 mm rounds ripping flesh from the Algerian troops. One soldier was slammed against the back of the Land Rover while the other two danced under the hail of fire before collapsing to the ground.

Nokhtari rose from his position as the Land Rover's driver tried to cover the escape of his officer and the unidentified civilian. The man swept the area with gunfire, striking a GIA gunner in the chest before he was mutilated by return fire from three Galils. The driver's head exploded in a bloody pulp of wet flesh and shattered bone, and his decapitated corpse stood erect for a few seconds before slumping to the pavement.

The Algerian officer reached for his side arm as he urged the civilian to run for the ship. Nokhtari rose to one knee, brought the stock to his shoulder and triggered a 3-round burst. The impact spun the officer away and dumped him prone to the ground. Nokhtari swung the muzzle of the weapon toward the fleeing man and triggered another burst. Two of the slugs chopped away at the man's legs and tripped him. He collapsed to the ground, his screams drowned by the cacophony of autofire.

The other three GIA fire teams fired and maneuvered like true, hardened professionals. Most of the Algerian troops didn't have to time to respond, their bodies torn apart by the fusillade of rounds chugging from the African- and Soviet-made weapons. The GIA terrorists quickly advanced on the ship, rushing the pier and slowly making their way up the pair of wide gangplanks.

Four troops from the frigate crew tried to detach one of the gangplanks as the Algerian guerrillas ascended, but Nokhtari's men were too quick. The crew abandoned the idea in favor of a defensive posture. They withdrew concealed weapons from their loose-fitting garments and began to fire upon the advancing attackers.

Even in the darkness, Nokhtari could see the resisters were professional soldiers. They carried H&K MP-5s—the preferred close-quarters weapon of American Special Forces and antiterrorist units. Given the scope and nature of their facade, and the tactics they were using to repel the attack, Nokhtari was certain they were facing U.S. Navy SEALs. This only served to confirm his original suspicions. The deceptive war-mongers of his own government were working in concert with the enemies of Islam. He hated the Americans and a mo-ment of pride stabbed his heart as he watched his men bravely counter the heavy fire from the freighter crew.

Nokhtari rushed to the civilian and ensured he was alive, then began to direct half of his men to repel the resistance while the remainder dealt with the crates. Time was quickly running out. He whipped out his radio and gave the signal to the waiting trucks. A large bay door began to slide upward, assisted by two men pulling on a heavy chain. When the door was clear, the pair of stolen military trucks roared from the large warehouse and rushed to the dock.

The GIA terrorists not engaged began to dolly the crates down the gangplanks while their counterparts covered them. The steady barrages of gunfire began to wane as Nokhtari's men dispatched the enemy with vengeful fury.

Nokhtari grabbed the injured man and dragged him across the dock to the abandoned Land Rover. He ordered two of his men to lift the prisoner into the back of the vehicle as he con-tinued to supervise the loading of the trucks. The unmistak-able sound of a whistle overtook the dying reports of autofire. Nokhtari watched intently as a pair of flares erupted from some point aboard the freighter and shot skyward. Moments later the entire dock was bathed in bright light as the star-clus-ter flares burst across the sky. He closed one eye as his men continued to work furiously around him.

A fresh burst of gunfire rang out as another cluster of crew members from the freighter appeared and began to combat the GIA invaders. Nokhtari knew their time was up. If they didn't leave now, Algerian army reinforcements would arrive before they could make good their escape. They would be trapped, and any hope of success would be extinguished there on the docks.

Nokhtari brought the radio to his lips and tersely ordered a retreat. The officers commanding the GIA terrorist teams immediately directed their troops to beat a hasty withdrawal.

It wasn't as tactically organized as Nokhtari had hoped, but there would be time to assess that later. Most of his men would split up into groups of two or three, disappear into the night and make their way back to the operations base in a day or two. Some of the local members would return to their lives in the city, keeping their ears open for any information that could further the GIA-Djihad cause.

Nokhtari whirled and ordered the trucks to take off. The terrorists loaded the last of their goods into the rear of the trucks and then hopped aboard. Nokhtari returned to the Land Rover and jumped into the passenger seat, while one of his men waited behind the wheel. The GIA terrorist started the engine at his leader's command, whipped the nose around and pointed it toward a road that led west out of the city.

Each vehicle would take a different direction. This way, if one was captured, the others stood a greater chance of eluding Algerian military and police forces. Not that it mattered—they would resist anyone who tried to detain them.

Nokhtari knew his men were completely devoted to their cause. Those who had resisted the new alliance with the Djihad or turned themselves in under the Algerian president's amnesty program had already been weeded out. Only the best and most dedicated members remained with the Armed Islamic Group.

And Mamduh Nokhtari was proud of their success this night.

1

Dakar, Senegal

The Executioner had followed his enemies to North Africa, and they knew it.

Murderous hatred etched in the faces of the six men converging on his position was Mack Bolan's first clue to this fact.

The second clue came in the form of various weapons the attackers produced from under the folds of their caftans. The blued finishes of Glocks and Model 61 Skorpions played starkly against the cream and white of the traditional Arabic-type robes the men wore.

Bolan *had* been feeling out of place. Now he felt right at home as he whipped the Beretta 93-R from beneath his light blue windbreaker and prepared to meet the threat.

One of the Arab gunmen toting a Skorpion tried to outflank the Executioner while the rest rushed him head-on. It seemed obvious the man was unaware his adversary had seen that trick one too many times. The soldier snap-aimed in the enemy's direction and squeezed the trigger, a 3-round burst of 9 mm rounds spitting from the muzzle at a rate of 375 meters per second. The semijacketed hollowpoint slugs punched through the gunmen's chest and slammed him into a large fruit cart. He tumbled to the ground amid a heap of dates, prunes and kumquats.

The remainder of the gunners spread out as they continued their approach, obviously deciding to take a more conservative approach. The sound of gunfire sent people running in every direction, some taking a definite route away from the sudden violence while others banged into one another.

Bolan tried to keep the innocents out of the line of fire, pushing one mother and her two children aside just as a pair of his adversaries opened up with their Glocks. He barely managed to dive away from the deadly 9 mm fire. He sought cover behind a large basket filled with some kind of handcrafted ironware, thumbed the selector to single mode for better control and squeezed the trigger.

The first round took the closest man in the forehead, blowing a small chunk of bone and flesh out the back of his head. The man dropped his weapon as he staggered into his partner. The impact sent the other gunman's shots wide, and the Executioner took advantage of the lapse. He sighted carefully down the slide of the Beretta, took a deep breath and fired twice. Both rounds landed square on target as the 158-grain SJHPs blew out the heart and one lung. Pink, frothy sputum gushed from the gunman's mouth. His eyes rolled into the back of his head as he collapsed onto the street in a cloud of dust.

Less than thirty seconds had elapsed, and the enemy had already suffered fifty percent losses. It was clear to Bolan that his attackers had counted on a swift and clean kill. Now they were trying to bring him down amid the crowds and sheer pandemonium. They had made the ultimate mistake in regard to their enemy—they had underestimated him.

Now Mack Bolan was about to show them the error of their ways.

Another opponent jumped onto a nearby basket in an attempt to get a clear shot and fired down on the Executioner's position. In turn, he had only succeeded in presenting himself as a clear target without endangering the innocent civilians. Bolan leveled his pistol in a two-handed Weaver's grip and squeezed the trigger twice more. The rounds took the terrorist in the stomach and knocked him off his feet. He landed on the street with a dull thud.

Another gunman nearby saw the closing odds and realized he would never survive an encounter with the cold-eyed stranger who fought like a devil. He turned and ran down the street, merging into the running crowds before Bolan could readjust his aim for a clear shot.

The last would-be killer managed to come around behind Bolan, and only the scream of a child diverted the Executioner's attention. He whirled in time to see the short, lithe terrorist push the little girl aside with exasperation, backhanding her when she couldn't get out of the way because of the pressing crowd now gathered to watch the show.

As the hardman swung the Skorpion 61 in the Executioner's direction, the soldier clenched his teeth, smoothly raised his pistol and shot the man twice in the face at point-blank range.

The headless corpse turned in an odd, tight circle before toppling to the ground.

Bolan turned to see if the little girl was all right. An awkward hush had now fallen upon the crowd as the Executioner walked to where she sat in the dust. She couldn't have been more than four. She looked up at him, and the chubby, dirty cheeks scrunched against deep brown eyes. Bolan realized that a smile was formed on her fattish lips as she made some comment in her native language.

The Executioner holstered his weapon, reached down and picked her up. He ruffled the black hair corn-curled tightly against her head, and she threw her tiny arms around his neck. Only a moment passed before a woman in a green sarong and bone-tooth bracelet rushed to Bolan and held up her arms with a cry of distress. He handed over the child and strode from the crowd.

A WARM, SULTRY BREEZE shook the palm trees towering above the street. Darkness had come to Dakar and the Executioner tried to merge with it, become one with its essence. He could hardly feel at home in the strange surroundings. Everything about the place seemed old and run-down.

As Bolan entered the café, a worn face surrounding dark eyes caught his attention. The man's skin didn't stand out amid the crowd of patrons, but the warrior knew that face. Yakov Katzenelenbogen had described it to the last detail.

The man sat at a corner table, deep lines of suspicion lining the corners of his eyes and mouth as he watched Bolan approach. The dust and sweat of the day's heat caked his clothing and hands.

Bolan walked up to the small table and looked around before seating himself across from the man. He quickly adjusted his chair so that his back wasn't exposed to the entrance. The soldier said nothing for a long moment. He simply folded his hands on the table and stared back at the challenging gaze until the man finally broke into a wry grin.

"Good evening, Mr. Blanski," Lemuel Jakom said cordially. "Welcome to Dakar."

Bolan smiled. "I guess you got the message."

Jakom looked around furtively before lowering his voice and replying, "From what I've heard, we have certain mutual acquaintances who got the message, as well."

"Meaning?"

"I was told of your encounter. Today. In Matahari Square?"

Bolan nodded curtly. "So much for not drawing attention."

"Locals, perhaps?" Jakom pressed.

"No." Bolan shook his head, then added, "Too well equipped for natives. Arabs carrying Skorpions and Glocks. And they were just as out of place as I was."

Jakom shrugged and frowned. "That does not sound good."

"It wasn't. For them."

Their conversation was stopped short at the approach of a waiter. The man eyed Bolan with concern but Jakom laid a hand on the man's thigh and shook his head. He said something—Bolan was guessed it was Swahili—and the man nodded. He didn't seem convinced by Jakom's words, but he sidled away from the table immediately and disappeared into the haze of cigarette smoke.

The Executioner wasn't quite as ill at ease as when he'd first entered the café. Most of the men in the room were predominately of Negroid descent. Had Bolan been on a mission of this sort in Turkey or some of the North African countries, he would have experienced much more discomfort. The Caucasoid and Arabic peoples congregated mostly in the upper continental regions, however. Black Africans made up the majority of the population, but there was no shortage of Europeans, Asians and Arabs to be sure.

In any case, it was this fact that had led to his statement about his attackers being "out of place."

"That is Manu," Jakom explained, inclining his head in the direction of the waiter. "He is a trusted friend."

"No offense, Jakom," Bolan replied, "but trust is something that comes very hard in my business."

"I understand."

"You know Yakov from way back, I guess."

"Many years," Jakom replied with a deep sigh. "We served together in the Israeli corps."

"So I heard."

"Yakov speaks very highly of you. He told me that you are a man to be trusted and admired."

"He's my good friend," Bolan replied with a noncommittal nod.

Jakom leaned forward. "Tell me, please, what has brought you to Senegal?"

"In a word, theft."

"May I ask of what nature?"

Bolan realized that he would have to entrust sensitive information to Jakom if he could earn the same in return. The numbers were running down, and he knew it was no time to be vague. He didn't know the people or the area and had no idea how to proceed. There was no time to let his adversaries come to him, and he had no reason to believe they would make another attempt on his life. It made more sense for them to cut their losses.

Thus, Bolan would now have to take the offensive and find them.

"Four days ago," he began, "a cache of electronic triggers was stolen from my country. They were part of a disarmament shipment being transferred from the Rocky Flats nuclear storage site in Colorado to Los Alamos, New Mexico. My intelligence sources led me here. I'm certain the thieves were a U.S. faction operating under the direct support of the GIA."

Jakom nodded intently. "The Armed Islamic Group. I know these criminals and terrorists well. They are vicious animals who care nothing for peace and order."

"Recent information," Bolan continued, "suggests they might try to get these triggers to their headquarters in Libya. Security along the bordering countries here is tight. I know *who* they are and *what* they plan to do. I just don't know how."

"The African authorities are vigilant in their fight against groups like the GIA," Jakom concurred. "This group used to have close ties to the Islamic Salvation Army."

"True," the Executioner interjected, "but many of them surrendered to the Algerian president's amnesty program."

"Ah, yes. The 'civil reconciliation.' An admirable program that I now feel created more problems than it did solutions, despite overwhelming public support. The GIA and the Salafist Group have continued to fight against this reform. Every year hundreds, even thousands, of people are murdered during Ramadan. This is the month of fasting in Algeria."

"I know," Bolan replied. "It's also usually the time of greatest bloodshed."

"And it will only continue to grow worse."

Bolan's eyes narrowed. "What do you mean?"

"This new issue you have brought to me. Of the triggers?"

"What about it?"

"There has been a rumor growing in this area." Jakom looked around and in hushed tones continued, "Many believe it is simply another way to spread propaganda and panic throughout Africa. My own sources have told me otherwise.

It is possible that the GIA has forged a new partnership with a terrorist group rooted in the Islamic population of Egypt."

"And who are they?"

"They call themselves the Da'awa wal Djihad, which literally translated is Appeal and Struggle. They have apparently split from an Egyptian group. Together with the GIA, they have wiped out entire villages and conducted campaigns against the governments in Libya, Niger, Algeria and even members of the Mali army."

Bolan swore softly under his breath and shook his head. The very thought of such a far-reaching terrorist group concerned him greatly. A cold, hard knot settled in the pit of his stomach. The combined strength of the GIA and Djihad could result in a destructive conflict vast enough to throw more than half of Africa into chaos.

"There is more," Jakom continued. "A few evenings past, an arms shipment secreted into Algiers by your government was intercepted by an armed unit. Some of the members involved in the assault are known to be active members of the GIA."

"It's funny you mention that," Bolan replied. "Something else has brought me here. The disappearance of a man named Robert McKarroll."

Jakom nodded. "He had information regarding Egyptian Djihad involvement in the attacks on American embassies. Yes, I know about his disappearance, because I helped plan the mission to rescue him from the Djihad. He was to be taken out with the freighter that brought the arms. He disappeared along with the weapons, I am afraid."

"Well, I've got to find him and bring him out. So I guess that makes it twice as important I find out who I'm up against and where they're operating."

"If you are certain that these triggers were brought here," Jakom said, "then the concerns Yakov voiced to me are well-founded."

"Explain."

"There is no question that several terrorist bases are secreted throughout the Niger desert. This is as true now as it

was years ago. The GIA and Djihad have established an un-
precedented foothold in northern Africa. Hundreds of sight-
ings have been reported, but few come forward out of fear of
reprisal. It is possible those triggers will be used to equip
weapons of mass destruction."

Bolan nodded slowly. "That's my concern. Rumors aside,
I'm afraid those weapons could be turned against my country."

"Or against *any* country, Mr. Blanski," Jakom reminded
him gently. "And it is now clear why Yakov sent you to me."

"Because you know where these bases are?" Bolan surmised.

Jakom snorted with a look of disbelief. "I wish that were
true. If it were that easy, I would have acted by now. No, I am
talking about the fact that we are on the eve of one of the greatest sporting events on earth."

"You mean the Dakar Rally?"

"Of course."

Jakom stopped talking as Manu returned with two small
cups filled with a dark, hot liquid. The waiter set the drinks in
front of the men, said something and then quickly walked away.

Jakom's eyes flicked in that direction, but he kept his voice
steady. "Do not look at the door. We are being watched by
newcomers who do not belong here."

Bolan's right hand left the table and settled inside his windbreaker. He wrapped his hand around the cold butt of the
Beretta, but Jakom stopped him with a harsh look.

"Do not show your side arm. We would both die before you
could shoot. Just relax and listen. As long as we are in here,
we are safe."

Bolan returned his hand to the table and gripped the small
porcelain cup. The heat from the drink nearly burned his
hand, but the Executioner ignored the pain. It took his mind
off wanting to look, to react. He hated feeling trapped but he
also knew he had to trust his Israeli benefactor. Jakom had
trained and fought at the side of one of the best warriors
Bolan had ever known. It would do him no good now not to
heed the man's advice.

"You were going to tell me about the rally," Bolan prompted him.

"Yes. I was elected as an adviser with the Amaury Sports Organization. This is the group that organizes the race. The course this year is the same as it was in 2000. I have kept informed of the ongoing activities where groups like the GIA are concerned throughout the past year. Despite my warnings, and those of the French authorities, the sponsors are not willing to listen."

"You believe there's a threat to the rally?"

"Without question."

"Then why won't they listen to you?" Bolan asked.

"You must understand that millions of dollars were spent to shorten the 2000 rally. Hundreds of vehicles and countless crew members were airlifted from Niamey to Sabha, in southern Libya. Most did not believe there was any real threat then, and they are strongly resolved to that thinking now. Even though there have been more killings."

"So the race must go on as planned," Bolan concluded.

Jakom nodded glumly. "We cannot convince them of the dangers. There is too much money at stake."

"And unfortunately that money is more important than lives to these people."

"It is very political, the Dakar Rally. It is also a capitalist venture of astounding proportions. This year they have chosen to spend their money in massive security measures. A dozen or more countries have pitched in to provide added protection, including Britain, France, America and even parts of Asia."

"That's going to be of little effect against terrorists," Bolan stated. "Even in an international event like this, governments are still bound by the rules of territorial conduct and jurisdiction."

"Perhaps," Jakom conceded. "But it is possible they would not attack if they stood to gain something by this."

"What do you mean?"

"If you are correct about these triggers, and given your earlier observations regarding the increased antiterrorist programs throughout Africa, it is entirely possible that the men you seek may try to smuggle their contraband to its intended receivers via the Dakar Rally."

Jakom's insight astounded Bolan. He hadn't considered this new possibility for a moment, but it made complete sense. If the GIA-Djihad alliance was planning something on a large-scale basis, it would be difficult to keep such plans secret. What would serve their purpose more than to move the triggers via the world's greatest cross-country race?

The plan seemed almost too simple.

The terrorists could deliver the triggers into the hands of their superiors under the very noses of a global crowd. The delivery was a cinch since it would take place amid the combined protection of the mightiest powers on Earth. Security would be so tight that the GIA-Djihad could transport the triggers without fear of theft by competitors or reprisal by the very authorities bent on their failure. These facts would also make it twice as hard for Bolan to find them and defeat their plans, as he would be under constant scrutiny of those same security agencies.

"Yeah," Bolan agreed. "It's damned foolproof."

"I do not envy you, my friend," Jakom said. "You have your work cut out for you, I think."

"How many vehicles run in this race?" Bolan asked quickly.

"Given all the classes, about eight hundred. However, at least one-third of those are too small to carry the triggers."

"Unless they split up the shipment," Bolan told him. "If something was to go wrong, they wouldn't take the chance of losing the entire cache."

"This is probably so." Jakom seemed unable to repress a mischievous grin. "You Americans have a phrase, I believe. Do not put all of your eggs into one basket, no?"

Bolan nodded his agreement.

"How do you intend to find the men who have stolen your triggers?"

"I'm not sure." Bolan shrugged and let out a frustrated sigh. "Any suggestions?"

"You will stand out to them as a spectator. Perhaps you might pose as an American newsman?"

"No dice," Bolan replied, shaking his head. "I don't have the time to gather resources and I can't risk that kind of exposure. American sportscasters are a tight-knit group. I'd never fit in."

"Then I must suggest you have only one alternative."

"What's that?"

"You must pose as an entrant."

"In the race?" the Executioner asked with disbelief. "And how do I manage that? I don't have wheels or a sponsor."

Jakom's eyes twinkled. "No, you do not. But I have both. And since you are a friend of Yakov's, and I am in a unique position to help you, I can provide you with what you need. But I warn you, to drive this race takes unbelievable skill and talent. Have you ever done anything of this sort?"

"Driving in a cross-country rally? No." Bolan's hard blue eyes flashed challengingly. "But we have another saying in my country. There's a first time for everything."

Jakom's reply was grim. "Perhaps, Mr. Blanski. But I will pray to Yahweh that it is not your last."

"Yeah," said the Executioner.

2

Niamey, Niger

Darkness faded and replaced the senses of Admiral Robert McKarroll with the harsh light of an overhead lamp.

The U.S. Navy officer had no idea where he was or what had happened to him. Everything seemed like a blur. How long had he been unconscious? Hell, he couldn't even remember *how* he'd lost consciousness. He tried to lift his arm and look at his watch, but he couldn't move his hand more than a few inches in any direction.

As reality continued to creep into his psyche, McKarroll realized he was lying flat on his back, manacled at the wrists and ankles by heavy straps. The inside of his mouth tasted as raw as the leather that bound him, and his eyes wouldn't stop tearing. He tried to lift his head only to find that his forehead was strapped down, as well. A sudden rush of pain hit him in the legs and washed over his body in waves of nausea.

And then he remembered.

The events on the Algiers dock came back to him like a flood of water. He'd just climbed down from the back of the Land Rover under armed guard when the shooting started. McKarroll could remember the looks of surprise and terror on the faces of the Algerian army troops as they fell under an unceasing hail of gunfire. He recalled rushing toward the officer in charge of the detail, the man yelling orders for him to run, his mad dash for the ship and the shots that felled him.

Oh, God, he was a prisoner once again! But of whom?

The sound of a heavy metal door opening broke through like an answer to his thoughts. Perhaps he would now find out just exactly who had subjected him to such pain and degradation. Well, he would demand his immediate release. He would tell them nothing. By God, he was an officer in the mightiest sea power on Earth. They would release him or there would be hell to pay!

"Good morning, Admiral," a crisp, heavily accented voice said. It echoed in his ears like thunder although he knew the speaker wasn't talking loudly.

They'd obviously drugged him—painkillers or maybe even truth serum. Had he talked in his drug-induced stupor? Had he told them everything already and now they were just here to torment him some more? Hell, he didn't even know who they were.

It was probably better to remain silent for the time being.

Something stung his face, and he only realized that the speaker had slapped him after he heard the echo of the blow in the dank chamber.

"I do believe you are being rude, Admiral McKarroll," the man scoffed. "You will answer and show me some courtesy."

McKarroll mumbled something through the thickness of his tongue and tingling in his gums. Whatever he'd said was not intelligible. What the hell had he tried to say, anyway? Did he actually try to reply to his captors? Nothing made any damned sense to him. Yeah, he'd definitely been drugged.

"That's much better," the speaker replied. "Ayman, untie our guest's head so that he may see us."

McKarroll scrunched his fists and eyes in anticipation of another blow but it never came. The tension against his forehead dissipated and he immediately became aware that he could turn his head. His neck muscles were terribly sore, and the pain in his legs was nearly unbearable.

A tall, dark-haired man stood near him. He was dressed in

desert camouflage fatigues and wore a scarlet turban. A bandolier of ammunition was slung across his chest. A web belt encircled his waist and a pistol was tucked into a holster in cross-draw fashion. His skin was dark, dusty with the dirt and sand of the desert, and a thick beard covered his face. Beads of sweat gleamed against his nose, and a smell emanated from him resembling bitter herbs.

"Wh-who are you?" McKarroll finally managed to say, the question followed by a dry cough.

"My name does not matter," the man replied. "However, since it will die with you I see no reason to hide the fact. I am Mamduh Nokhtari, leader of the united Islamic resistance."

Although Nokhtari's words came through like a tape run at one-quarter its normal speed, McKarroll understood every word. A chill ran down his spine, and he couldn't believe his ears even while he replayed Nokhtari's announcement in his dulled mind. The Armed Islamic Group had united the FIS and countless other organizations throughout northern Africa. While McKarroll knew of Nokhtari by name and reputation, this was the first time he'd ever laid eyes on the terrorist leader.

The Navy man's escape from the Da'awa wal Djihad was obviously to be short-lived. Countless people had risked their lives to pull him from the clutches of the Djihad terrorists, and now he was, if not in the most literal sense, once again their prisoner.

Part of the news he'd planned to pass along to his government was the recent alliance between the two organizations. Their combined numbers were said to exceed seven thousand, and they had infiltrated nearly every region north of the central plateau.

Moreover, something disastrous was boiling in the proverbial pot, but McKarroll had no idea of the intended target. All he knew was that these were the same maniacs responsible for repeated attacks against U.S. holdings within Africa, including firebombings of embassies, American tour groups and news agencies from at least half a dozen U.S.-allied countries.

Many believed that things could only get better under the increased security measures implemented through the united efforts of Africa's respective governments. But McKarroll knew better than to put his hopes in those measures, since they stood to have as little effect as throwing rocks at a carrier fleet. In the long and short of it, increased security was nothing but window dressing. Terror groups like the GIA and Djihad would not rest until they had either achieved their ends or were completely eradicated.

"You are now a prisoner of the united Islamic resistance, Admiral," Nokhtari spit. "And as such you are not entitled to the same treatment as a prisoner of war. We do not show mercy to the enemies of Islam."

"Stop it," McKarroll replied drolly. "You're scaring me."

"I should have expected such a response from a man like you," Nokhtari snapped. He nodded to a hulking man next to him.

The man whom McKarroll assumed was called Ayman stepped forward and slapped him again. His teeth threatened to jar loose from his mouth, and his eyes felt like a pair of craps dice rolling inside his head. The blow wasn't that hard, even coming from the beefy hands of a man the size of this guy. Nonetheless, the combined effects of trauma and drugs almost sent McKarroll back into unconsciousness.

Unfortunately, he could feel his heart begin to thud inside his head and he gasped. There was nothing to explain the sudden change in his condition. Something caused him to look down the length of his body. He saw a small man with a pencil-thin mustache and white coat withdraw a syringe from his arm.

"What are you giving me?"

Nokhtari grinned a death's-head grin. "Just something to wake you up. To make you a bit more cooperative."

Cooperative, right, McKarroll thought. He knew this technique all too well.

It was one of those he'd been trained to endure during BUDS. As a former Navy SEAL, McKarroll knew all the tricks in the book—he also knew how to resist most of them. It would take more than the regular administration of amphetamines to pry the answers from him. Although his captors would probably use other tried-and-true methods like repeatedly slapping his stomach with a belt, or applying a vice clamp to his testicles.

And that would be just the beginning.

McKarroll stared at Nokhtari and snickered in spite of the euphoria. "You can inject me with all the speed you want, flyshit. You can try your sleep deprivation. Play the games you want. You can even kill me and leave my dead carcass in the desert. But it will be a cold day in hell before you break me!"

Nokhtari's eyes narrowed and the smile disappeared. "We shall see, Admiral."

Six hours after beginning work on McKarroll, Nokhtari still didn't have any of the answers he needed. The American Navy officer was going to be tougher than Nokhtari had first predicted. He ordered his men to prepare McKarroll for transport to their base of operations in the Niger desert. Nokhtari knew he would have every modern method of torture at his disposal there. If McKarroll knew anything of value, Nokhtari would know it, as well.

Every man had his breaking point. And if by some chance McKarroll died without talking, so much the better. This would serve a dual purpose in the plans of the GIA leader.

Once McKarroll was loaded into the back of a small truck that served as Nokhtari's command vehicle, Ayman drove them to a deserted area outside of the city.

A chopper painted desert tan awaited the men and their exhausted prisoner. It was an Egyptian army conversion of the Mil Mi-8 Hip helicopter. The first models were produced in 1967 by the former USSR, but quickly saw service in the air forces of many South Asian and Middle Eastern countries. This Hip-E model was powered by twin Isotov TV-2-117A turboshafts and could exceed 250 kilometers per hour. It was equipped with four rocket pods that fired 57 mm rockets, as well as AT-2 missiles. Not to mention the nose-mounted 12.7 mm machine gun.

The Hip-E was a gift to Nokhtari from his Egyptian partner, and he prided himself on the sleek assault chopper. It could hold a crew of thirty-two troops, and it was ideal when circumstances necessitated a quick flight across the desert.

As they flew to their base of operations, a growing sense of excitement coupled with impatience burned in Nokhtari's heart. He anticipated seeing Fuaz again, spending time in the element with which he was most familiar.

Nokhtari had spent the better part of his life in groups like the GIA—as had his father. It was as much out of a sense of heritage as it was honor that he served the revolutionary forces bent on returning Algeria to the control of the Islamic people. The Algerian government had betrayed the Islamic religion for a political democracy and its beliefs. At every level, the Algerian president and his advisers were controlled by perverse ideals of the West. Nokhtari viewed the United States as his mortal enemy and the single greatest threat. The European nations with their common market ran a close second.

The resistance of Nokhtari's people was fueled only by their desire to counter such manipulation. He had never considered himself a fanatic, and he had no wish to die for something so idiotic and simplistic as the name of God. No, there was a greater cause here. He was fighting for a way of life, just as his brothers in the mujahideen had done against the Soviets. If his people didn't continue their campaign of rebellion, complacency would take over and all would be lost.

This was a crucial time for the GIA.

Nokhtari aspired to methods different from those of his predecessors or of his friend and Islamic brother, Hassan Fuaz. Bombing embassies and tourist buses or machine-gunning bazaars didn't send a clear message, to Nokhtari's way of thinking. The GIA, *his* GIA, was a military force to be reckoned with. Their aims were founded upon self-ruling Algeria as much as geopolitical and religious principle. This philosophy didn't advocate terrorizing the innocents and casually spilling the blood of his own people along with that of the Westerners.

Fuaz called that kind of warfare "acceptable losses" under the pretext that a certain number of Islamic citizens died because they were in the wrong place at the wrong time. Nokhtari fiercely disagreed with that theory. Preservation and support of the cause would only come from those same people by careful selection of targets. What good did it do to hamper the Western influence in North Africa if the very people you fought for fell beside the enemy?

Nonetheless, Nokhtari could understand the basis for Fuaz's views. In some strange way, he could even empathize with them. But he couldn't bring himself to implement such strategies with callous disregard for his own. That was the only true difference between the two men. Fuaz was a man thirsty for blood, regardless of its owner, while Nokhtari was a preserver of it.

Nearly an hour passed before the helicopter touched down at the base. Ayman and one of the four GIA soldiers accompanying them off-loaded McKarroll's unconscious form, which was manacled to a wood-and-canvas litter. The remaining troops assisted the pilot in setting up a camouflage net over the aircraft once the rotors had stopped. It would blend into the barren terrain of the Niger desert, and prevent any heat-seeking or infrared systems from detecting its position.

For all practical purposes, it appeared the pilot had set them down in the middle of nowhere. Only the sound of sand scraping against metal broke the quiet of the desert as a portion of the ground suddenly erupted about twenty meters from the LZ.

Six armed troops wearing desert-stripe fatigues and purple scarves scurried from the bunker entrance. They rushed to assist Ayman with the litter.

Nokhtari smiled at the efficiency of the men. There was no question in the man's mind that the troops of the Da'awa wal Djihad excelled beyond those of even his own force in every way. Most of those members left in the GIA were little more than freedom fighters who had left wives and children behind because they believed in the cause. But Hassan Fuaz's men came from quite a different breed.

Nokhtari left them to their work and entered the bunker alone. He descended the stone steps into the cool ground beneath. The bunker was dimly lit by large candles mounted on the wall. Circular cups of polished brass behind the candles enhanced the rather crude lighting. Installing electric generators was costly and inefficient at best, not to mention the increased risk of discovery such a luxury might produce.

The entire facility was buried beneath the sand. It had taken almost four years and a lot of money to construct the 2,500-square-meter bunker. The engineers and builders performed all of their work at night, under the most extreme conditions such as sandstorms and cold. Many died or suffered injuries, but their labors paid off in the long run.

The facility could comfortably house more than two hundred soldiers and command staff from both the GIA and Djihad. It boasted a fully equipped armory and infirmary, as well as an electronic communications and computer lab. These additions were powered by solar collectors hidden among the outcropping of a nearby butte.

Yes, tremendous skill and forethought had gone into the site selection.

Nokhtari made his way through the halls to Fuaz's quarters. The furnishings beyond the entrance were hardly meager. Convenience pervaded Fuaz's living arrangements, and he surrounded himself with every imaginable luxury. It seemed an oddity, considering the rather archaic surroundings. Nokhtari's associate had spared no expense in cluttering himself with those accommodations reserved only for kings.

Colorful panels of nearly translucent satin hung from the walls and ceiling. Fine tapestries hung from the walls that surrounded a king-size bed that could easily sleep four—and usually did, as Fuaz had two wives and two concubines.

One area was set aside with a desk and chair carved from pure cedar. Plush chairs were scattered throughout the room and adorned by plusher pillows and body-sized throws. In one respect the decor was almost East Indian, by design, and that left a peculiarly bad taste in Nokhtari's mouth. Yet he knew of his friend's first love as a soldier and leader of Islam, so he couldn't bring himself to begrudge Fuaz what few luxuries he chose.

As Nokhtari quietly took a seat, an aging but muscular man stepped from the curtained area where Nokhtari knew a toilet and heated tile bath were housed. Heavy perfumes rolled from the refreshed figure, a mixture of odd scents in light of the fact they emanated from a man attired in the garb of a soldier.

The man smiled with genuine warmth as his dark eyes flashed in the lamplight flickering from a desk near where Nokhtari was seated. The man hastened to Nokhtari, who stood and hugged him in a true fashion of mutual respect and brotherhood.

Gray hair had replaced the once stark black in the man's younger days, and a slight layer of fat was detectable around the neck and cheeks. But there was no mistaking the strength and power in the shoulders, arms and hands. Authority seemed to radiate from the wrestlerlike physique.

"Welcome to Meccafatwa, my brother," Hassan Fuaz said. He gripped Nokhtari's shoulders and echoed, "Welcome home."

"God be with you, my friend," Nokhtari replied tiredly.

Fuaz nodded and then gestured for his friend to return to his seat. The Djihad leader sat on the edge of his desk and crossed the muscular arms. A flash of concern crossed his face—at least it appeared to be a look of concern. Perhaps it was curiosity mingled with consternation. In any case, Nokhtari wasn't about to read anything into it.

"You look exhausted, Mamduh," Fuaz noted. He raised his eyebrows and cleared his throat.

"It has been a long day. I've brought back the American that escaped from you. He was, shall we say...uncooperative?"

"Yes, that bastard McKarroll," Fuaz replied with an angry nod. He rose and put his hands on his hips, his face registering disgust. "You leave him to me now, my brother. I will deal with this man."

"I do not think he knows much. Or perhaps he has been well trained to resist our interrogation tactics."

"He is of little concern," Fuaz cut in with a dismissive wave. He spit into the dust and sand collecting on his floor and added, "He could not have told our enemies much. He was never directly privy to our plans."

"I would agree. But he does know of our alliance. And something brought him to Egypt to infiltrate the Djihad. The Americans must be concerned, or they would not have sent him."

"I think," Fuaz admitted, "that he stumbled onto us rather than purposefully."

"It does not matter to you?"

"No. He will not live to see tomorrow."

"You do not think it would be valuable to keep him alive?"

Fuaz fixed his longtime friend with a harsh look. "Alive? For what purpose? He has repeatedly meddled in our affairs!"

"True," Nokhtari replied calmly. He'd become quite accustomed to Fuaz's sudden outbursts and found no reason to fear the man. He considered himself an equal. In some ways, he even thought of himself as superior, although he would never have dared voice this particular viewpoint.

"I will give it some thought," Fuaz finally said with grunt. Nokhtari let the subject close.

Fuaz sat behind his desk and propped up his feet. He lit a cigar after offering one to Nokhtari, who turned it down. Nokhtari wasn't particularly fond of them and only occasionally indulged himself with a cigarette. He had to admit that the Europeans were good for something.

"How are things proceeding at the lab?"

"Perfectly well," Fuaz said with a congenial smile. "Our scientists are the best to be found. Definitely suited to work in biological warfare." He sucked deeply on his cigar before looking directly at Nokhtari. "Will we have the triggers on time?"

"They leave Senegal tomorrow morning. If all goes as planned, they will arrive in Nioro du Sahel in three days."

"Excellent. You will then take them to Djado?"

Nokhtari inclined his head. "Of course." After a long silence, he asked, "What of the American that followed my men. Have you been able to identify him?"

"No," Fuaz replied, shaking his head with frustration. "It is as if he doesn't exist. He is definitely a professional. We underestimated him when setting up an ambush once. We will not repeat the mistake. By dawn he will be dead. I have assurances from my personal team."

"Then I should have no trouble getting the triggers to you."

"Well done, my brother. Our people will be ready by then, and the new strain of bacteria will have reached a stage that we might immediately implement one lot against a target of our choosing."

"Good. Do you have any thoughts as to where we should start?"

"Of course," Fuaz replied. He didn't seem hard-pressed to conceal his almost maniacal glee. "We shall start with Algiers."

3

Mack Bolan returned to his hotel in the southern part of Dakar.

Two men followed him.

The soldier couldn't be sure if they were the same men from the café, since he hadn't seen them to begin with. But that hardly mattered. If they were looking for trouble, then they had come to the right place.

He entered the hotel and risked a glance in time to see them cross the street and take up a position where they could watch the hotel. Bolan almost smiled at their sloppiness. He was certain they would make their move before the night was through. They would wait until he was asleep, obtain a key by greasing the clerk's palm, sneak into his room and try to slit his throat.

Bolan went to the closet as soon as he was in his room and changed into his blacksuit. It was time for a reconnaissance.

Jakom had given him the address of a house occupied by an old man connected to people within the various intelligence communities. Security agents from a half-dozen countries had relied on this man known only as the Kateb. Literally translated "writer," the nameless mystery man seemed to know everything about everybody, and he'd gotten his name because of scrolls he kept secreted away and written in an ancient language only five or six linguists in the world could translate.

The whole story didn't wash with Bolan, but Jakom insisted on the Kateb's reliability. If the Israeli's word was good enough for Katz, it was good enough for Bolan.

The Executioner tucked his Beretta into a shoulder harness, donned black combat cosmetics, then pushed the rattan blinds aside to see if the two men were still there.

They were.

Bolan shook his head and left the hotel room, first checking to see if the way was clear. He walked quickly but silently down the hallway to a window that would provide his escape. He stuck his broad-shouldered frame through the narrow opening and looked up to see the roof ledge about five feet above.

The soldier got both feet placed firmly on the windowsill, then jumped straight up, his fingers biting into the sandstone ledge. His combat-hardened muscles were taut as he pulled himself up and swung his legs over the top. He rolled into his landing and crawled far enough to the rear so that he could stand without being observed by the lookouts below.

Once he'd regained his feet, Bolan leaped to the next roof, then onward along the line of buildings until he reached the street where the Kateb lived. Many of the buildings were nearly butting against one another, clustered together due to Dakar's overcrowding problem. It was really not that much different from most of the cities in Senegal. That was where the work could usually be found, and thus that was where people wanted to live.

Bolan dropped down in a narrow alley between two single-story houses and crouched. He could make out an occasional form moving past the alley entrance, but he was too far into the shadows to be noticed. A half moon hung in the hazy African sky, providing minimal light.

Violent crimes and burglaries weren't terribly common in that part of the world. The penalties were very severe for anyone caught stealing or breaking into a home. The people in power didn't believe in probation—the Executioner couldn't say he blamed them. The average person didn't have a lot to begin with. The thought that someone would try to steal what they did have was ludicrous.

A thief was marked for life—usually by a stump where the hand used to be.

Bolan waited nearly fifteen minutes to see how many people passed by. Only three in that time period, which made his odds pretty good. He edged to the alleyway entrance and un-leathered his Beretta. He let his eyes rove over the abandoned street. In the distance, he could hear a group of men and women singing some kind of native song. Bongo drums and a harp-like instrument played uneven rhythms in accompaniment.

The Executioner let his eyes follow each house front until they came to rest on the one that Jakom had described. It wasn't as nice as the others, and this surprised him. He figured that the Kateb was a sort of wise old shaman type with a sharp intellect. One with money squirreled away that he could have at least paid to someone to maintain his house.

Perhaps the Kateb didn't get out much.

The soldier couldn't shake the nagging sensation that something—despite the outward of appearance of the Kateb's residence—wasn't quite right. It seemed almost too quiet, and the hairs began to stand up on the back of his neck. Bolan could just hear the silence. It was eerie and out of place. Sure, there was the music and the distant if scattered sounds of a dog barking, a horse snorting.

Yet...something was still amiss.

Bolan checked both sides of the street to ensure it was empty before crossing quickly and swinging the Beretta into play as he reached the front door. There was no alley between the Kateb's house and the adjoining structures, which meant no place for Bolan to watch and wait. Suddenly, he heard the sounds of a woman's protests within the house and the gruff response from a male voice. It sounded like an argument or interrogation—as if somebody was in trouble.

CALANDRE FAUNA COULDN'T believe her hard luck.

She'd come to see the Kateb and instead found trouble in the form of three Arab men in desert-camouflage fatigues. She wouldn't have known who these men were except for the pur-

ple scarves encircling their necks. They were members of the
Da'awa wal Djihad, one of the most feared terrorist organizations in all of the Middle Eastern and North African countries.

Fauna had doubts as to exactly what had brought them to
the Kateb. Perhaps they were after her because she was seeking information on terrorism in general. With only six months
in the field as a French intelligence agent, even her extensive
training hadn't prepared her with the knowledge and expertise necessary to operate against the trio of hardened Egyptian terror mongers.

"What are you doing here?" the man snapped in English.

Fauna thought about acting as if she didn't understand but
decided it wasn't time to be coy. Especially when she considered the fact that the two men behind the speaker were toting 9 mm Tokagypt pistols. Fauna thought of her own pistol,
a Belgian-made Browning BDA .380, tucked in the waistband
of her khaki shorts and concealed beneath a short-sleeved
blouse. She wasn't stupid enough to try for it.

Fauna knew these men would shoot her dead with one
false move.

"I—I am here on p-personal business," Fauna said, feign-
ing wide-eyed innocence. "Please do not hurt me."

"You are American?" the brute demanded.

"No, I am French."

The three men didn't notice the slight movement of the
door behind them, and Fauna did what she could to keep her
eyes off the specter that entered silently. The man was tall,
muscular and dark haired with the coldest eyes of blue she had
ever seen. She struggled to stifle the increased thudding in her
chest, and she felt as if her heart might leap out at any moment. She somehow managed to keep her face impassive.

The big man in black cocked back the hammer of the
Beretta in his fist and placed it against the head of the terrorist closest to him.

"Put your weapons down and don't move," he whispered.

The leader whirled and reached for his pistol a moment before he realized his mistake. The intruder squeezed the trig-

ger and took out the first of the Djihad terrorists, splattering the leader with blood and brain matter.

Before the two men could react further, the newcomer shoved the other terrorist aside as he aimed center mass at the leader's chest and stroked the trigger twice more. Fauna dived from her position directly behind him in time to avoid the pair of 9 mm Parabellum rounds that drilled through the leader's chest and ripped out fragments of his spine.

Fauna saw the remaining terrorist recover and swing his pistol toward the dark wraith before she could draw her own pistol.

She screamed a warning.

The big black-garbed commando already saw it coming. He drove a combat boot in the unsteady terrorist's direction, catching a knee before following up with a front snap kick and knocking the pistol from the terrorist's grip. He stepped forward as his screaming opponent collapsed and grabbed a handful of the guy's shirt. He shoved the smoking barrel of the Beretta against the terrorist's forehead and had the man pleading for mercy before Fauna could even blink.

The woman felt stupid as she realized the battle was over before it had really begun for her.

"GIA or Djihad?" the big man asked coldly. He thumped his pistol muzzle against the terrorist's head for emphasis.

Fauna was astounded by the question. Whoever this man was, he appeared to already know something about what had brought Fauna to this place. Was he perhaps a bodyguard for the Kateb? Maybe he worked for the CIA, or possibly security for one of the nameless European interests in-country at that moment. Whatever the explanation for his identity, Fauna was certain about one thing. He was definitely an American.

"He is Djihad," Fauna whispered.

The stranger snapped a hard look in her direction. Those hardened, icy features were somehow both handsome and frightening. They epitomized Fauna's most irrational fears, and she felt at that very moment as if she were looking at

Death itself. There was no mistaking the fire-and-brimstone stare of her savior. He was like some angel of vengeance.

"I'll get to you in a second," the man replied.

He turned his attention back to the terrorist. "I know what you're up to, and I know someone from your organization took those triggers from my country. Where are they?"

"I will say nothing."

Fauna could actually see the soldier's hand tighten around the pistol as he pressed the barrel harder against his prisoner's forehead.

"I'll ask one more time. Where are the triggers?"

"You will learn nothing!" the terrorist roared, suddenly producing a combat knife from a hidden thigh pocket on his fatigues.

The echo of his reply died under the soft chug of the Beretta. The man's head snapped backward as the back of his skull exploded. The corpse fell backward and died in that position, only a twitch or two coming from the hand holding the knife. It clattered to the ground.

The man moved quickly to the door, peering outside a moment before closing it behind him. He turned with his weapon held at the ready in Fauna's direction.

"What's your name?" he asked.

Fauna stood slump shouldered, her BDA .380 hanging loosely at her side, and stared at the frightening tower of black that loomed above her. Muscles bulged beneath the one-piece suit he wore, and black smears hid most of his less prominent features. His hair was still stark black, but visible lines radiated from the grim eyes and the corners of his mouth.

"Who are you?" Fauna managed to ask at last.

"I asked you first," the man said, shaking his head. Then he shrugged and added, "My name's Blanski."

"Calandre Fauna." She held out her hand, but the man ignored the gesture. "You may call me Calee. You are American?"

"Yeah. And based on the accent, I'd say you're French. Probably DGSE here for the Paris-Dakar rally."

Fauna was completely amazed at his insight. He was more

than just a hired gun. The guy was a professional. A professional *what,* she didn't know, but that was okay because she had an inkling she'd find out soon enough.

What most surprised her was that Blanski pegged her as a member of the Direction Générale de la Sécurité Extérieure. Many people assumed the Sûreté was an espionage agency but they were mistaken—Sûreté was concerned only by criminal activity within the country. The DGSE was a subordinate to the French Ministry of Defense. Members were officially considered military personnel—soldiers assigned to the Forty-fourth Infantry Regiment in Orléans—but that viewpoint was changing radically. Fauna was just one example of a civilian employed in covert military operations.

The DGSE replaced the External Documentation and Counterespionage Service in the early eighties. Its primary goals were to collect, disseminate and provide military intelligence, as well as strategic defense. Fauna was in the direct employ of the operations division, having received her training as a field agent at a top-secret facility in Roscanvel. She'd transferred to operations after more than three years as a computer analyst and cryptographer in the technical division, assigned to the Bouar base in the Central African Republic.

It was her familiarity with the region, customs and people that had landed her a chance for field duty in a political hotbed of violence, tension and international terrorism. There were definitely no warm feelings between the French and Islamic peoples, particularly given the French government's support of Algeria.

But nothing had prepared Fauna for this kind of horrific and violence.

"It is true," she managed to choke out, not able to keep from looking at the dead men lying around Blanski's feet. "I am with French intelligence. And you are CIA?"

Blanski shook his head. "Freelancer. I'm looking for a man called the Kateb."

He gestured around the room and added, "You probably came for the same reasons I did, so I won't bother to ask why you're here."

Well, Blanski was a straight shooter and Fauna saw no reason to be dishonest.

"How did you know these were Djihad?" he asked.

"Many hours of study. My people believe that the Da'awa wal Djihad is planning a major operation in Africa. We do not yet know the exact nature of this plan, but we are certain they have allied themselves with Algerian guerrillas."

"You're real warm," Blanski offered with a nod. "Actually, they aren't just guerrillas. They're GIA."

"Oh, no," Fauna whispered, putting a small hand to her mouth. "I should have fought back against these men. I should not have cowered."

"Heroics in the face of those odds proves only two things—you're not bulletproof or smart," Blanski advised. "You did what you should have."

Fauna inclined her head in genuine gratitude. At least Blanski had manners. He didn't look down on her with some sense of machismo—that "poor little French girl needs to be rescued" shit. Maybe they could work together to accomplish their tasks.

She voiced her thoughts.

"No, thanks, lady. I don't need a partner. Nothing personal."

"But surely you're here to prevent this kind of filth from destroying your people."

"That's exactly why I'm here. But I do it alone."

Fauna narrowed her eyes and studied the mysterious stranger with righteous indignation, tossing her left hand on her hip as she shoved the pistol into her waistband. Blanski just returned the look with an icy gaze of his own, although Fauna swore she could make out the briefest tug of a smile play at the corners of his mouth.

She looked down at the corpses. "I will not get in your way, Mr. Blanski."

There was no reply.

And when Fauna looked up, Blanski had gone as quickly and quietly as he'd appeared. Fauna rushed to the door, but only a silent, deserted street greeted her. The big handsome man with the ice blue eyes had simply vanished.

MACK BOLAN WAS angry with himself.

He was wasting time looking for mysterious old men and rescuing young, impetuous females who didn't know better. The whole situation was going to hell right in front of him. The longer the missile triggers were missing, the less his chances of finding them.

The Executioner never considered himself a crusader. His cause was one of duty. And right now that duty called for serious action. It was time for a frontal assault. The men who'd followed him to his hotel were definitely not the religious fanatics he encountered at the Kateb's house. Although they had made a sloppy error by allowing Bolan to peg them as tails, they were much cooler and wiser in comparison to the trio of idiots he'd just dispatched.

Something didn't make a bit of sense here.

Islamic extremists steal a dozen or so triggers from Rocky Flats and beat feet back here to Africa. Which, it just so happens, is on the eve of the one of the world's most infamous sporting events. While Bolan agreed with Jakom's theory that smuggling the triggers under the noses of everyone was brilliant, it didn't explain the ulterior motive.

Where were they headed? What kind of missiles were the triggers going to be installed into? Why not use them right there in the U.S. if Americans were the targets?

The questions were piling up as fast as the bodies of dead terrorists. There was no question in Bolan's mind that the Djihad and GIA were under the direct support of Osama bin Laden. Bin Laden's three fatwas were the mainstay of the present Islamic terrorist movements both within the Middle East and abroad.

He viewed these as religious rulings. His declaration of war called for the radicalization of existing Islamic groups and the creation of those where none existed. He advocated the destruction of the United States, which his paranoia led him to believe was against any Muslim reform. Most of all, bin Laden supported many of the Muslim fighters in countries such as Afghanistan, Somalia, Tajikistan and Yemen, and he called on his Islamic brothers to do the same.

In the early part of 1998, bin Laden formed the Islamic World Front, an umbrella organization bent on resisting what he called "Jews and Crusaders." The Executioner knew that the Da'awa wal Djihad belonged to this organization, but he didn't have enough intelligence on who pulled the strings within the Djihad. Many of them were Afghan veterans from the mujahideen war against the Soviets.

The Djihad had several training camps, staffed by those same veterans who were steeped in the ideals of Islamic fundamentalism. In most respects, they were well trained and well armed. The only thing Bolan couldn't factor into the equation was their rumored alliance with the Armed Islamic Group.

Well, he'd need some answers before the race.

The soldier checked his watch as he returned to the roof of his hotel. Only about six hours remained until he was supposed to meet Jakom at the starting point for the rally. The man had promised to have credentials, clothing and Bolan's vehicle. Jakom hadn't wished to reveal what kind of wheels Bolan would actually be driving.

"You will not be disappointed, Mr. Blanski," Jakom said. "That much I can assure you."

The Executioner knew that running this race would be completely worthless if he couldn't figure out who had the triggers. Eight hundred vehicles were no laughing matter. A lesser man would have said the job was impossible, but the Executioner wasn't such a man. He lived for impossible jobs—especially when it meant the lives of innocent people. He would have driven a thousand rallies if it could save even a half-dozen lives. Not to mention that the GIA-Djihad alliance was one that had to be stopped.

Bolan returned through the window and went back to his room.

The door was still shut tightly and locked. He opened it while standing to one side, then snatched the Beretta from shoulder leather and proceeded through. He moved quickly and quietly, careful not to turn on the lights or expose himself. A quick check confirmed the room was empty and undisturbed.

Bolan went to the window and looked down. The two men were still there, watching the front of the hotel and smoking cigarettes. Neither one of them appeared to be in a hurry, nor did it look as if they were even focused on Bolan's room. Perhaps they'd been instructed to only observe him for now. Death might come later, or maybe sooner.

Either way, Mack Bolan would be ready to meet it head-on.

4

Stage One—Dakar to Tambacounda

As the light of first dawn reached the African morning like golden tendrils snaking their way through the high savanna trees, a hushed excitement permeated the air.

Mack Bolan could feel the energy as he walked toward the low metal building with a rusted roof. Clouds of dust caked his clothing, the aftermath from a score of vehicles that passed. There was an unbelievable assortment of machines present for the race. Everything from four-wheelers in the dune-buggy class to motorcycles were headed toward the starting line.

Bolan knew that the Paris-Dakar Rally was the world's most famous transcontinental off-road race. Statistics revealed over thirty nations would be represented this year, which made Bolan's job a bit easier. He would be less likely to find the triggers in the trunk of some Swede's car than in the cab of a truck belonging to a dark-skinned Arab.

Not that he could typecast his enemy. They were clever, and Bolan knew he had to be suspicious of everybody—all were guilty until proved otherwise. It was the only way he could operate if he wanted to beat the odds.

Through the dust and faint light, Bolan quickly made out the stout form of Lemuel Jakom outside the building.

Jakom shook the Executioner's hand enthusiastically when Bolan reached him.

"Good morning," he boomed with anticipation. The Israeli clapped his hands and added, "Are you ready to see your toy?"

Bolan shrugged. "Lead on."

Jakom led him into the building and toward the rear. The metal structure was surprisingly clean and well maintained inside. It was also air-conditioned, a commodity few could afford given the socioeconomic status in the region. The cool air felt good against Bolan's face, though, and he wasn't about to complain.

Through a back doorway, the building opened up into a fairly large and impressive garage. It was perhaps six car lengths deep and at least three wide, with plenty of room between each one. Bare-bulb lights hung freely from the high, beamed ceiling. Ages of dust coated many of the objects in the garage, but there was a large workshop off to one side with a complete set of tools neatly arranged on a table. Their silvery finishes gleamed with oil and loving care.

In the center of the huge bay sat the outline of a pickup beneath a heavy cover. Jakom walked directly to the vehicle and began to loosen its protective covering.

"If you would, please," he said, nodding toward the clips on the back end.

Bolan walked over to the vehicle and began to loosen the straps. They were cinched tightly against the vehicle with the type of pinch-operated fasteners that slid along the rope when pressed, and locked into place when pressure was released.

It took a minute or so to get all the fasteners loose, but when they pulled the cover away Bolan had to admit it was worth it. It was a midsize Dodge Ram 1500 with a short bed and heavy-duty, oversize tires. A lift kit had obviously been installed, and Bolan estimated at least an eight-inch rise both front and rear.

The chrome gleamed in the lights and nearly blinded Bolan. It covered the front and rear bumpers of the truck, along with a matching brush guard and overhead spotlights. The base coat was a sparkling navy blue from the doors to the rear, overlaid by large white stars, and red-and-white stripes ran down the hood. There were various other advertising monikers along the sides and across the windshield Paris-Dakar Rally was emblazoned in glitter-gold lettering.

Bolan whistled with amazement and looked at Jakom. "Kind of stands out, doesn't it?"

"Oh, my friend," Jakom said with a chuckle, "this is nothing compared to many of those you will be racing against. More than half of the entrants in this year's rally are French. They will be expecting this kind of thing from the Americans." He waved his hand to encompass the truck and added, "You would be out of place if you didn't have all of this."

"All right," the soldier replied noncommittally. "But you know it might get nasty. I hope you weren't planning on me bringing this thing back in one piece."

"Hardly." Jakom tapped the hood lightly. "Beneath here is the kind of engine they put into sports cars. It is capable of tremendous speed and power. I caution you to be careful, though. The laterite is slick and the pistes are narrow. You will need every bit of skill and concentration at your disposal."

"That's still no guarantee," Bolan shot back.

"I know what you are thinking, Mr. Blanski," Jakom intoned.

"Do you?"

"But I can assure you," he continued without missing a beat, "that there are no strings attached. I am here to help you in any way possible.

"For years I watched the evil and violence that the Djihad spread among both my people and their own. Most of us wanted to live in a peaceful society. But it was not to be. And so I joined the IDF, just like Yakov, to fight for what I believed in. I can now say with surety that not only did we survive, but Israel is a happier and better country for it today."

Jakom smiled at Bolan, and his eyes twinkled almost mischievously. "So you see, Mr. Blanski, I understand perfectly. And I support you in your cause to fight for your own country and its ideals."

"I wish my motives were as pure," Bolan replied truthfully. He had a lot of respect for Jakom. More than enough that he wasn't going to lie to the guy. "But this mission's about more than honor. It's about the continuous horrors committed at the hands of vermin like the GIA and Djihad. If I can't return the triggers safely, I'll destroy them right along with the thieves. But one way or another, I won't finish this until every last one of them is buried deep in the sand."

Jakom nodded with understanding. "Then I pray that Yahweh goes with you, Mr. Blanski. And I wish you all success."

"You, too." Bolan shook hands with Jakom and then asked, "What about my identification?"

"It is in the truck, along with the entry papers and some appropriate attire. You will also find the equipment you requested." He looked at Bolan's shorts and windbreaker and raised his eyebrows. "I do not think your tourist cover will last long."

Bolan looked down a moment and then chuckled. "Yeah. I guess you're right."

THE FIRST STAGE of the race was scheduled to run from Dakar to Tambacounda.

It didn't really start all that dramatically. A time was simply allotted between the vehicles, and they would take off three and four at a time. The heavier vehicles were the last to go, with the midsize first and the motorcycles in the middle. This gave every entrant some advantage, and they figured it all came out fair in the end.

It would be a long trip through this first stage—over two hundred miles—but hardly a challenge as long as Bolan could take a leisurely drive. After all, winning the race didn't really matter to him one way or the other.

But living to tell the tale did, and it appeared one group in a Toyota Land Cruiser converted to an open top had other ideas. The vehicle roared up next to Bolan about an hour into the drive. One of the dark-skinned men riding in back made his plans for the Executioner well-known when he popped up through the top and leveled a Model 61 Skorpion at him.

The soldier seized a sudden advantage that appeared and ran his new wheels up a nearby embankment to circumvent one of the narrow pistes straight ahead.

"Now, let's see what you can do, baby," he whispered.

The powerful Ram truck pushed its way over the top of the crumbling dirt wall and jounced along several hard ruts left by heavy rains earlier in the month.

Bolan tugged the part-time lever into four-wheel drive, downshifted, then swung the truck around. He bounced in his seat as the impact threatened to jar his teeth out of place. He came back down another piste wall and quickly maneuvered the Ram up to the enemy's rear. He fought the wheel every second to control the vehicle as its light back end fishtailed over the laterite.

Bolan could barely see through the cloud of dust but he managed to hook an arm out the window, a .44 Magnum Desert Eagle clutched in his fist. The big weapon boomed with repeated shots as Bolan fired on his would-be assailants. One round slammed into the terrorist toting the Skorpion, the 240-grain slug punching a hole in his throat and blowing out a chunk of his neck. A sudden turn tipped the dead form off balance and the body sailed from the Land Cruiser.

A second man in the back seat rose, holding some kind of weapon. The Executioner couldn't identify the man's gun through the thick dust and blinding sun, but he didn't really care. He wasn't about to let whatever it was get used on him. Bolan threw the gear shift into fifth and scooted up beside the Land Cruiser just as a sharp piste narrowed ahead.

The enemy driver tried to slam Bolan into the wall, but he chickened out with the effort when he almost lost control of his own vehicle. Bolan slowed slightly and nosed the front of his bumper guards against the rear end of the Toyota as it rounded the narrow piste. The vehicle was too high profile to handle the corner and flipped over, ejecting the one man and crushing the front-seat passenger beneath it before coming to rest on its wheels.

Two other camouflaged soldiers emerged over the top of

the Land Cruiser as the stunned driver somehow managed to pull away and race after the Executioner.

Bolan swore to himself, aggravated that his plan hadn't worked. He would have to find another way to defeat them. The chase continued for some time through the narrow turns as quarry and hunter finally emerged from the bush and crossed the savanna. The soldier could remember Jakom pointing out this section on the map. This long stretch of the race had even more pistes with laterite.

Bolan decided to try to lose them by sheer power and speed. The Land Cruiser didn't have nearly the engine beneath its hood as the Ram 1500.

The Executioner would have the advantage there.

The idea was sounding better, then he suddenly dismissed it. As crazy as it sounded, he needed contact with the enemy— he had to find those triggers and he couldn't do that by running from them. It was time to take the fight to them and see if he could capture one alive.

Bolan deviated slightly from the course, ignoring the entrance to the piste runs and continuing across the higher land. The Land Cruiser followed, and Bolan kept just far enough ahead to make shooting at him impractical.

At the last second, the Executioner spotted a furrow cut into the land that led into the pistes, and he took it. He brought his vehicle to a jarring stop and quickly jumped out with a satchel in hand. Heavy dust and some mud and oil coated his racing coveralls. They were styled in the same fashion as the vehicle's paint job: blue with stars, and red-and-white stripes at the knees, shoulders, elbows and across the back.

In less than a minute, the Land Cruiser would be there. Bolan raced back to the furrow and quickly pressed himself to one side. He yanked two M-26 HE grenades from the satchel and pulled the pins. As the roar of the engine resounded nearby, Bolan let the spoon fly on one, then the other a few seconds later.

He tossed the grenades into the furrow.

The driver would have to slow his vehicle considerably to

enter the pistes. The grenades erupted just as the Land Cruiser crossed over the furrow. The first explosion sheared off the bumper, and the second blew out the rear tires, sending the back of the vehicle into an end-over-end flip. The three occupants started to climb out, but the gas tank ignited and two men in the rear were caught up in a wash of flames.

Bolan rushed forward to assist the driver, who was struggling to extricate himself from the burning wreckage. The Executioner yanked the man out of the truck by the collar and dragged him across the sandy, brush-covered ground. The guy screamed, holding one leg that was bleeding from a large gash in the calf.

Bolan dropped the guy when they were safe distance and put the muzzle of the huge Desert Eagle in his face.

"You've got just one chance to talk to me," the Executioner growled. "Take the chance."

"They would k-kill me if I did," the man stammered.

"I'll kill you if you don't. You have nothing to lose at this point."

"I do not work for—for them," the man said.

Bolan could see that this was a native African with dark skin and a thin, drawn face. The guy was probably just hired as a driver—he'd had nothing to do with the actual people behind the assassination attempt. Membership in groups like the GIA or Djihad would have been out of the question for this man. The color of his skin said it all, and Bolan figured he was finally going to get some answers.

"Who is 'them'?"

The man pointed to the burning Land Cruiser. "Those men work for Hassan Fuaz. He is very feared and respected."

"Feared maybe," Bolan snapped. "Not respected."

"These were some of his best men," the man said. "When he finds out about this, he will be angry. He will send many after you, and they will kill you."

"Not hardly," the soldier snorted, jerking his head at the Land Cruiser and adding, "Especially not if these were some of his best. What I want to know is what this Fuaz is up to."

"I do not know this," the man said. "All I know is that there are those in this race that are delivering something to his associates."

"So they are using the rally as a front," Bolan murmured more to himself than his prisoner.

The man nodded emphatically. "Yes."

"What are they taking to him?"

"I do not know this."

"Okay, then, who are they meeting? Who are these associates?"

"I do not know that, either. I just know where."

"Then where?" Bolan asked with exasperation, waving the Desert Eagle to illustrate his impatience. "Don't make me play twenty questions."

"They are supposed to meet in Nioro du Sahel the night after the morning."

Bolan nodded. "That's in stage three. Less than two days from now, when we leave Kayes and head for Bamako." He looked at the man and added, "They plan to make the switch during the forest run."

"Possibly," the man replied fearfully. "I know that there are Djihad forces waiting in Nioro du Sahel. This is true."

The Executioner pinned the man with an icy gaze. "Get out of here. You've earned your freedom. Find some new friends."

"I cannot go," the man cried. "My life will not be worth cow dung by morning. It is my destiny to help you. I knew you would come."

"What are you talking about?" Bolan asked.

"I think it would be better for us to leave here now, American."

"No dice. Explain what you mean."

"Am I not the one you sought out?" More quietly, he added, "I am called the Kateb."

5

The sun was setting when the first of the rally vehicles began to arrive in Tambacounda. The streets were in complete disarray, and every hotel and guest house was crammed. The bars and pubs—or at least the African equivalent—were jammed with celebrants and rally crews alike.

The atmosphere reminded Calee Fauna very much of the Mardi Gras held each year in New Orleans. She attended the French Quarter quite often in her visits to the United States. Many didn't realize how much intelligence the French gathered from their allies. In the espionage business, there was no such a thing as friendship. Nobody could be trusted; this was a lesson Fauna had learned hard.

The lesson came in the form of a man—one much like the one named Blanski. He'd been an agent for MI-6 and assigned to a multinational case that found its roots through a terror organization headquartered in Paris. Fauna was fresh out of training as a cryptoanalyst and worked closely with him. She fell in love and he eventually broke her heart. Now she found it very difficult to trust in her business, and doubted she would ever fall in love again.

The sound of a firecracker jolted her back to the present. Fauna scolded herself for daydreaming. There would be time for that later. Right now she waited patiently for the arrival of a certain big, dark-haired man who she knew was posing as an entrant. She raised the binoculars again and inspected another plethora of vehicles as they arrived at the stage-one finish line.

"Any sign of him yet?" the man next to her asked softly.

Fauna lowered the high-powered field glasses and shook her head.

She turned her eyes in the direction of the voice. The darkened room hid the handsome features of her liaison, Talbot Dutré, but it seemed she could still see him. Dutré had never made it a secret he lusted after her. There was no real love there, although he always referred to her as his darling. It was a rather presumptuous term of affection, but she'd stopped scolding him long ago.

After all, he really didn't mean anything by it.

"He will come," Fauna said matter-of-factly, although she wasn't really sure deep down if she believed it.

"You sound uncertain," Dutré observed.

"He has something to gain by coming here."

"If our intelligence about this Blanski is correct," Dutré retorted, "he will come anyway. Even if he doesn't have anything to gain by it."

Fauna narrowed her gaze. "You are so cynical sometimes, Talbot."

She could see him only smile in the half light and she turned her attention back to the field glasses. A small cloud of dust caught her attention in the last of the sunset and she raised the binoculars with strange anticipation. Her heart began to beat faster as she saw the truck. It was decorated with the stars and stripes of the American flag. Unmistakably, it was Blanski's vehicle.

"Still nothing," she whispered. She swung on her heel, tossing the binoculars to Dutré as she walked past him. "Continue to watch. I am going to get something to eat."

"Excuse me," Dutré said harshly.

Fauna stopped in her tracks, certain that her ruse had been uncovered. She turned slowly and waited for him to say something about the deception but he only frowned.

"Perhaps I am hungry, as well."

"Well, what would you like?"

"Some of the fried bread with lamb that they serve down the street would be delicious."

"Consider it done."

"Bless you, my darling."

Fauna left the apartment and descended the stairs like a rocket. It would take some time for Blanski to get past the check-in points and find a place to park his vehicle. That would give her time to find and track him. When the time was right, she would contact him with her information. The information she hadn't been able to deliver the other night.

Fauna couldn't even understand why she wanted to involve the American at this point. As she pushed her way through the crowds, determined to complete her mission, the anger welled inside her. Blanski had made it quite clear he didn't want to cooperate, let alone work with her. But something kept pushing Fauna to make it work.

Blanski was more than he appeared to be. He was more than just a freelancer, as he put it. He was a specialist. He was a man who fought like five men, and moved with a precision and grace that spoke of no wasted energy. He was like a giant cat that stalked prey with stealth and silence, but he attacked with the ferocity of a pack of starving wolves. The way he'd dispatched the three terrorists at the Kateb's and then disappeared without a trace still had Fauna's mind reeling.

The French agent eventually made her way to the check-in points and inquired of one of the security officials as to the truck. The man nodded and pointed to the Ram as it was entering its assigned parking area. Security guards would keep the staging areas patrolled, both to discourage vandalism and other such debauchery. Some could strip vehicles of invaluable equipment in seconds, so the protection was heavy.

Fauna stole through the parking area, keeping clear of the guards, and soon she saw Bolan's vehicle. He was just putting the cover over the truck as she approached, but her attention was distracted by the sudden flash of movement in her peripheral vision.

She turned in time to see the two men in caftans rushing toward her, large knives clenched in their fists. She shouted a warning to the big American, then turned into a fighting stance to prepare for the attack.

When the first man reached her, she stuck out her foot out as she sidestepped and blocked the knife thrusting toward her belly. She swung outward and spun the man in circle, stopping at the last second to throw him back in perfect judo style. The guy collapsed in the dust and his partner tripped over him in his haste to finish the young woman.

Before either man could recover, Bolan was at Fauna's side. The second man got to his feet and stood uncertainly as the Executioner imposed himself between the Frenchwoman and the attacker. The man tried a straight-jab feint, then an outside thrust, but Bolan knew the trick.

A large fighting knife suddenly rasped from a hidden sheath as the soldier blocked the thrust. He brought the point of the knife in an upward jab into the soft point of the jaw. The blade continued through the tongue, roof of the mouth and finally penetrated the skull, cracking bone before it punctured the brain. The terrorist's body went rigid for a second before dropping to the dusty earth.

Bolan left the knife in place, whirling to face the other attacker, who was rising to his feet now. The remaining opponent circled his quarry, and the Executioner pivoted. Those ice-blue eyes watched every move.

Fauna was afraid to get involved because it might distract the big American. She waited with her hand on the butt of her pistol.

The caftan-clad terrorist continued to size up his opponent, but Bolan didn't let it faze him. He appeared totally focused. Concentrating. Waiting for an opening.

It finally came as the Arab roared a battle cry and rushed forward. Bolan went low and scooped up his enemy in a fireman's carry, making sure to grab the wrist of his opponent's knife hand. He turned in a half circle before falling backward with all of his weight. Ribs cracked audibly in the evening air, and Bolan rolled away and onto his feet.

The terrorist screamed in agony as the soldier walked calmly back to him and snatched the knife he'd dropped. He raised the weapon to bury it in the man's chest but a calm, soothing voice from behind Fauna stopped him.

"Do not do it, Mr. Blanski," the man said. "You would then be no better than those you seek to destroy."

Fauna drew her BDA pistol and whirled only to find herself staring into the ageless face of a stranger. The man was filthy, practically dressed in rags. Fauna was speechless for a moment, but she could immediately see he wasn't a threat.

"Put your weapon away," the man said softly. "I mean you no harm."

"Do as he says," Bolan ordered, tossing the knife away.

Fauna looked behind her and slowly lowered the pistol.

"What the hell are you doing here?" Bolan demanded as he approached her.

"I told you," she shot back, "I am seeking the same thing you are."

Shouts of surprise and footfalls reached their ears.

"It would be wise for us to leave now if we wish to avoid any unpleasantness," the older man suggested.

"Let's go," Bolan ordered.

The three of them merged with the darkness.

"THERE IS no question that the Da'awa wal Djihad and GIA are working together in this," Fauna announced.

She sat with Bolan and the Kateb in a small restaurant on the outskirts of Tambacounda. The place was dark and smoky, but noisy with people. Faces in the crowd represented almost every major nationality, so it was the perfect place to be inconspicuous. The Kateb drank tea, while Fauna and Bolan nursed beers.

"What makes you think so?" Bolan probed.

The Executioner already thought he knew the answer, but he was interested now in what she had to say. Fauna had the ability to gather intelligence that Bolan didn't. It was a better course of action for him to use this to his advantage at this point. Perhaps her people could pinpoint the exact location of their operations in the Niger.

"Because we've positively identified members working together. Plus, the weapons recovered from those men you encountered at the Kateb's were linked back to an arms shipment stolen in Algeria a week ago."

Bolan nodded. "My own sources confirmed it was a GIA operation."

"Firearms stolen by the Armed Islamic Group," the Kateb interjected, "end up in the hands of members from the Da'awa wal Djihad."

"The evidence is overwhelming," Fauna continued. "And let us not forget that both the Djihad and GIA have threatened to commit acts against this race."

"Maybe, but I believe that's just a cover."

"Why?"

Bolan knew he'd shown his hand too soon. There was no way to back out of it now. It looked as if he would have to give something to get something. It was a small price to pay.

"Members of the GIA stole missile triggers from my government. I tracked them here."

"But you said you were a freelancer," Fauna countered. "You said you were not CIA."

"I'm not."

"Then what organization are you from?"

"I'm not free to discuss that."

There was a long silence, and the three sat drinking for a minute while the buzz of conversation increased with uproarious laughter and then dwindled again.

"Any thoughts as to what they plan to do with these triggers?" Fauna asked.

"I thought they would take them to some base of operations within America, but they wound up in Africa."

"Perhaps they are for use against an African government," the Kateb ventured.

"Or maybe they could not transport whatever it was they wanted the triggers for," Fauna added.

"Yeah, but what?" Bolan countered. "Plutonium is available almost anywhere on the black market these days. It's stable to transport as long as it's not linked to anything. Sneaking parts of nuclear weapons into a country is easier than the entire thing."

"Plus the fact," Fauna replied, "I doubt they plan to launch them from their secret base in the desert somewhere."

"Never assume," the Kateb hissed.

"What?" Fauna asked.

"You are assuming they plan to use the triggers for nuclear weapons."

"Well, yes, of course. What else could they have in mind?"

"Chemical bombs," Bolan finally said. He looked hard at the Kateb, then Fauna before adding, "Maybe even biological."

"Oh, God help us," Fauna whispered. "But against who? The United States? As you said, they could have simply done that within your country."

"Terrorists usually do things with the purpose of making some statement. Like implementing radical fundamentalist policies or building support for new political regimes."

"The GIA has always been concerned with political reform in Algeria," the Kateb offered. "This might be their target."

"Or one of them," Bolan agreed wholeheartedly.

Thus far, the soldier was extremely impressed with the Kateb's knowledge of the goings-on in Africa. Jakom had underrated the man's value in this. He was a veritable gold mine of intelligence and information. It was no wonder the man had established such a reputation in the central plateau.

Bolan knew he could be trusted. After their little encounter in the Senegalese savanna, the Executioner had cleaned and dressed the Kateb's wounds, and taken him along in the truck. He explained to Bolan that he'd posed as a hired hand to further penetrate their organization so he could collect more information for his writings. It didn't make a tremendous amount of sense to Bolan, but then it didn't really have to.

The soldier had come to realize in getting to know the man

that the Kateb was making his own contributions in his own way. He kept a wealth of information on these groups and their operations in Africa so that someone down the road—somebody like Mack Bolan—could utilize it to help eradicate the enemy. Intelligence was the single greatest weapon in any soldier's arsenal. The more he knew about his opponents, the bigger his advantage.

"Let's say your assumption is correct," Fauna interjected, "and the GIA does plan to use some sort of mass-destruction weapon against Algeria. How would the Djihad fit into this?"

"My dear girl," the Kateb said easily with a chuckle, "the Da'awa wal Djihad would fit into any plan that called for reestablishment of Islamic ideals in a country founded on Western democracy."

"In other words," Bolan explained, "they'll do it because it involves American principles."

The Kateb nodded his agreement. "This is part of Osama bin Laden's ultimate plan. He wishes to demoralize and dishonor the Western world in any way that he can. He hates whites, both Americans and Europeans alike. To people like Hassan Fuaz, leader of the Egyptian Djihad, you have fallen from the pure faith in God."

"It's hard to digress from something you never believed in to begin with," Fauna shot back.

"Doesn't matter," Bolan snapped. "Remember that the GIA and Djihad are first and foremost terrorists. Ultimately, they don't give a damn about human life. They know one job. Terror, plain and simple. Well, their time has come, and that's why I'm really here."

"I see," Fauna countered. "You're just here to wage a personal war."

"Right."

"Seems like a hard way to go through life, Blanski."

"It suits me."

"I'll bet."

The Kateb appeared to watch this exchange with interest, then stifled a yawn. "I have done what I could here. This is now for those less aged than myself." He stood and bowed to both of them. "I wish you God's speed in your quest."

"How will you get back?" Fauna inquired.

"I will find my way, just as you will find yours. Goodbye to you both."

As he left the restaurant, Fauna gestured wildly toward him and said to Bolan, "Aren't you going to stop him?"

"No."

"Why not?"

"Because he's a free man," the Executioner growled. "He has to go his own way. That's something I understand well."

"What is with you, Blanski?"

Bolan scowled as he took a slug of his lukewarm beer and replied, "What's with *you?* In this game the enemy's playing for keeps. I do the same, and I don't force my views on anybody. If someone wants to walk away, who am I to stop them? Anybody who wants to get involved gets the same respect."

"Except for me?" Fauna shot back, raising her eyebrows and flashing him a triumphant grin. Her expression left Bolan with the feeling she thought she'd obtained some victory with the statement.

"Afraid I don't follow."

"You told me last night you didn't want me involved."

"No, I told you I didn't want to work with you. Big difference. If you want to get involved, go for it. I work alone. It's as simple as that."

"Well, you're not going to be able to get rid of me."

"Fine."

"Good," Fauna said uncertainly. She seemed puzzled by his sudden change in attitude. "I think."

"Have you bothered to ask yourself," Bolan said, changing the subject abruptly, "why somebody's trying to kill you?"

"What do you mean?"

"Well, those clowns tonight certainly weren't after me, and I don't think they were waiting for me at the Kateb's last night. There's one common denominator linking both of them."

"And that is?"

"You."

It hadn't occurred to Fauna until just then, and the look of realization on her face said it all. Bolan had run every angle and he wasn't sure himself, but it was part of what he planned to find out. At least with Fauna close to him, if the GIA was trying to eliminate her then that would put the Executioner closer to finding the triggers.

Somewhere out there, among hundreds of vehicles parked on the edge of Tambacounda, was the pot of gold he sought. A pot that wasn't connected to a rainbow but rather to trail of blood and intrigue. Eventually, the soldier knew he would reach the end of that trail.

And then he would destroy the enemy once and for all.

6

Stage Two—Tambacounda to Kayes

The Executioner arrived at his truck early the next morning in time to see Calee Fauna tuck a duffel bag under the leather cover stretched across the bed. He eyed her with some indifference for a moment and decided how to broach the subject of her little transgression.

Obviously, something he'd said last night had led the young woman to believe they were now partners. Bolan wanted to keep Fauna close, but not *too* close. He certainly didn't intend to have her ride with him, but he wasn't too sure how to make that clear. He thought he'd made his case last night. Apparently, Fauna thought otherwise. Bolan could already feel the argument coming even as he opened his mouth.

"And what are you doing?"

"Just bringing a few necessities."

"For what?" Bolan demanded.

"For our little trip."

"Our little trip?"

"Now look, Blanski," she protested immediately, "I know what you're going to say. You work alone."

"Right."

"And you don't need me slowing you down, and getting in the way, and all of that shit."

"Right again."

Now she understood—this wasn't her fight. Bolan couldn't really blame her, though. She was spunky, determined and up to her neck in this stuff. That's what bothered him the most. He understood why the GIA-Djihad movement considered him a threat, but he wasn't so sure about Fauna. How she even fit into this thing was a mystery that grew more puzzling by the minute. Within thirty-six hours, there had been two attempts on her life.

Bolan couldn't believe that her encounters with the terror group were mere coincidence. Something stunk about this thing. She hadn't admitted she was a member of the French intelligence agency, but she hadn't denied it, either. It seemed she'd come by much of the same information as Bolan, although where she'd gotten it was anybody's guess. Most of the time, the GIA operated discreetly. They weren't used to attracting so much attention and operating in the open for everyone to see.

Perhaps they had underestimated Bolan, and they were preparing to employ other more subtle methods.

One thing was certain—they would now believe there was a distinct connection between him and Fauna. Bolan couldn't operate without her being around, and if he ditched her she'd just track him down and bust into his operation at some other inopportune moment. No, it was best to keep her close.

Real close.

"All right," he finally conceded, "you're in. But we do things my way. Got it?"

"Check. Your way."

"I mean it, lady," Bolan warned, jabbing a finger at her. "One misstep and I'll dump you at the next half-civilized outhouse." He nodded in her general direction and added, "You armed?"

She smiled. "And dangerous."

"Yeah, right," he replied with a lopsided grin, finding himself unable to keep a straight face. "Let's go."

The two climbed into the Ram, and Bolan fired the engine. Power roared beneath the hood. The truck was a marvel of automotive engineering, a real credit to its makers. The manufacturer had originally used the Magnum engine in the Viper

RT/10 to test its new platform team concept. Bolan knew the aluminum block was normally reserved for heavier-class trucks, such as the 2500 and 3500, but they wouldn't have functioned as well in the African terrain.

The 8.0-liter V-10 was the largest and most powerful engine available in American sports cars. It was a 460-hp workhorse with integral fuel rails cored into the castings. The dual-throttle bodies and multipoint injection system controlled mixture and flow. It was mounted to one of the stiffest sport-truck chassis ever constructed, and many of its internal features were taken directly from Formula One engines.

Bolan never fancied himself an auto mechanic, but he knew the truck's basic specifications. Not to mention the fact that Jakom—as a member of the Amaury Sports Organization— would have access to the finest equipment and maintenance crews available. Their ride was definitely powerful and reliable, both attributes Bolan knew he would need in the untamed wild of the central plateau.

The Executioner steered his truck through the maze of rally crews working to get on the road. He submitted his credentials to officials at the starting point, and within a few minutes he was given the green light to proceed.

"So what's the plan, Blanski?" Fauna asked when they were under way.

"I've ruled out about half the vehicles right off the bat." They're either too small or the particular drivers don't fit within parameters."

"Unless," Fauna stated, "they're carrying these triggers and don't know it."

Bolan shrugged. "Possible but not likely. The beauty of this is that I don't think I'm going to have to search as hard as I originally thought."

"What do you mean?"

The soldier downshifted as he entered the first set of piste turns on the west side of Tambacounda. This section would take concentration, and Bolan gestured for her to be silent while he negotiated the grueling course.

The laterite was softer here—not from the rains nearly as much as from the sheer thickness of it. It formed in layers of deposits and was commonly used as a building material. The laterization process took place from the weathering of rocks in tropical climates. It was boggy when wet, and atmospheric exposure left behind concentrations of iron and aluminum oxides that were like thick gravel when dry. Most accidents in the rally were attributed to high speeds over the laterite.

When the route eased some, Bolan continued, "I'm betting on the fact that when I'm close to them, it'll make them nervous enough to try again."

"That could take some time."

"I know," he admitted, "but I don't have much choice. I can't effectively search that many vehicles. I took a walk after we left last night and did some looking around. We're getting hot."

"How hot?"

They roared up on the back side of an older vehicle that was powering through the laterite-strewed pistes with very little effort. Bolan immediately identified the vehicle's shape as an Italian-made Fiat. The all-steel body featured a rear cargo area that contained a bench seat along one side with room for up to five personnel and space for three more in the front cab. The vehicle was commonly used as a forward ambulance for the Italian army, but Bolan had seen many attributed to peacekeeping forces when he was in Lebanon. The engine wasn't that large, maybe eighty horsepower, but it could ford at two feet, had a range of nearly four hundred miles and could travel up to seventy miles per hour.

The most interesting part about the vehicle was the camouflage-clad terrorist who opened up with a Skorpion machine pistol from a kneeling position in the rear cargo area.

Bolan swung the steering wheel hard right and brought the Ram into a bone-jarring turn. The heavy-duty tires screeched in protest as the differential whined to compensate for the sudden change in the 4.1 axle ratio. The light back end swung around in a J-style turn, and Bolan double-clutched to bring the gearshift into Reverse. He slammed the wheel in the opposite direction and the nose of the truck continued around until they were facing forward again.

He launched the Ram from second gear. A quick inspection didn't reveal any vital parts of the vehicle had been hit by the autofire.

"Shit!" Fauna cursed.

"Very hot," Bolan murmured, cranking through the gears to overtake the Fiat.

The Executioner slowed some and looked at her. "You think you can drive this thing without killing us?"

Fauna's expression was one of uncertainty, but she answered, "Of course."

"Then get over here."

The French DGSE agent immediately jumped into his lap and took the wheel. The smell of her perfume and closeness of her warm body was a slight distraction to the Executioner but he put it from his mind.

Once Bolan was sure Fauna had control, he slid out and over to the passenger seat. He reached over the console into the rear of the cab and quickly snatched one of the items Jakom had secured for him back in Dakar.

Bolan quickly checked the action of the Belgium-made FNC.

The weapon was the dream child of Fabrique Nationale, creator of the popular FN FAL and its less popular successor, the CAL. It was made from steel and alloy stampings, gas operated with a rotating bolt. The Executioner had requested the weapon because he knew, given its widespread use in the area, how easy it would be for Jakom to obtain. That particular model was equipped with a plastic folding stock and was capable of single, 3-round burst or automatic fire.

Bolan leaned out the window and snap-aimed to align his sight post along the back of the Fiat. He flicked the selector to full auto and triggered a long burst. Unlike the FAL, the weapon was quite easy to control on full-auto. The FNC chugged in the soldier's hands as 5.56 mm NATO rounds rocketed into the back of the opposition's light-duty vehicle. Several rounds hammered through the terrorist's chest. The impact twisted him into an odd position and dumped him on his back.

Bolan readjusted his aim and tried to take out the tires, but the Ram truck suddenly skewed to one side. He ducked inside the cab and fired a dirty look in Fauna's direction. He watched her biting her lip, drawing blood, as the truck fishtailed in a particularly thick section of laterite.

Bolan held his silence. It did no good to yell at her—she was doing the best she could and he didn't want to risk breaking her concentration.

She quickly regained control of the vehicle and before long they were closing on the Fiat again. The pistes were narrow at this part of the course. Bolan groaned inwardly. If it wasn't the slick laterite then it was the narrow twists or high, canyonlike walls of the route.

Bolan waited until the Fiat was close enough, then leaned out and fired 3-round bursts at the rear tires. One of the shots finally punched a clean hole through the right rear, and the Fiat nearly toppled over, its rear end swinging back and forth like a giant pendulum. The Fiat finally scraped to a halt against one of the piste walls.

Fauna barely managed to stop the Ram in time to avoid a collision and passed by on the other side, lightly scraping the opposing wall herself. She brought the Ram to a halt fifteen feet ahead of the Fiat and nearly around a very tight turn in the pistes.

Three men bailed from the cab of the Fiat. The terrorists were dressed identically to their dead comrade, but they all wore purple scarves like the men Bolan had encountered in the Kateb's house. This clearly marked them as members of the Da'awa wal Djihad, and that meant there was a good chance they had the triggers in the back of the Fiat.

"Check their wheels!" Bolan ordered Fauna as he jumped from the truck. "I'll take care of them!"

Two of the Djihad trio fanned out to spray the Executioner with covering fire while the third scrambled up the unstable wall of the piste. Dirt and loose rock crumbled under the terrorist's weight, and he dropped to the ground in a heap of dust.

Bolan triggered the FNC, the weapon still set for 3-round bursts, and blew off the head of one of the terrorists. The Djihad gunman's body staggered backward and collapsed on his comrade who had tried to escape up the piste wall.

The Executioner dropped to the earth and rolled in time to avoid a hail of 9 mm stingers that spit from the muzzle of a Galil being toted by the terrorist still on his feet. The big American got to his knee and lined up for target acquisition, but a Mitsubishi truck beat him to it. A rally driver rounded the corner and jammed on his brakes, swerving to avoid the gun-toting terrorist, but there was no room to maneuver around the grounded Fiat.

The sport truck smacked head-on into the gunner and sent him airborne. Bolan watched as the body somersaulted high through the air, struck the ground headfirst, then rolled out of sight over the edge of the piste wall. The last enemy troop had pushed aside the messy, bloody corpse of his fellow terror-monger and was on his knees with a Skorpion machine pistol in hand.

The driver of the Mitsubishi started to get out, but Bolan shouted a warning. It was a moment too late as the terrorist's weapon stuttered in the hot morning air. The echo of the shots hadn't died before Bolan watched the driver dance in place, and then collapse to the ground.

Bolan pointed the muzzle directly at the murderer as he thumbed the selector switch to full-auto and squeezed the trigger. Ten rounds of 5.56 mm ammo tore flesh from bone and ripped large holes through vital organs. Bolan could see dust chug from the wall on the other side as the rounds continued through the body and embedded themselves in the African terrain. The terrorist's body dropped and lay still as blood poured from multiple wounds, mixing with the red-brown dirt.

Bolan slowly regained his feet and walked over to study the carnage a minute. Flies had already begun to settle on the terrorists' bodies. He double-checked the driver, pulling the man's racing helmet from his head and checking the pulse.

The man was Asian—probably Japanese—and he didn't look more than twenty years old.

His heart ached for the innocent driver who was just trying to win a race. This young man had paid the ultimate price—he'd given his life for the thrill of speed and adventure. Another senseless death, and the Executioner couldn't help but feel responsible. There were countless victims of his war. All he could do was numb the pain with the realization that he'd saved many more lives than he'd lost.

But that never completely took the hurt away. Nothing could ever do that.

"Blanski!" Fauna called.

Bolan turned from the grisly scene and rushed to the rear of the truck, where Fauna's attention seemed to be focused. She was looking at something, and the soldier realized why the odd expression when he peered over the edge of the box she'd secured. Inside was nothing but a few rocks and piles of desert sand.

Fauna shook her head with disbelief. "I don't get it. Where are the triggers? I thought for sure they'd be here."

"That's just what they wanted you to think," Bolan replied quickly. "And me too."

"Who?"

"Whoever's responsible for delivering them to this Hassan Fuaz."

"You mean—"

"Yeah. This was a decoy."

Nioro du Sahel, Mali

COLONEL MAMDUH Nokhtari sat at a table with Ayman in a deserted eatery attached to their hotel.

Nokhtari was anxious for news of the triggers. Word had come that Fuaz was on his way to the secret lab where the new bacterial agent neared completion. The thought of a biological weapon made Nokhtari a little nervous, although he wouldn't have disclosed this to his Egyptian counterpart. The scientists working for Fuaz had spent many hours perfecting the newest addition to the GIA-Djihad arsenal. Nonetheless, Nokhtari didn't want to be anywhere near the missiles when they were ready for practical testing.

The GIA leader was savoring the roasted goat and bits of wild rice mixed with vegetables that were piled before him on a steaming plate. He had a large hunk of unleavened bread brushed with salted olive oil and was about to sample his first morsel when one of his field officers appeared at the door.

Ayman rose from the table and lumbered over to the officer. The man whispered a message, and the bodyguard nodded several times, then dismissed the man. The huge Algerian moved back to the table and sat himself in front of his water glass. Ayman wasn't eating and he sat respectful and silent, obviously not wishing to disturb Nokhtari with the officer's news.

After several bites of the meal, Nokhtari wiped his mouth and returned the napkin to his lap. "What is it, Ayman?"

"You must eat first, sir," the huge bodyguard admonished his leader.

"Don't tell me what I must do," Nokhtari snapped. "I know what I must do. What is it?"

Ayman seemed uncertain at first.

Nokhtari realized he'd been a little hard on his faithful servant. Few people knew that Nokhtari had a form of diabetes; it was controlled through diet for the most part. Nokhtari could easily have afforded the medicines to control his blood sugar, but he didn't wish to dump Western-made chemicals into his system, and injecting pork-based insulin was out of the question.

"What is it?" Nokhtari repeated more gently.

"Hassan's men are dead."

Nokhtari finished chewing and swallowed hard. He washed the meat down with a glass of water, then gestured to Ayman to pour him some more from a nearby ceramic carafe. As he piled another bit of the goat on the bread, he continued his inquisition.

"How many did we lose?"

"All of them," Ayman replied.

Nokhtari dropped the bread on his plate and stared at the dark, towering form of his assistant. "Those were Hassan's personal troops. His elite guard, Ayman."

"I know this, sir," the man replied softly. "It is a tragedy. I am saddened by the loss of our brothers."

"What about the triggers? Are they safe?"

Ayman nodded. "The decoy you sent worked perfectly. They should arrive here tomorrow afternoon. Perhaps ahead of schedule."

"If they make it to the rendezvous site."

"What do you mean?" Ayman asked with a puzzled expression.

Nokhtari rose and began to pace around the room, crossing his arms and drumming his fingers against his chest. He performed several rotations, Ayman watching him with interest. Finally, he stopped and faced his subordinate.

"It was this American who was responsible for their deaths?"

Ayman nodded.

"So it is still possible he might discover the real team."

"Yes, sir, there is a possibility. He has allied himself with the Frenchwoman that Master Fuaz ordered us to eliminate."

"Then we must still consider him an active threat. Where is he now?"

"He and the woman are following the course to Kayes. They should arrive some time tonight."

"I want you to send a squad of our men to finish the infidels once and for all. We can no longer risk their interference in our plans. Particularly the American. I am not too worried about the woman. Our contact will take care of her. But the American must die. I want him ashes in the wind before the moon rises. Is that clear?"

Ayman rose from the table and bowed. "It shall be as you wish."

DUSK HAD SETTLED upon the oasis of Falémé. It was a popular watering hole for the rally's drivers, where they could get fuel, rest, food and just about anything else they might need. The oasis sat in a pass at the base of the Mandingue Mountains, the border of Senegal and Mali.

Bolan and Fauna took their break away from the rest of the rally crews on an outcropping near the oasis exit. The Ram was completely hidden from view by ground and only partially visible from the air. The two sat side by side, drinking their water sparingly from the canteens Bolan was carrying and watching the sun reflect off the rugged Mandingues, painting their sides with red, orange and sapphire hues.

"It's beautiful, isn't it?" Fauna asked Bolan.

"Yeah."

She turned to look at the Executioner, but he pretended not to notice. His mind was preoccupied with the task ahead. "It's views like these that make me forget how dangerous this world is. And how evil."

"Without evil there's no good," Bolan replied. It was a statement he'd made thousands of times before.

He found himself believing it more every time he said it. He'd experienced almost every kind of imaginable injustice in his War Everlasting. The cold reality of the world left no room for compromise, and this was a lesson learned long ago by an impressionable soldier in Vietnam. A soldier they called the Executioner—but one they also called Sergeant Mercy. The only compromise in Bolan's life was the internal one, the one where he'd learned to balance the good with the bad.

When it came to the enemy, there could be no compromise...only action that was swift and final.

"How far do we have to go?"

Bolan noticed the sudden change in subject but decided not to mention it. It was actually a welcome relief. "About eighty miles, give or take."

Fauna stood and ran her hands along her backside. "Feels like I've been sitting forever."

"Yeah," Bolan replied with a chuckle, "that thing gets to ride like a tank after a while, huh?"

She turned and smiled at him. "You said it."

A small chunk of jagged stone jutting from the boulder next to her exploded, severed from its host, but Bolan never heard the shot.

Fauna jumped backward and lost her footing. The Executioner reached out and saved her from a long drop. He pulled her by the hand and raced toward the cover of the truck. They reached the small ledge immediately above the roof, and Bolan jumped down, landing with catlike grace before reaching up and assisting Fauna off the ledge.

Two more rounds plowed through the ledge where she'd sat only a moment before, sending sharp bits of stone and clouds of dirt into the air.

"Hurry up!" he ordered. "Get in!"

The pair bailed off the roof, landing on their respective sides, and jumped into the cab. Bolan started the engine and spun tires to beat a hasty retreat from their cover. He maneuvered the Ram full speed down the sandy slope to the course trail. The truck nearly rolled as the warrior downshifted and turned onto the makeshift route. Within minutes, they had put considerable distance from the oasis.

"Whew!" Fauna spit. "That was too close."

The Executioner gripped the steering wheel and kept his eyes on the road ahead.

7

Stony Man Farm, Virginia

Aaron "the Bear" Kurtzman, resident computer whiz and electronics expert hunkered in his wheelchair and stared at the computer screen. Harold Brognola, director of the Sensitive Operations Group, stood behind him and stared at the same screen.

Neither man was happy.

"There's no doubt about it, boss," Kurtzman said, leaning back and cracking his knuckles. "Mack is definitely in Africa. I'd recognize his handiwork anywhere."

"How can you be sure?"

"Members of French security put a tail on him as soon as he got into Senegal, although we're not sure why yet. They said he took out a group of Arabs who attacked him, then went to meet with a member of the Amaury Sports Organization. Then he checked into a hotel and was there the rest of the night."

"The agents who claim to have seen him didn't get any photographs, did they?" Brognola queried. He turned as he posed the question and sat in his chair at the small table nearby.

Kurtzman turned, a surprised look on his face. "Are you kidding? He probably took pictures of them."

Brognola shook his head and chuckled at the wisecracking Kurtzman. "I figured Striker would track those missing triggers stolen from Rocky Flats somehow. I just didn't know he'd end up in Africa."

"Well, our people at the CIA confirm that he was there, and that he was kicking ass and taking names."

"As usual."

"Yep." Kurtzman turned back to the computer and tapped a button. Brognola couldn't see the new bit of information that popped up, but Kurtzman had probably read it by the time the big Fed made that realization.

"There are any number of reasons why he could be there," the computer expert continued. "According to our intelligence, the place is crowded because of the Paris-Dakar-Cairo Rally. That means lots of people, and since tensions are high right now in Africa, particularly the northern and central regions, that means great business for terrorists."

"Makes sense."

Kurtzman turned his chair away from the computer and faced Brognola. "That also means he might have traced the triggers to Senegal."

"Okay, let's assume for the moment he did. What about the disappearance of McKarroll? Have we been able to put the responsibility on anyone yet?"

"Armed Islamic Group," Kurtzman replied quickly. "No doubt about it."

"How do we know?"

"They were well armed and well organized, not to mention that the follow-up investigation traced the leak about our shipment to the Algerians back to GIA insurgents."

"Somebody talked."

"Exactly."

"The Oval Office thought it might be McKarroll," the big Fed chief interjected, "but I squashed that theory quick. He didn't know a damned thing about that shipment."

"What's the status on him, anyway?"

"Presumed dead. He was snatched up during that arms-shipment raid. And if you're correct in your assessment about the responsible parties, I'm guessing either the GIA's holding him for information or..."

Brognola could hardly finish the statement, and Kurtzman nodded his understanding.

"For the moment," Brognola continued, clearing his throat, "we're more concerned with what McKarroll had discovered. Rumors were flying that the GIA was gearing up for something big. But they weren't planning on doing it alone."

"Right," Kurtzman said with a nod. "I've already worked that angle."

He rolled himself over to a nearby printer and retrieved a small stack of papers. He filed through the first couple of sheets, soaking up the information and finally letting out a grunt when he'd apparently found what he was looking for.

"My first thought was to break down every known group operating in Algeria, as well as Mali, Libya, Niger and Chad."

"That's a pretty thorough list," Brognola remarked offhandedly.

Aaron Kurtzman never failed to amaze the Stony Man chief. The guy was unbelievable with his computers and machines, obtaining information at the push of a button. He could pull just about anything he wanted on practically any subject in the world. Then it was just a matter of sifting through what he'd gleaned to separate the chaff from the wheat.

Kurtzman's actions some time back against the crazed Kach-Kahane Chai terrorists, who tried to overcome military installations through computer technology, only served to raise Brognola's level of appreciation. Kurtzman was an invaluable asset to the Stony Farm project, and one of the most intelligent people he'd ever known.

Before either one of them could say another word, a third member in Stony Man's arsenal came into the room. Her stride would have left most thinking she walked on air, but to anyone that knew her—and the two men knew her well—she practically carried the weight of an entire country on her shoulders. Or at least the security thereof.

It was immediately apparent to Barbara Price that the two men were watching her intently, and the change in her expression read uncomfortable.

"What are you two staring at?"

"The jury's still out on that one," Kurtzman cracked.

"Very funny," she shot back, wrinkling her nose at him before turning to face Brognola.

Price waved a file folder as she dropped into a chair. "I tallied that stuff Aaron asked me to on our terrorist groups. You're not going to like it, Hal."

"Give it to me."

"There's no question that some terrorists are operating heavily in North Africa, particularly around the race. Personnel within the Amaury Sports Organization have been told that members loosely linked to the GIA have threatened to attack drivers, crews and whatever else they can. Apparently, this is in retaliation for some imagined actions taken against them by the Algerian military."

"But there haven't been any recent incursions against the GIA by the Algerians," Kurtzman protested.

Price looked at him and shrugged. "I know. That's why I said 'imagined.' But there's also something else we haven't considered here."

"What's that?" Brognola asked.

"The GIA's main goal has and probably always will be twofold. First, return Algeria to Islamic rule. Second, incite a revolution among the people of North Africa and establish one religion across the continent."

"Basically," Brognola finished, "they want to implement Osama bin Laden's declarations of war."

"Exactly."

"Okay, I'm with you so far. What else do we know?"

"Well, there are several groups that could be involved with the GIA. Many of these were ruled out by the Accountability Review Board that investigated U.S. Embassy bombings in Nairobi, Kenya and Dar es Salaam back in 1998."

Price pulled a list from the file folder and began to read. "That leaves four major terrorist organizations, any one of which might be working with the GIA. There's the Salafist Group for Preaching and Combat, also known as the GSPC, which was a primary opponent to President Bouteflika's reconciliation programs."

"But most of their actions are centered around Algeria," Kurtzman supplied helpfully.

"Right," Price agreed. "Same story with the Islamic Salvation Army, which is an armed wing of the FIS. Although their operations are more widely spread."

"So it's possible either one of these groups could be working with the GIA," Brognola replied, "but not likely."

"Okay, so that leaves two Egyptian groups. There's the Jamatt ul Jihad, which was founded by Aiman al-Zawahiri."

"Al-Zawahiri was a major player in launching the FIS," Brognola interjected. "He was one of bin Laden's most trusted allies. But he's more of a figurehead now, with very little real power."

"Plus his group is primarily concerned with Muslim power in Egypt and considers Israel the center of what he calls the great conspiracy to wipe out Islam and its allies."

"So who does that leave?" Kurtzman inquired.

Price clucked her tongue and pulled a second sheet and a photograph from the folder. "A group calling themselves the Da'awa wal Djihad." She set the photo on the table, and the two men leaned forward to see it. "They're led by this man, Hassan Fuaz. He's a renegade, a fugitive from Egypt and one of the most influential cell leaders in the Islamic World Front. He derives much of his support from bin Laden."

"What do we know about him?" Brognola inquired.

"Trained by the CIA during the Afghan war against the Russians in the early eighties," Price said, reading from the piece of paper. "Combat veteran of the same and a respected leader. This guy's been involved in almost every major operation in Africa. His group is highly specialized, well equipped and very dangerous."

"Sounds like our man," Kurtzman said.

"He may very well be." A familiar voice resounded through the room.

All eyes turned to see the hard visage of Colonel Yakov Katzenelenbogen.

"Katz!" Kurtzman howled.

Katzenelenbogen walked over to Brognola, and the two men shook hands warmly.

"Thanks for cutting short your vacation, Yakov," the big Fed said, gesturing to a chair.

"I wouldn't have missed this," Katz replied.

Brognola noticed the sudden looks of expectancy from his crew. "I asked Katz to come back. Obviously, he has special knowledge where this is concerned, and I wanted his technical expertise."

When the group was seated again, Katz looked grimly around the room. "The man you're talking about? I know him. Professionally speaking, of course, but I know his tactics and his work."

Price looked quizzical. "How's that?"

"Phoenix Force and I encountered him on a mission, although not directly. It was when we went up against a man named Kaborya, a revolutionary and leader of a Palestinian Rejection Front cell that had joined up with the Iraqis."

"My God," Kurtzman breathed. "I remember that. It was quite a few years back, but we had all of you globetrotting against that group."

"Yes," Brognola added. "They nailed American, British and French embassies before we finally got them under control. And their actions against Wonderland nearly resulted in disaster."

"Correct," Katz continued. "I later got it from some old friends in Israeli intelligence links that Hassan Fuaz might have not only trained Kaborya at the mujahideen camps, but it's entirely possible he helped support their actions in Yemen."

"Well," Price said with a sigh, "there's no question that many Islamic resistance groups all congregate under the same roof. It's part of bin Laden's fatwas that they unite themselves toward the betterment of Islam."

"No argument there," Kurtzman echoed.

"The same link I had then just recently contacted me," Katz said. "He's concerned about a recent alliance rumored between Fuaz's group and the GIA. He's certain they've secreted a base somewhere in the Niger desert, and he's equally sure they're planning something big."

"Do you think they're planning a demonstration at the Dakar Rally?" Brognola inquired.

"No. I think that they did that this time around as a front. They want to divert the focus away from their real aims."

"Any thought on what those might be, Katz?" Price asked.

"I think I have a good idea. The man I've been talking to is a former colleague from my time in the IDF. His name is Lemuel Jakom. When Striker called me about this business in Dakar, I sent him to Lemuel."

"Do you think he can be trusted?" Price asked.

"I wouldn't have sent Striker to him unless I was certain of that, Barb," Katz admonished her. "The ideology and strategy of Fuaz is pretty complicated, but I don't want to oversimplify things, either.

"The organization of the Islamic Front basically comes down to two primary goals—radicalization and unity under Osama bin Laden's leadership. The Al-Qaida is a network of organizations like the Egyptian Jihad and Egyptian Armed Group, the Partisans Movement of Kashmir, the Advice and Reform Commission and the Pakistan Scholars Society."

"Just to name a few, eh?" Brognola griped.

Katz nodded. "Really. The biggest threat from this is, of course, that it combines all the organizational levels within these groups, as well. That's what moved them from a constituency to an actual operation. The results have spelled doom for countries ill equipped in handling Islamic resistance. And it's left every government in Africa petrified."

"So you think that the union between the GIA and Djihad is part of this whole Al-Qaida thing?" Price asked.

"Absolutely," Katz replied. "Lemuel believes they are trying to smuggle the triggers across the country during the Dakar Rally. And Striker is now in the middle of this thing and doing everything possible to stop them."

Brognola grunted and then turned to look at Price. "Barb, you mentioned there was something about this whole thing I wasn't going to like. What did you mean?"

Price swallowed hard. "I was afraid it might be the Da'awa wal Djihad joining with the GIA. We're talking thousands of terrorists here, Hal. And they're all moving toward the completion of mass-destruction weapons."

"Good God," Brognola said, turning his attention back to Katz. "We're talking a major operation here."

"Most likely," Katz replied somberly. "And there's very little we can do about it at this point."

"I wonder if it would be a good time to call in Phoenix Force," Brognola said.

"I wouldn't do that just yet, Hal."

"Why not?"

"Because Striker is on this, and he's not expecting any company however welcome they might be. Do you even have any idea of his present whereabouts?"

"Not really."

"Then I wouldn't go jumping the gun and sending in the team before you know what's really going on. They could all wind up dead and so could Striker."

"I could probably utilize our satellite networks to begin a search for him, Hal," Kurtzman offered.

Brognola nodded immediately. "Get on it. Pronto."

"Check."

"Is there anything you want me to do?" Price asked.

"Well, for the moment we'll play this Katz's way. He knows this game better than I do. But it wouldn't hurt to put the Phoenix Force on alert, and make sure the guys are available at a moment's notice. Also, talk with some of your contacts at the NSA. See if we can't get more on this Da'awa wal Djihad's base out there in the Niger desert."

"I'm on it."

When Price and Kurtzman were gone, Brognola fixed Katz with a mournful expression. He couldn't stifle his feelings of helplessness. He knew that Mack Bolan had a right to pursue his own missions without outside interference. But the head Fed was absolutely certain Striker was about to walk into something bigger and larger than anticipated.

He wanted to help the Executioner any way he could.

It was blatantly obvious that Katz was feeling the same way. He could see it in the old Israeli's eyes. When you were part of a team for that long, and then suddenly you were out of the action, it probably seemed as if nobody needed you. Of course, that wasn't the case, but Brognola knew beneath that hard exterior was an extremely soft and caring man.

It was funny, but Brognola had never thought he would use the word *gentle* to describe Yakov Katzenelenbogen. But at that moment it was the one word that came to mind. The guy was just itching to see some excitement again. To relive the experiences and the thrills of belonging—of being involved in something when he could make a difference. Especially when it might come down to Mack Bolan's life or death.

"I know what you're thinking, Yakov," Brognola said with a half smile. "And you can't risk it."

"Actually, I was thinking about volunteering to take a little trip. I hear Africa's beautiful this time of year."

"Oh, bullshit," Brognola boomed. "You're just looking for an excuse."

"I know I can help him," Katz said quietly. "What he probably needs most right now is intelligence. And you have no other way of getting it to him."

"The French are tailing him for some reason. We could pass it through them."

"And you feel that's reliable?" Katz argued. "I wouldn't trust them to deliver a pizza, Hal, let alone sensitive information such as this. Besides the fact, Lemuel's involved in this up to his elbows, and there's little doubt he's going to need my help."

"No offense, Katz," Brognola replied, "but if we aren't sure where to find Striker, what makes you think you can?"

"Because I know that area inside and out. And I know what his plans were. You don't have much of a choice, Hal. I'm going to go to Senegal one way or the other. You might as well use that to your advantage."

"Oh, hell," Brognola finally said with a deep sigh.

Djado Mountains, Niger

Hassan Fuaz arrived at the rendezvous point nearly twenty-four hours before Nokhtari was scheduled to arrive with the triggers.

The laboratory was dwarfed by the Meccafatwa base, but it was equally well hidden and no less impressive. It was buried in the foothills of the Djado mountain ranges in the Niger wilderness known as the Ténéré Desert. The nearest town was Seguédine, which was about seventy-five kilometers to the southeast.

The entrance to the mountain complex was camouflaged by a large rock formation that Fuaz referred to as the Islam Gateway. Access to the lab was accomplished by electronic card and code key, a doubly effective security measure that insured his people could work undisturbed. Fuaz, escorted by two members of his personal guard, slid the key into the lock and punched in the sequence of seven numbers. The huge metal door slid aside and they entered the lab.

The hum of generators was barely audible, secured by thick metal walls equipped with sound-muffling insulation. The cool air actually chilled Fuaz and he fought to repress a shiver. The Egyptian was acclimated to the heat of the desert and a life spent in the dry, arid climates of North Africa.

Nonetheless, the scientists in the lab insisted that the interior of the complex had to be kept at an exacting twenty degrees Celsius, and Fuaz saw no reason to argue the point.

His people knew what they were doing.

Fuaz walked through the complex and soon reached the demonstration area. The room itself was about forty square meters. Three metal seats with straps occupied the center of the room, spaced approximately three meters apart. Only one door provided access to the test chamber. The rest of the chamber was sealed, and small ports for the gas protruded from the corners. In just a short time, this was where the test subjects would be brought and Fuaz would be able to experience the fruit of their labors.

Once he'd inspected the test chamber, Fuaz and his men proceeded to the incubation lab. Four men and two women worked feverishly around a small cubicle that was completely surrounded by plate glass three inches thick. In the center of the cubicle was a small vial containing about a liter of blue-green substance that resembled slime. The gellike fluid within that vial held some of the deadliest biochemical toxin ever created.

One of the women, who was dressed in a white one-piece lab suit, turned at Fuaz's entry. She was Arabic, with long dark hair and unusual blue eyes. Her name was Dr. Hasna Qaseem, and she was the project leader of Fuaz's scientific team. Qaseem was the daughter of a former colleague, and was educated in the finest American and European schools. The woman wasn't of pure Arabic descent. Her father had served with a lieutenant in Osama bin Laden's army, and for a time she'd acted as one of his concubines.

Fuaz wasn't completely comfortable with a woman in charge of this project, particularly not one who wasn't from pure Arabic heritage. Nonetheless, she was a devoted follower of the Al-Qaida cause and one of the most brilliant biogenetic engineers in the world. Fuaz could forgive her impurities while he needed her so desperately.

"God be with you, Hassan," she said, bowing and kissing Fuaz's hand. "We welcome you back."

Fuaz raised an eyebrow in surprise. He knew that Qaseem truly despised him deep down and her reverence was little more than a showpiece. She was as deceitful as she was beautiful—a combination that made her even more dangerous. Qaseem's loyalties were neither with Fuaz nor the Da'awa wal Djihad. She was completely loyal to bin Laden, however, and so the Djihad leader was required to keep her alive and treat her with the utmost respect. Anything less would have enraged bin Laden and would likely result with Fuaz losing his head.

"How are your plans proceeding?" Fuaz asked quietly.

The woman turned away as she spoke, studying the chemical within the vial. To not look at Fuaz when speaking was something no one else in the room would have dared to do. Qaseem was different in this respect. She cared little for protocol beyond the pleasantries of her initial greeting.

"We are well ahead of schedule, I think," she replied. The tone in her voice was cold, haughty. "We shall begin the testing shortly."

"And the delivery devices?"

"They are prepared," she said, then turned and added, "except for the triggers. Will Mamduh be delayed with the delivery?"

It was Fuaz's turn to grin coolly. The bitch wasn't the least bit concerned with the arrival of the triggers—not when it came to Nokhtari. Fuaz knew of their little trysts and secret meetings. They were lovers, although Nokhtari thought he could keep this a secret. Fuaz had eyes and ears everywhere within his operation. This prevented any betrayal. While he both loved and admired Nokhtari as a brother and loyal associate, he also understood the needs of a man. He had them himself from time to time. But he couldn't understand why Nokhtari insisted on keeping his relationship with Qaseem a secret.

After all, Fuaz had no designs on Qaseem. The half-breed Westerner could pleasure anyone that she pleased, as long as she did as instructed and worked to further the cause. The minute she overstepped her bounds, though, would be the day she was returned to bin Laden for unworthiness. Fuaz secretly relished that day, for he knew it would come.

"The American hardware will arrive early tomorrow evening," Fuaz countered. "You do not have to worry about this. Mamduh knows exactly what he is doing."

Qaseem smiled deviously and said, "I know that he does."

"Now, I must take my leave and clean up. I will see you at the demonstration. I am most anxious to view the results of your work."

"You will not be disappointed," Qaseem said.

"I hope I will not," Fuaz replied.

The Djihad leader smiled when he saw Qaseem's expression of surprise. Good, the threat had been implicit enough. While Fuaz had no real authority over Qaseem, he was the appointed overseer of the entire project. Everyone within the organization ultimately answered to him, and he wielded that power to his every advantage. Qaseem would be treated no differently than anyone. It was the success of Al-Qaida that took precedence above all else. No one within the organization was above reproach, and everyone was expendable.

Fuaz had already come to accept this, but Qaseem thought more of herself.

Before she could say another word, Fuaz turned on his heel and marched from the lab. He proceeded along the corridor until he reached his assigned quarters. He ordered the guards to stand outside his door as he entered and walked to a waiting basin. The water was warm, and after a shave and sponge cleaning that wiped the sand and dirt from his face, Fuaz proceeded to the demonstration area.

Three of the scientists were already seated, and they stood when Fuaz entered. He acknowledged each of them in turn, then waved them back into their seats. His guards posted themselves at the door as Fuaz took a chair that afforded him a perfect view.

From the observation room, he could see the test subjects were already seated and strapped into their respective places. Fuaz had personally selected these men for testing.

One of the men was Umar el-Wasim, a chief negotiator to the Algerian president. The man had been captured during a GIA raid and he'd outlived his usefulness. The second was an Egyptian native who'd entered the organization as a mole, planted by Fuaz's government. His selection as a test subject was based simply on vengeance for his actions against the Djihad, and Fuaz would most certainly enjoy watching him die.

The third man was a last-minute candidate. Admiral Robert McKarroll struggled against his bonds but to no avail. Fuaz disagreed with Nokhtari's assessment that the man's life might be worth something to the organization. McKarroll's death warrant had already been signed by the United States government, and if they hadn't sent someone by now to rescue him, they weren't going to. So it only made sense to see how this American held up against the new virus.

Qaseem entered the viewing chamber a moment later and reported, "All is prepared. Make yourselves comfortable."

"It will take some time for the virus to affect them, will it not, Doctor?" Fuaz asked.

Qaseem shrugged indifferently. "Not as long as you might think. I would imagine we should start seeing initial effects within the hour."

"That is quite impressive," Fuaz replied with surprise.

"Part of the compound we have developed contains high quantities of serotonin."

"What is this?"

"It is a compound derived from the amino acid tryptophan. It affects the blood vessels in the body and also works as a neurotransmitter—"

"I do apologize, Doctor," Fuaz interrupted, "but I would appreciate it if you could simplify these things for those of us that are less learned."

Qaseem looked as if she wanted to scream at him, but she held her tongue. Fuaz was quite satisfied with himself that he could engender such a response from the normally reserved scientist. It gave him immense pleasure to aggravate this woman, who obviously considered herself superior in intellect to him. Not that it mattered—she was a scientist but knew nothing of the complexities and intelligence required to lead men in battle.

"An example of a neurotransmitter would be adrenaline, the substance that increases heart rate and blood pressure. Serotonin inhibitors are contained in such drugs as lysergic acid diethylamide. In this case, it speeds the process of infection and has an increased effect on the nervous system. This makes it very dangerous and quite impossible to control once it spreads."

"Excellent. Thank you," Fuaz replied.

"Actually, you will see very few effects for the first eight hours," Qaseem added. "The purpose of this demonstration is to illustrate how the subjects will initially show no ill effects from the exposure."

"In other words, when we use this against the general populace," Fuaz said, "they will not know they've been infected?"

"That is correct."

Fuaz clapped his hands and rubbed them. "That is absolutely ingenious, Doctor. I am most pleased with your results. You may proceed with the test."

Qaseem nodded curtly, then turned to a microphone on a nearby control panel. She flipped a switch and ordered the unseen crew members standing by to start the test. There was a small rumble in the room as the pumps started up, then a few minutes later the gas began to seep through the ports into the test chamber.

The three subjects looked around them, probably more concerned about the sounds they were hearing than about anything visible. According to Qaseem's earlier reports to Fuaz, the gas would be odorless, colorless and tasteless. Fuaz had to admit that there was nothing abnormal present from where he sat. About ten minutes went by before the humming stopped.

"You may begin decontamination, then enter the chamber for blood tests," Qaseem said into the microphone. She turned to Fuaz and the other scientists and said, "Now we must wait. This concludes the demonstration."

"Will those men be contagious?" Fuaz asked, unable to contain the trepidation in his bass voice.

"If our initial calculations are correct, and the chemical properties of the compound are accurate, the blood tests should confirm they are highly contagious." Qaseem stared hard through the viewing window at her human guinea pigs. "We should start seeing more practical results within a few hours."

"What exactly will happen?"

"We can never be sure, since this is a different and more potent strain of the original virus," Qaseem replied. "More than likely, however, they will develop a fever. This is followed by a rash that develops into pustules. The fever will most likely be transient, but when it returns the rash will have become infected with bacteria. Eventually, the bacteria will reach the lungs, heart and brain. By the time someone figures out what is happening, millions will be dead."

Qaseem turned her stare to Fuaz, and the bloodthirsty look in her eyes chilled him. The look wasn't nearly as soft at it usually was, and Fuaz could see something behind those blue eyes that scared him. There was something deathly violent and cold in that frozen stare. It was almost as if she were picturing him as one of the victims, and although Fuaz wouldn't have admitted it or shown his discomfort, he definitely didn't like it.

He didn't like it one bit.

"And I would imagine that millions more will be infected," she concluded.

"Is there an antidote?"

"Of course, and I shall see to it that all of our people are inoculated once we have verified the efficacy of the virus."

"Where is this vaccine located?"

Qaseem let out a laugh that dripped with derision. "Oh, no, my dear Hassan. That is my guarantee that I stay alive. Do you think me stupid?"

"Not at all," Fuaz replied congenially, "but I could order you to tell me."

"And I would tell you to go to hell!"

Her outburst surprised everyone, and her colleagues quickly jumped from their chairs and left the two alone.

Fuaz was completely taken aback by her reaction. She was rapidly becoming out of control, and the Djihad terrorist was unsure of how to deal with her. Perhaps it was her relationship with Nokhtari that made her so bold, perhaps something else. She was right, of course. Possession of the only antidote to this new, monstrous creation *was* the only thing that could keep her alive. Nobody in her position would have casually thrown away such a powerful advantage.

There was no question about it. Despite how much Fuaz disliked her, Qaseem wasn't ignorant and she wasn't a fanatical fool. She was a scientist and, like any other scientist, she probably thought things out quite thoroughly before proceeding. The hardest thing for Fuaz to accept was that this insolent woman held his own livelihood in her hands, as well. That couldn't continue, because as long as it did, Qaseem wielded the real power.

"There has not been a case of smallpox in the world since 1979. It is considered eradicated," Fuaz finally said. "An antidote was found before, and it can be found again."

"Not anymore," Qaseem replied quietly.

THE CITY OF Kayes was a beehive of activity.

Like Tambacounda, it was packed with rally crews, press members and sports aficionados. A group of scantily clad women hovered around one of the French drivers on the road leading into the city, posing with the man for pictures and begging him to sign autographs. One of the women, a blond bombshell dressed in khaki shorts and a pink halter top, waved at Bolan as he passed. She really wanted him to stop and sign her picture, or maybe add to the collection of markings on her arms and legs, but the Executioner decided to pass. The less attention he drew to himself the better.

Bolan reached out and gently shook Fauna, who was sleeping soundly next to him. She opened her eyes slowly, then sat up in her seat. For a moment, she squinted and looked around, obviously unsure of her surroundings. The day's activities suddenly flooded her worn, exquisite face and she turned to look at Bolan with a crooked smile.

"We are in Kayes?" she asked softly.

"Yeah. We need to find some hole where we can clean up and get some rest. Tomorrow's going to come awfully early." The Executioner proceeded past the staging area and continued deeper into the town.

"Where are you going?" Fauna said quickly. "You passed the parking zones."

"I need to do a soft probe," he explained. "See if I can find those triggers."

"If any of the rally officials catch you in town with this truck, they'll disqualify you," Fauna advised. "I don't think—"

Bolan pulled the Ram into an alleyway and killed the engine. He turned in his seat and studied the French beauty with resolute skepticism. Fauna winced inadvertently as he fixed her with the harsh gaze, and he was satisfied his sudden change in demeanor was having the desired effect.

"All right, it's time to cut this nonsense," Bolan snapped, jabbing a finger at her. "Who's trying to kill you and why?"

"I don't know," Fauna replied in protest. "I'm as much puzzled by this as you are."

"You're working for the DGSE."

"That is true."

"What was your mission here?" he pressed.

"I was here to provide security for the race," she said. "And to gather intelligence that might lead us to discover what the GIA is up to. I've already told you what I know."

"No, you haven't. First, I find you at the Kateb's with Djihad members just about ready to cut out your tongue. Then there were the two Arabs in Tambacounda, followed by an obviously amateur sniper taking potshots at the oasis."

Fauna looked through the windshield of the truck and sighed as her eyes reflected the lights of Kayes.

Bolan could see the conflict there—she was trying to decide how much she should tell him. He could understand her reticence, but that didn't mean he agreed with it. As far as he was concerned, the espionage game was up. Her cover was blown, somebody wanted her dead and all of these facts were somehow directly tied to the GIA-Djihad alliance.

"It's time for you to start leveling with me," Bolan warned. "Otherwise, I'm going to leave you here and you can fend for yourself."

When Fauna turned to look at Bolan, he could see the tears welling in her eyes. "You are treating me as if I am the enemy."

"It may seem that way," the Executioner replied more gently, "but your cover's blown and it's hampering my mission. I can't help you if I don't know what I'm up against."

"Okay, I will tell you the truth." She took a deep breath and plunged forward before she lost her nerve. "My specialty is electronic communications. I have not been a field agent that long. I was assigned to the race because certain members of my government are concerned someone is feeding vital intelligence on our security measures to bidders within the GIA movement. They believe that this individual could be the man I'm working with."

"So," Bolan interjected, "someone else is here and you're keeping an eye on him."

"Exactly. I'm thoroughly convinced that they are wrong about him." She paused a moment, wiping her eyes and adding, "Or at least I thought they were."

"Who is it?"

"His name is Talbot Dutré. He is also a member of our agency, and he has been operating in the African theater for the past two years."

"Where is he now?"

"I left him in Tambacounda. He has no idea where I am or who you are. I'm sure of that."

"Yeah," Bolan replied, "well, I'm not so sure. Did it ever occur to you that he might be the one sending all of these hit teams?"

"For what purpose? He has no reason to consider me a threat," Fauna countered quickly. "My cover is still intact."

"Not if your people are correct and he's working for the GIA," the Executioner said matter-of-factly. "Look, he supplies secrets to someone within this group on your security measures. You're sent to Africa and he gets suspicious. Did you tell him about me?"

"Only that you interfered with Fuaz's men at the Kateb's."

"So you think this guy can't put two and two together?" Bolan asked, feeling incensed that she had decided to spring this on him now. "I'd be willing to bet that these men really are onto me, and it's just convenient you're with me."

"I do not understand."

"They can kill two birds with one stone, Calee," Bolan said angrily.

The roar of a chopper's rotors suddenly filled their ears.

The soldier grabbed Fauna's arm and yanked her from the truck as the sound of electrically powered autofire roared from the Hip-E helicopter's 12.7 mm nose gun. The machine gun spit rounds at a cyclic rate of 450 per minute, and the heavy-caliber ammunition that traced around them exploded into flame against the walls.

Bolan swore as he barely managed to avoid the fire. Chunks of superheated stone and metal threatened to burn them into ashes. The machine gun was firing armor-piercing incendiary rounds, and one hit could easily end it for both of them.

The Executioner raced down the alleyway for the street at the far end, practically dragging Fauna behind him. She tripped twice trying to match his long strides before they reached the end of the alley. The chopper raced overhead and pivoted to meet them head-on.

Bolan pushed Fauna behind a stack of thick steel drums as he yanked the Desert Eagle from his hip holster and took aim at the chopper's tail rotor.

The pilot opened up again, and Bolan only managed to get off a single shot from the .44 Magnum pistol before ducking behind the drums. Hot lead pelted their makeshift cover, knocking the top drum off its base and sending it halfway down the alley. The autofire died abruptly, and Bolan risked a glance over their cover.

In the darkness, heavily armed men began to descend from the chopper.

9

"Move!" Bolan ordered, shoving Fauna back in the direction of the truck. The soldier looked over his shoulder as they sprinted for the Ram.

The cloud cover had moved aside to bathe the street in moonlight. In the reflection off the street, Bolan could make out the GIA commandos dressed in black fatigues. Most of them carried R4s, a South African version of the Galil assault rifle. The R4s were adopted as the new standard weapons of the Defense Forces, and were modified to chamber 5.56 mm ammunition.

In any case, they were deadly in the hands of the GIA terrorists, and the Executioner wasn't about to stick around and find out just how deadly they could be.

He and Fauna reached the truck as the chopper dumped the last of its troops, then lifted away. There was no way for the Hip-E crew to accurately lay down more of the 12.7 mm fire without taking out their own troops, and Bolan meant to take advantage of that tactical error.

As Fauna jumped into the Ram, Bolan quickly inspected the vehicle's exterior. A few holes and several scorings marked the bed where the heavy API shells from the machine gun struck the Ram, but the vehicle still looked serviceable.

Well, they would find out soon enough.

The soldier jumped behind the driver's seat and started the

engine, which roared beneath the hood. He hardly let it drop to an idle before slamming the gearshift into second. Gravel spat from the tires as Bolan headed directly toward the charging assault crew from the chopper. The Hip-E was now traversing its same course across the alley and heading toward the truck.

"What the hell are you doing, Blanski?" Fauna screamed.

He ignored her question as he powered through the gears. The GIA terrorists seemed unsure of what to do. Obviously, this wasn't what they had expected from their quarry, and they weren't quite prepared to open up with their weapons. With no time to lay down defensive fire, the first three in line could do little more than jump out of the way in time to avoid the automotive missile.

Two more bringing up the second wave weren't quite as fast. One of them managed to trigger his rifle, starring the windshield before the polished chrome of a bumper guard wrenched the R4 from his hands and knocked him aside. The impact slammed the GIA gunman into the alley wall, smashing cranial bones into his brain and killing him instantly.

His counterpart leaped away and tried to fire into the cab, but Bolan opened the door in time to hammer the weapon aside. The Executioner fishtailed and the rear bumper snagged the terrorist's fatigue trousers. The gunman was yanked off his feet and dragged down the length of the alley before crashing into a series of wooden beams protruding from the wall. The splintered wood grabbed the man and ripped him from the bumper, breaking ribs and both legs in the process.

Four more GIA troops had set up a perimeter at either corner of the alleyway exit and they opened up with their R4s. Muzzles winked in the night as the terrorists flooded the alley with 5.56 mm slugs. Bolan pushed Fauna's head down while ducking behind the cover of the dash as best he could.

"Hang on!"

The Executioner passed through the group and entered the street, jamming on his brakes and snatching the wheel hard left. He then downshifted before releasing the brake, depressed it again as he double-clutched and righted the pow-

erful Ram. The chassis held firm as Bolan accelerated away
from the troops and headed for the open road.

"You almost killed us!" Fauna shouted.

Bolan looked hard at her. "No kidding."

She ignored him and asked, "Where to now?"

"I don't know, but we're not out of the woods yet," he said
through gritted teeth. "We still have to deal with that chopper."

As if on cue, the helicopter thundered toward them, cruis-
ing at speeds that made Bolan feel as if they were standing
still. He had to find some kind of cover and quick. Their
chances of evading the heavily armed and highly maneuver-
able helicopter were about nil. There was nothing more difficult to fight than an enemy with air superiority at its disposal.

The chopper zoomed past them, its machine gun blazing.
Dirt, sand and rock were blown upward by the autofire, adding
to the cloud of dust already created in the truck's wake. The
aircraft raced past them and whirled for another run as Bolan
left the roadway and made for the open country. The Ram was
fast and well built, but it wasn't *that* fast and the body couldn't
take a tremendous pounding from artillery-grade weapons.
The Hip-E was a tremendous machine, capable of turning
light armored vehicles into scrap metal given half a chance.

Before Bolan could think up another plan, the night around
them was lit as bright as day and an explosion nearly flipped
the vehicle on its side. Flame whooshed past the Executioner's
shoulder and he could feel the intense heat from the blast as
a wall of orange flames licked hungrily against the Ram's
frame. He looked back just as another rocket sailed from the
side-mounted launchers.

Bolan knew the chopper was equipped with quite an armament, and he had to admit that the GIA was serious. They
wanted him dead, and there were no two ways around it. He
spun the wheel to the right and avoided the rocket by about
forty yards. It was a good thing they weren't heavier, since
most of the 107 mm ammunition and above in modern aircraft was either heat, infrared or laser guided.

The soldier made for a stand of trees barely visible in the

distance. He couldn't risk killing his lights, since he needed them to negotiate the rough terrain. Things could get sticky at a moment's notice and he didn't need to drive over a piste wall and bury them before it was time—the GIA would probably do that soon enough.

"We're going to die, aren't we?" Fauna asked in a shaky voice.

Bolan shrugged as he kept the accelerator jammed to the floorboard. "It doesn't look good."

They continued in a straight path for the trees. Fate seemed to be with them as they didn't run into any insurmountable obstacles. Bolan missed a few boulders by scant inches, but he kept the vehicle under control. They were maybe seventy yards from the tree line when a gigantic explosion erupted to their right and a massive ball of hot flame melted the paint on the passenger side and shattered the window. Most of the heat dissipated, but a few waves of thermal energy singed some of Fauna's hair.

"Oh, shit!" she said in a most unladylike fashion, practically jumping into Bolan's lap. "What was that?"

"Swatters," Bolan grumbled.

"What?"

"AT-2 Swatter missiles."

"Missiles?" she echoed. "What kind of missiles?"

"The kind they use against tanks," Bolan explained gruffly as they reached the trees and plowed into the miniforest. He killed the lights.

Fauna just stared at him with her mouth agape.

The AT-2s were Russian-made missiles that ran off UHF radio guidance command link with three possible frequencies. They armed at 500 meters, which explained why the Hip-E hadn't pursued the Ram. The AT-2 actually contained a hollow-charge HE capable of penetrating almost twenty inches of homogenous armor, and was propelled by a solid-fuel rocket with a range of up to 3000 meters. All of that was packaged into a missile barely four feet in length and roughly two feet in diameter.

Bolan and Fauna bailed from the truck and rushed deeper into the woods. The Executioner had his equipment with him, including the Desert Eagle and Beretta 93-R, both with plenty of spare clips. He also had the FNC clutched in his fist, and there were grenades and C-4 explosives in the backpack he'd kept in the cab of the truck.

They ran nearly a hundred yards before crouching in the darkness and waiting silently. They could barely hear the chopper's rotors, and it sounded as if the big machine was moving farther away.

"What are they doing?" Fauna finally whispered, although there wasn't really any reason to keep her voice down.

"Probably picking up their troops," Bolan replied.

"Shouldn't we get out of here?"

Bolan seriously pondered her question. There was no time to get back to the truck and leave before the chopper returned. The GIA would pick up on their trail, and the weary pair would be right back where they started. If they hoofed it out of the woods, they'd be on foot and without any kind of cover or concealment. As long as they stayed in the trees, the enemy would have to land the helicopter and disperse in a search pattern.

They could saturate the woods with rocket fire, but Bolan figured whoever was in charge was too smart for that. Why burn down that much foliage on the off chance of hitting the target? No, if the Executioner was correct, the enemy would bring its men to sweep and clear the woods.

Based on what he'd seen so far, the GIA troops weren't nearly as competent as those members of the Da'awa wal Djihad he'd run up against. Their movements weren't as calculated and the men seemed less prepared for the rigors of combat. The difference in training showed, and Bolan couldn't help but wonder why the Djihad would have allowed such a ragtag group to weigh it down.

Either way it didn't much matter. Bolan would see how they dealt with someone who could fight back. For decades the Armed Islamic Group had thrived on blowing up innocent people and assassinating unarmed politicians. Now it was time to see what its men did when going up against a well-armed, professional soldier. There was only one thing holding him back. He needed to get Fauna out of the line of fire.

"I want you to take off," Bolan said. "Get into Kayes and lay low until I come find you."

"Not a chance, Blanski," she argued. "I'm staying with you."

"No, you're not," Bolan countered. "The agreement was you do it my way. And I'm telling you to split."

"And what if you don't come back?" she asked quietly.

"Then you'll know I'm dead. If that's the case, I want you to get in touch with a guy named Jakom. He's attached to the Amaury Sports Organization. Tell him what happened. He'll know what to do."

"But—"

"Dammit, Calee, no buts," Bolan cut her off coldly. "Just get the hell out of here. Now."

The sound of the helicopter's engine and the rotors slapping the night air reached their ears. The Executioner didn't have to say another word. A simple jerk of his head was all Fauna needed. She reached over quickly to kiss the soldier on the cheek, and then she was gone.

Bolan pushed any thoughts of her from his mind and waited for the enemy to come. He rushed to the edge of the wood line and peered at the sky. Moonlight danced off the Hip-E as it drew closer by the second. One of the things he knew he had to do was to give Fauna a little time to clear the woods and get as far away as she could.

When the chopper was close enough, Bolan used a tree for cover and raised the FNC. He triggered the weapon in quick, short bursts to prevent the pilots from gaining acquisition from the muzzle-flash. After several controlled shots, he burst from his cover and ran down the length of the wood line, traversing it by nearly a hundred yards before dropping behind another tree and repeating the process.

The Hip-E's machine gun went into action, spitting out covering fire in his general direction as it came in low for a landing. So far, the GIA terrorists were performing just as he'd expected. Whoever was in charge of this little expedition was fairly predictable to this point. Bolan would have little trouble taking the terror troops now. They were in his element and playing his game.

Yeah, it was his turn to sweep and clear.

The chopper landed and began to power down as the troops debarked and fanned out. They moved toward the woods in leapfrog fashion, and amid the group was a huge man dressed in identical clothing to his troops. He was obviously the leader and Bolan set the phosphorescent tri-dot sights on his huge frame. He brought the weapon snug against his shoulder, took a half breath and squeezed the trigger.

The hammer fell with a deadened click. Misfire!

Bolan jacked the slide to the rear, extracting the round and chambering a new one even as the troops dropped to the ground. Bolan rolled away from his cover and pressed deeper into the woods as the enemy opened fire. A plethora of 5.56 mm rounds chopped away at the area above him, some of the ammo interspersed with rounds producing brilliant red tracks of light.

He dropped to the ground and almost smiled as he crawled back toward the group at a forty-five-degree angle.

His enemy was using tracer rounds, and that was very much to the soldier's advantage. It obviously hadn't occurred to the terrorists that tracers, while they helped with accuracy, tended to give away position. The idea of putting tracers at every fifth round was fine in the heavier-caliber weapons because the cyclic rate of fire wasn't nearly as high. But it was insane to do so with small-caliber weapons, especially if you weren't firing at the enemy in short bursts.

Bolan slowly moved up on the terrorists' right flank as the leader kept calling for them to cease-fire. He closed one eye, lined up the sights on three separate positions and opened up with the FNC. Mixed cries of pain and distress echoed through the night, some of them drowned out by the reverberation of Bolan's autofire.

Experience told the soldier he'd scored several hits against his enemies, and that was definitely a step in the right direction. Sections of tall dried grass crunched and swayed under the troops as they tried to crawl for better cover.

Bolan reached into his backpack and retrieved two DM51 grenades. The German-made bomb had become a recent favorite in the Executioner's arsenal. Developed by Diehl of Röthenbach, the grenade body was hexagonal in shape and covered by a lightweight plastic sleeve. It used over two ounces of PETN explosive that propelled 6,500 2 mm steel balls a range of ten meters in every direction.

It was the ultimate in offensive and defensive weaponry, and quite useful in the hands of a trained user.

Bolan yanked the pins and tossed both grenades into the group's center. Shouts and curses were followed by horrendous twin explosions as the immediate area was lit up. The Executioner's ears rang with the concussion, but he was far enough away to avoid any permanent hearing damage. Given his many years of combat, he wondered by what miracle he wasn't already deaf.

The soldier jumped from his cover and moved along the perimeter of the tree line back toward his truck. Screams of horror and shouted commands barely came through over the bursts of autofire from maybe two or three of the R4 assault rifles. The Executioner had nearly reached the truck when he realized there was still one task to complete.

He edged out of the woods and crouched as he ran in a semicircle to enable an approach to the helicopter on its unprotected rear. When he was within twenty-five paces, Bolan dropped to his belly and crawled the rest of the distance.

He reached the underbelly of the large gunship and quickly withdrew a one-pound block of plastique. He tore half of it away, primed it with an electronic blasting cap at its center and molded the puttylike explosive to the airframe. He risked getting to his feet and applying the remainder in a similar fashion to the highest point he could manage on the tail rotor.

Once the task was accomplished, he sprinted to where he'd left the truck and jumped behind the wheel. Even as he engaged his lights and pulled away from the woods he could hear the engines power up on the chopper. Bolan was maybe halfway back to Kayes when he saw the attack helicopter lift smoothly into the air and assume a pursuit course.

The Executioner purposely slowed the Ram and waited for the enemy to catch up. He wanted to make absolutely sure that the radio-controlled detonator now clutched in his palm was within signal distance. As the chopper closed the gap, Bolan slowed even more and counted off the seconds in his head.

The first muzzle-flashes of the 12.7 mm gun became apparent and that was his signal. He flicked the switch and squinted his eyes in preparation for what would come next.

No more than two seconds elapsed before the rear compartment of the Hip-E suddenly blew apart. The HE plastique tore through the fuselage even as the second batch on the tail assembly exploded. The helicopter spun wildly out of control—the entire back section awash in flames—then hit the ground and exploded. Secondary blasts incinerated the gunship, and metal shards erupted sixty feet into the sky, propelled by the helicopter's volatile fuel.

Bolan waited a moment and blew out a ragged breath of satisfaction before putting his truck into gear and continuing toward Kayes. Now he would have to track down Fauna amid the crowded streets and hotels of the city. Knowing the French DGSE agent as he did, she had probably headed for the main road and hitched a ride with one of the crews coming in.

He stopped to consider the possibility she hadn't gone far and it might be easier to head back toward the woods and meet up with her on the other side. Bolan dismissed the thought. His chances of locating her quickly in the dark were slim, and if there was one thing he didn't have at the moment it was time.

She could take care of herself for the time being. Now was his chance to locate the crew smuggling the triggers to Fuaz's crew in Nioro du Sahel. He had to identify the crew before the race tomorrow morning or it would be too late. Even once he'd neutralized the thieves, there was still the threat from Dutré, not to mention mopping up remnants of the GIA and Djihad movement.

It wasn't merely enough to find the triggers. The threat from the terror groups still existed, and Bolan knew he would have to find the heart of the group and cut it out before things could return to some normalcy within North Africa. His mission was hardly nearing its conclusion.

And Mack Bolan saw nothing but hellfire in his future.

10

As the Executioner entered Kayes, he noticed headlights in his rearview mirror appear from a side street.

Someone was following him.

Bolan was exhausted, his battle with the GIA terrorists had worn him down. In his sour mood, he knew a further confrontation was not a good thing. Then again, the passing of a few streetlights afforded a view of the sedan's occupants and that intrigued him. It was the two men who'd been watching him at the hotel in Senegal.

Yeah, it was time to find out who these men were.

Bolan turned onto a side street, killed the lights and went EVA. He crossed the street and dashed into the shadows of a small recess. He made a quick evaluation of the block, which was quiet and deserted. That would make his job much easier.

A minute elapsed before the car came around the corner and nearly passed the truck. The driver slowed, putting his foot on the brake, but then apparently thought better of it and decided not to stop. The car rolled very slowly past Bolan's Ram 1500, and the attention of both men was centered on the battle-scarred vehicle.

The soldier jumped from his hiding place and sprinted to the driver's side of the car. Bolan had the Desert Eagle in his fist and he stuck the barrel against the driver's head, reaching into the car and putting the gearshift in neutral.

"Kill the engine," he said coldly.

The driver did as instructed, and one look from Bolan told the passenger to keep his hands where they were clearly visible. There didn't seem to be any question in either man's mind that the Executioner would decorate the inside of the sedan with the driver's brains if he were provoked for any reason.

Bolan quickly studied his adversaries. They were definitely European, both with dark hair and stinking of cologne and foreign cigarettes. A slight bulge beneath their suit jackets left no doubt they were armed. Bolan ordered the passenger to take out his pistol and drop it from the window while the warrior relieved the driver of his own weapon.

The Executioner studied it for a moment before he recognized its familiar lines.

The imprint on the slide read: Manufacture d'Armes Automatiques and a marking at the top of the grip confirmed Bolan's assessment. It was a Model D MAB, and it surprised Bolan that his man would be carrying such a unique weapon. It went a long way to identifying his tails, but somehow he wasn't the least bit surprised by this revelation.

"You're working for the French government," Bolan announced simply. "Why are you following me?"

Neither man said a word. They just sat there and gave him dumb looks as if they didn't understand.

Bolan smiled and shook his head, then began to speak to them in French—what little he knew. "Let's try this again. Who are you and why are you following me?"

The expression on the passenger's face revealed that he considered the Executioner a complete fool and he smirked, raising his hands as if the two men were completely innocent.

"Okay," Bolan said in English, "we can play this one of two ways. You see, this pistol here is an MAB. It fires the 7.65 mm Longue cartridge, which I know is only used by the French. That means you're French and I know who sent you. Talbot Dutré, right?"

The two men tossed each other astonished looks and Bolan knew he had them.

"You know Monsieur Dutré?" the passenger asked.

"Not personally," Bolan replied easily.

He knew the men were unarmed now so he brought the .44 Magnum hand cannon away from the driver's head, but still kept it in view. Perhaps if he took less of a hard line, he could obtain some of the answers he sought.

"Did Dutré put you onto me?"

"Yes," the driver replied, glad he no longer had the gaping muzzle of the Desert Eagle pressed to his head.

"Did you know he's working for the Armed Islamic Group?" Bolan snapped. "That he's betrayed you and your country, and arranged for the potential slaughter of thousands or maybe even millions of innocent people?"

"What do you mean?"

"The woman who was with me, Fauna."

"Yes," the driver interjected, "we were informed that it was she who was a traitor."

"And who told you that?" the Executioner shot back. "Dutré?"

"Y-yes," the driver stammered. "How did you know this?"

"Because your superiors assigned her to him in the first place. This guy is playing two ends against the middle, and I don't like it. It took me some time to put it all together. If you've been onto me since I got to Senegal then that means Dutré has, as well."

The two men began to talk it over with each other in French before the passenger—who was obviously the senior agent—spoke to Bolan again. "It is possible what you are saying is true. But we were never informed that Dutré was under suspicion. We were told to watch Calandre Fauna."

"Probably because she had her doubts about Dutré."

"This would make sense," the man replied with an emphatic nod.

Bolan handed the MAB back to the driver, who immediately holstered it, and then the Executioner secured his Desert Eagle.

The passenger opened the door, reached out to retrieve his own weapon and checked to make sure it wasn't damaged before holstering it. He turned his attention back to Bolan and smiled.

"I am Vicq," he said. He gestured to the driver and added, "He is Marmion."

Bolan nodded. "You can call me Blanski."

Vicq repeated the name before continuing. "We are sorry that this has happened. It would seem the relationship between our countries is not always as good as it should be, no?"

"No, not always. I'd be willing to bet," Bolan suggested, "that Dutré has information on my mission. Is he here in Kayes?"

"Yes, he arrived earlier this afternoon," Vicq replied.

"Will you tell me where he's at?"

"We will do more," Marmion offered. "We will take you to him."

Bolan shook his head. "No dice. I need your help with something else."

"How can we help you?" Vicq asked.

"I can deal with Dutré, but I need you to find Fauna. We had to split up after a little run-in with the GIA."

"We saw this. We are sorry that we could not interfere, but it would have caused us many problems."

"Understood, but we all stand something to gain if we can work together. The GIA-Djihad movement is as much of a threat to your people as it is mine, particularly given French interests in Algeria."

"Very well," Vicq replied. "Tell us what you need us to do."

A QUICK CHECK of his watch confirmed that dawn was only an hour away.

The Executioner knelt on the rooftop of a tall, single-story home directly across from the guest house. From his present position and the information Vicq had given him, Dutré was staying in the darkened room now directly across from his line of sight.

Kayes, like many cities in Africa, was divided into strict economic areas. Some parts boasted large houses in well-maintained neighborhoods, while others were as old, crowded and dirty as some of the ghettos in America.

Things had changed drastically from traditional times, when the vast majority of Africans were farmers and herders. They had once roamed the huge African expanse, raising crops and livestock, with manufacturing and crafts carried on as part-time activities. Increased European colonization resulted in a modern-day Africa with both a subsistent and exchange economy. Yet no white face could break tradition, and most Africans maintained commercial or cash-crop farming; it was common labor throughout the continent.

In many respects, Kayes was the center of that break between agriculture and manufacturing, given its unique geographical position. It was practically at the center of four small countries, and while trading between the African nations was limited due to commerce with industrialized nations, Kayes stood out as the place where all could bring their wares. At that time of morning, however, there was no buying or selling going on.

The Executioner knew it was time to make his move.

He was ready for action, dressed in his blacksuit with the trusty Beretta in shoulder leather and the .44 Magnum Desert Eagle riding on his right hip. He'd traded the FNC for an M-16 A-2/M-203 combination. It was a miracle to him that Jakom had even been able to secure such a weapon, but in another way it made perfect sense.

Probably any weapon was available in Africa for the right price.

Thus far Bolan had seen his opponents carrying quite an assortment of weapons—everything from Skorpions to the rarer Galil knockoffs known as R4s. It made no sense that Fuaz hadn't trained his men to become proficient with one weapon, and even less so that they all carried different kinds into combat. Interchangeable weapons in close-quarters firefights were an important facet of team operations. If a combatant ran low on ammo, he could always police up spare clips from dead comrades.

The Executioner was probably overequipped for his little visit to Talbot Dutré's hotel, but he wasn't taking chances. Bolan withdrew a grappling hook from his backpack, and with several good swings he heaved the lightweight steel across the narrow street. It landed on the roof of the two-story guest house and wrapped itself around a water standpipe.

Bolan pulled on the high-tensile rope with all of his weight, but the hook stayed firm. He tied the working end of the rope around a similar pipe on his perch, then lowered himself over the edge and quickly traversed the rope hand over hand.

Thirty seconds later, Bolan was on the very thin and unstable ledge outside the window of the sandstone guest house.

Bolan risked a light push on the casement-style window. It slid inward easily, only the smallest scraping sound issuing from the move. It was actually no louder than a sigh, but it came off to Bolan as deafening in the dead quiet of the neighborhood. The soldier stepped gingerly off the ledge and entered the room.

The interior was pitch-black, and the Executioner waited for his eyes to adjust. As furniture and walls began to take shape, he swept the area around him with the muzzle of his weapon. He calmed his breathing, every sense attuned to possible dangers that might lurk in the corners. Another minute passed, and Bolan let the numbers tick off. No threat greeted him and he finally relaxed some.

The soldier's eyes adjusted and he planned his path to a closed door on the far side before weaving his way to it. He crouched and pressed his ear to the door. The sound of snoring reached his ears, but there was something too animated about it. Experience told Bolan that people who were asleep didn't breathe that regularly—these sounds weren't tinged with those irregularities.

Someone was waiting for him.

The sound of a car's engine roaring around a corner and stopping in front of the hotel captured his attention.

Bolan retraced his steps to the window and looked down in time to see Vicq and Marmion exit their car. Fauna was with them, and she urged them toward the entrance in hushed tones. As they entered the lobby, Bolan craned his head in time to see them draw their pistols.

What the hell were they doing here?

Something didn't add up and Bolan felt a sudden instinct to—

Duck!

A dark form came through the door and began to spray the room with automatic-weapons fire. Chunks of plaster and metal shards from cheap light fixtures erupted in all directions as the Executioner pressed himself to the floor. Glass from the casement window shattered under the onslaught of the chattering weapon, and its distinctive sound left little doubt in the Executioner's mind that he was facing the business end of a Soviet-made AKM.

Bolan rolled to his stomach, set his sights just above the muzzle-flash and squeezed the trigger. Ten rounds of NATO 5.56 mm SS109 slugs rocketed into the gunman as he stopped firing his AKM. The rounds punched through his upper torso, shredding flesh on their way before they lodged in the doorjamb. Blood sprayed in all directions as his would-be assassin danced with the impacts and then collapsed to the ground.

The room was abruptly bathed in light as three newcomers burst through the door. Perhaps they thought sheer numbers would shake their adversary, but the Executioner knew no such intimidation. Bolan took them out easily, blowing the first fatigue-clad terrorist's head off before he could find target acquisition.

The second and third gunmen sought cover but tripped on each other trying to avoid Bolan's fire. The soldier triggered another burst, and two of the powerful SS109 rounds punched through the foremost terrorist and struck his counterpart. Both men crashed into each other before they hit the rough wooden floor.

Bolan flipped off the safety of the M-203 grenade launcher as he got to his knees. He hip-fired the powerful weapon, the unmistakable chug from the weapon bucking in his hands with the kick of a 12-gauge shotgun. A 40 mm smoker sailed on a straight course through the doorway and impacted a wall a few feet in the adjoining room.

Bolan knew panic would ensue among any more enemy troops within the confines of that room.

The Austrian-made Arges RP92 grenade was a modern marvel. Not only did it produce smoke, but it was also a first-rate incendiary bomb. The nose was filled with red phosphorous. A pressure-sensitive fuse was the primary ignition source with a delay element in the base. When the impact fuse struck the wall, the red phosphorous would scatter, ignite the immediate area and generate a cloud of dense smoke. If no impact occurred, the eight-second delay element would then explode and produce the same effect.

Bolan moved toward the room even as the red phosphorous began to scorch the walls and sections of the floor. A small amount landed on a tattered rug, and it burst into flames that licked at the door immediately in front of it. The acrid stench of burned gun powder, cordite and the heavy smoke permeated the air.

The Executioner came through the door in time to see two figures rushing toward another window. He triggered his weapon. The heavy-caliber NATO slugs slammed into the small of one of the terrorist's backs. The fleeing gunman dropped his weapon as he arched his back and reached behind him. He dropped to his knees, then toppled to the floor.

The other man wasn't dressed like the rest of the slain enemy troops. He was attired in tan slacks, loafers and a white satin shirt. The man yanked open the casement window and stuck one foot out. A pistol was clutched in his fists, and he turned and fired a rapid double tap in Bolan's direction. The Executioner stepped aside as he saw the gunman aiming toward him, and the crazy shots went wide of their intended target.

The black-clad warrior dropped to one knee, raised the M-16 A-2 to his shoulder and fired a single round. The ball slug punched through the gunman's hand, separating three of the fingers as his weapon went sailing out the window. The man reached for his amputated limb and screamed in agony.

He nearly toppled from his perch, but Bolan reached him before he could fall.

The Executioner grabbed the man by the collar and hauled him into the room. He dragged the guy across the floor, fighting not to breathe as he heard his wounded quarry choking on the noxious gases produced by the grenade. Bolan kicked the door out, proceeding into a narrow hallway with his prisoner in tow. Shadows loomed across the stairwell at the end of the hall.

Dropping his load, he planted one foot on the man's back as he raised his M-16 to fend off the visitors. He lowered his guard some when he saw the French trio vault the top of the steps.

Calandre Fauna pushed past Vicq and Marmion. "You are okay!"

"Stay back," the Executioner warned.

"What are you doing?" Marmion asked.

Vicq displayed an expression of horror mixed with puzzlement but he stopped short of his approach and gestured for Marmion and Fauna to do the same.

"What is wrong with you, Blanski?" Fauna asked vehemently. "Have you lost your senses?"

"What are you doing here?" Bolan demanded. "That wasn't the plan."

It was Marmion who splayed his hands in surrender. "We knew Talbot had set a trap for you."

"And how did you know that, Marmion?" Bolan asked, raising his eyebrows.

Vicq and Fauna looked at Marmion with surprise.

"Yes, how did you know this?" Fauna echoed.

Marmion suddenly reached out and grabbed Fauna, sticking the muzzle of a pistol against her head and dragging her back toward the stairs. She let out a surprised gasp, then appeared to recover her center of balance and began to hammer against him with her elbows. He was a pretty big man, something Bolan hadn't really taken note of when he'd first encountered the Frenchman in the sedan.

Vicq went for his own weapon, but Marmion wheeled the pistol in the man's direction and pulled the trigger. The report from the weapon reverberated in the confines of the hallway. The 7.65 mm slug entered Vicq's windpipe and tore out a large section of his throat.

It was the delay the Executioner needed.

He raised his M-16 and fired two rounds that connected with Marmion's skull, shattering his head and blowing his brains out the back. He toppled away from Fauna and bounced down the flight of steps.

Blood covered Fauna's face and hair, but she only stared at Bolan in shock.

The soldier lowered his weapon, then gestured toward the man struggling beneath his foot. "Is this him? Dutré?"

"Yes," she said, barely audible.

Bolan inclined his head sharply in the direction of the mounting flames. "Get some water and put that out before we burn the place down."

Fauna nodded and quickly obeyed as the Executioner focused his attention on the bleeding, quivering man underfoot. He stuck the hot muzzle of the M-16 mere inches from Dutré's cheek and pushed down with his foot to make the threat clear.

"I know you're working with the GIA," the soldier grated, "so don't even try denying it."

"I—I am—" Dutré whimpered.

"Shut up. The triggers that were stolen from my government. Are they being smuggled in the race?"

"I don't know what—"

Bolan swept the barrel to the rear of Dutré's head and triggered a 3-round burst.

"Yes, yes, yes!" the French traitor bellowed.

"Straight answers from now on, or the next three go through your brain," Bolan warned. "Who has them?"

"Nokhtari's men are bringing them," he said quickly, the fear and accent making it difficult for Bolan to understand him.

"Who?"

"Mamduh Nokhtari. Leader of the GIA. His men are posed as members of the Ramat team from Libya."

"What kind of vehicle?"

"I do not understand—"

The hiss of the flames dying from Fauna's efforts to suppress them resounded through the air as Bolan repeated the question in clearer terms.

"They have a truck...much like...your vehicle, but it is green like the flag of the Libyan country. It has white writing on it."

"Is that all of them?"

"Yes. I swear," Dutré protested. "They...plan to meet Nokhtari near the Baoucle du Baoule. He is going to fly the triggers out."

Fauna had sidled up next to Bolan and she kicked Dutré several times, swearing at him in French and spitting on him. The rage that had welled up in her colored her cheeks, and she looked both ferocious and attractive in the half light of the hallway. Bolan didn't try to stop her as she unleashed the violent outburst on her traitorous companion.

"You are vermin!" she said, cursing him again. "You don't deserve to live. You don't deserve to call yourself a Frenchman!"

"That's enough," Bolan chided her, lifting a hand to restrain her from killing the man.

Dutré was now sobbing openly.

Bolan's voice reeked with disgust. "How does Fuaz fit into this?"

"He—he is the leader of Al-Qaida."

"The Osama bin Laden coalition?"

The unfathomable truth of it now came together for the Executioner in that instant. It was even worse than he'd thought. The GIA-Djihad alliance was only the smaller part of a much larger picture. Hundreds of thousands of Arabs could be involved in the conspiracy to turn the mass-destruction weapons against a whole score of various nations. Perhaps they were planning a demonstration on a worldwide scale, and the triggers were just the beginning of a more ambitious and disastrous scheme.

"What was in it for you, Talbot? Eh?" Fauna demanded. "Was it worth it, you bastard? Was it money?"

"I only wanted to make...things good for us."

"There is no *us*."

Fauna turned and walked away, adding, "I don't care if you kill him. Go ahead."

"Let the police deal with him," Bolan said. He clubbed Dutré behind the ear with the muzzle of the rifle and knocked him unconscious.

Fauna turned at the edge of the stairs. "The police are coming. And the race will start soon. We must find the GIA terrorists carrying the triggers before they rendezvous with their people."

Bolan sighed as he walked up next to her. "I'm sorry it didn't work out for you two, Calee."

"Come," she said, descending the stairs and not looking at him. "We have work to do."

Well, she was partly right.

The Executioner had work to do.

11

Stage Three—Kayes to Burkina Faso

Mack Bolan knew who was making the delivery—the only piece of the puzzle missing was exactly where.

The next stage would take the rally through the country of Mali and all the way to the town of Bobo-Dioulasso, a huge city in the country of Burkina Faso. This was the last short stage of the rally before the longer trips of five to six hundred kilometers began. It made perfect sense for them to do this thing now.

The Executioner meant to make sure that didn't happen.

One thing seemed fairly obvious: the GIA smugglers wouldn't divert too far off the course. They had to remain inconspicuous; otherwise security for the race would get nervous and start digging a little deeper into the goings-on of the Libyan team. Intelligence coupled with Talbot Dutré's confession told Bolan that this Mamduh Nokhtari was waiting to take possession of the triggers.

They wouldn't do an open delivery, which left about a ton of options.

Bolan was convinced they would make their play somewhere along the rally route bordering the Baoucle du Baoule. It made the most sense, created the least margin for error and wouldn't attract the slightest bit of attention. Under the cover of that national forest, Nokhtari could take possession of his precious cargo and move forward with whatever maniacal scheme he'd cooked up with Hassan Fuaz.

The one thing they weren't counting on was Mack Bolan.

The soldier had decided to take off while Fauna was in the shower. He couldn't risk involving her further. Her foul-up with Dutré was bad enough. She was a liability he neither wanted nor needed at this point. He had to do this alone. Besides the fact she'd agreed to play by his rules, and he was now making the call and deciding her involvement had ended.

Her mission was over anyway. Dutré would shortly be extradited back to his country, and the French would deal heavily with him. That meant Fauna had completed her objectives, and the rest of the business with the triggers was Bolan's responsibility. He appreciated the fiery woman's tenacity—and her help this far—but when it was time to call it quits, it was time.

That's just the way it had to be.

Bolan did a quick inspection of the Ram, careful to check fluid levels and the overall integrity of the body. Nobody had asked him about the holes, although one of the officials at the stage point eyed the body damage with a raised eyebrow. He looked at Executioner with a skeptical gaze, but the soldier just smiled and kept his cool. Finally, the official waved him through and he was off.

The first part of the stage out of town was a road, so the going was easy. The "Libyan" team was driving an all-green Nissan, with the official name of the country emblazoned across its hood and along the sides in flowing Arabic script.

Bolan figured it wouldn't be too hard to find the vehicle. He'd shadow them, play the role of rally entrant until they made their move.

Then he would make his.

He passed several vehicles along the road stretching east out of Kayes. Vegetation began to thicken along the route, and the laterite became progressively softer, taking on a muddy quality that made it hard to keep the Ram under control. Bolan paced himself, easing off the accelerator at the sharper turns.

Almost an hour elapsed before he caught his first sight of the green Nissan ahead.

Bolan stayed back from the group, watching them as they negotiated the winding course. Nioro du Sahel was about eighty kilometers north of the national forest's eastern border. That put the total run between Kayes and Nioro somewhere in the area of one hundred twenty klicks, which meant the course would soon turn south.

A stand of trees now lined both sides of the trail of compressed laterite, shrouding their early morning run in misty shadows. A humid breeze whipped through the cab of the truck as Bolan pressed onward, trying to keep his quarry in site. The foliage was particularly thick through this part of the run, an almost welcome change to the dry, desert browns and reds of the course to this point.

The Executioner realized just how well organized Nokhtari was. To take possession of the triggers at this point made perfect sense, and Bolan began to feel better in his theory. Yeah, the GIA group posing as Libyans would soon make its move. Bolan rounded a slight bend and saw the Nissan was slowing considerably.

He started to brake but then thought better of it. He pushed down the accelerator and coaxed the Ram's gearshift into fifth. Bolan gained more speed and blew past the truck, which had now stopped on the side of the trail. He needed to keep up appearances and not alert his enemy. If he showed his hand too soon, it was possible he'd blow his cover and bring the whole GIA force down on top of him. He needed time to get past them and double back to their last known position.

Bolan didn't even look at the three men who climbed from the Nissan's cab as he went past. He continued down the trail, making two more turns before pulling the vehicle over and entering a break in the trees. The Executioner broke past the forestry and finally brought the truck to a halt in a shallow about fifty yards inside the forest. He checked the rearview mirror to ensure he wasn't visible from the road.

Bolan stepped out of the Ram and zipped himself out of

the racing attire to reveal the blacksuit beneath it. The breeze felt good as it cooled him, drying the sweat resulting from wearing double layers in the tropical climate. The sun wasn't even visible through the canopy of thick trees overhead, but it was still damned hot.

The soldier began to gear up for his recon. He pulled a load-bearing harness from his pack and slid into it. The trusted Beretta 93-R was still in place beneath his armpit. He elected to leave the .44 Magnum Desert Eagle and backpack behind—they would only add unnecessary weight—and picked up the M-16.

He double-checked his clips, secured two M-26 fragmentation grenades to his LBE, then began hiking in the direction of the GIA terrorists.

YAKOV KATZENELENBOGEN surrendered to a warm hug by his old friend, Lemuel Jakom.

"Yakov, it is so good to see you are well."

"Thank you, Lemuel," Katz replied. "It is good to see you, too."

The two men proceeded from the docks of Cape Verde. A small unmarked motor launch had brought Katz from a U.S. Navy aircraft carrier on layover from maneuvers in the Atlantic. It was the most expedient and inconspicuous way for him to enter the country and allowed him to bypass the hassles of toting a passel of cover documents.

When they arrived at Jakom's sedan, Katz dropped his bags into the trunk. The two men climbed into the car, and Katz didn't speak until they were alone and well away from the dock area.

"Has there been any word from Blanski?" Katz asked.

He trusted Jakom with his whole heart, but he was careful to use the Executioner's cover name.

"There has been no word," Jakom said, "which not only surprises me but worries me, as well."

"Explain."

Jakom shrugged. "I understand he has had a few skirmishes since the race began. That is the extent of my intelligence at present." He merged with the light traffic zipping along the two-lane road leading from Cape Verde to its neighbor, Dakar.

"I told him to be careful," Jakom continued. "There is rumor of an alliance between the Armed Islamic Group and Da'awa wal Djihad."

"My people have confirmed this," Katz replied. "It is no longer a rumor."

Jakom tossed his friend a befuddled look. "I thought you had retired, my friend."

"I have," Katz said. "I'm here to help Blanski. It's, well..." Katz took a moment to find the right word. "It's personal."

"He is a good man, eh?" Jakom said, chuckling and jabbing an elbow at Katz.

The Israeli warrior blocked the shot good-naturedly and returned Jakom's smile. "Yes."

"Is this joint effort by the GIA and Djihad part of Al-Qaida?"

"I believe it is," Katz replied quickly. "Members of the GIA have brought missile triggers to Africa. That, combined with the rumors of their alliance with Djihad, makes a strong case. My people believe that Nokhtari and Fuaz plan to use the triggers in nuclear weapons."

"To construct atomic bombs is a tricky business, Yakov," Jakom countered. "None of the intelligence gathered by Mossad indicates either of these factions is capable of posing a nuclear threat."

"You could be right. Nonetheless, the U.S. government is taking the threat very seriously. I believe Blanski may not know what he's getting himself into. Sure, he wants to get the triggers back. He would even destroy them, if necessary, in order to prevent Fuaz or Nokhtari from laying their hands on them." Katz cleared his throat, then added, "Our concern goes much deeper than that."

"How so?"

"If the GIA-Djihad movement is this active, there's a strong possibility they've amassed enough weapons and manpower to constitute a small army." Katz pinned Jakom with a very stern expression. "I'm not just talking about a group of fanatics. I'm talking about a sizable force of organized soldiers, supplied with military-grade equipment and determined to destroy the Western world."

"Then it is more serious than I first predicted," Jakom admitted.

"The tendency for a massive confrontation is possible."

"It would seem that the Al-Qaida movement has become stronger through quieter means. You must admit they have done this rather subtly."

"Most of the opposing powers have known about Osama bin Laden's attempts to unite the jihad movement," Katz said. "It's just that no particular nation has had the wherewithal to combat them effectively. That is because too many politicians still believe you can negotiate with terrorists."

"Yet we have learned that lesson the hard way, eh, Yakov?" Jakom said coolly.

The Israeli nodded. "That is why our government has been effective against terrorists in the Middle East."

It was true and both men knew it.

The country of Israel had proved time and again that they knew how to deal with terrorists. From the Six-Day War to the airport rescue in Tel Aviv, the Israelis continually dealt crippling blows to a myriad of terrorist organizations. Yet they had some of the largest disasters within their own borders and it got difficult sometimes to differentiate the enemy from the innocent.

No country, no matter what its policies, was immune to the tentacles of terrorist groups like the GIA and Djihad. And every time one of bin Laden's Al-Qaida groups was victorious, it not only crippled the target nation but it also maimed the world as a whole.

"Basically," Katz said, "I'm here to help Blanski with intelligence. I have to get this information to him. It could be vital to his mission, and I need you to help me track him down."

"I am at your service," Jakom replied easily. "I will assist you any way that I can."

Katz nodded in grateful acknowledgment. He could only hope that they weren't too late.

CALANDRE FAUNA was fuming.

She scolded herself for not knowing better. Why she had ever allowed herself to trust Blanski she would never know. All men were alike. Damn! They would betray you and their mother at a moment's notice. All so they could just run off to prove how manly and virile they were. The whole idea was preposterous, and the machismo of men left Fauna disgusted.

They were supposed to be a team, her and Blanski. What would have possessed him to leave without her? Now she was stranded in Kayes without transportation or help. Oh, when she finally did find the American, she would give him a lecture he wouldn't soon forget. That, and possibly several swift kicks.

With her DGSE credentials and her orders listing her as security for the race, Fauna managed to get herself inside the mobile unit that utilized state-of-the-art satellite linking. The unit was paid for by a combination of fees from entrants, sponsors and press corps. Only those with the highest clearances were allowed anywhere near the expensive equipment, and the technicians that ran the unit were quite possessive about their toys.

Fauna could practically feel the apprehension when she entered the air-conditioned semitrailer. Several heavily armed members of the Afrikaans-French corps army stood guard throughout the rig. A couple of the soldiers leered at Fauna, who was dressed in teal stretch pants and a white midriff shirt. The arms of a light nylon pullover were tied around her waist, and the soldiers were concentrating so hard on the curves that they obviously failed to spot the Browning BDA .380 tucked away beneath the folds.

Fauna didn't mind, since it saved her having to explain why she was toting a pistol around and risk having it confiscated while she was inside the trailer.

"I need to track down a vehicle," she told one of the technicians.

"Yes, madam," the technician replied in French. "Do you have the entrant's number?"

Fauna had to think about it a minute before she could recall the entire number but she rattled it off quick enough. The technician punched it into his keyboard, and the vehicle's statistics were immediately brought up. The screen held there for a second, and then flashed onto a satellite view of the entire course.

"The vehicle is being driven by Monsieur Michel Blanski?" the technician reported uncertainly. "It is currently listed in the one hundred eighty-sixth place with—"

"That's fine," Fauna cut him off. "I know most of the details. I'm just wondering if you are showing a current location."

The technician punched in several buttons, then reported, "Based on his time of departure from the checkpoint, he should be in the Baoucle du Baoule area." He tapped another button, and a picture of the truck flashed onto the screen. "This is the last photo taken at 0650 hours."

"That's the national forest area, correct?" Fauna inquired.

"Yes, miss," the man said politely.

"Thanks," Fauna said. The DGSE agent immediately left the trailer and proceeded across the near empty staging lot.

She noticed a sporty two-door foreign job mounted on large wheels parked close to the roadway. An older man was working under the hood of a vehicle. She walked casually to it, looked inside and noticed the keys were in the ignition. She hated to steal the old guy's ride, but this was a matter of security and she wasn't about to let Blanski walk into a possible trap.

Fauna opened the passenger door quietly and slipped into the car. The man was just finishing his work and putting his tools away as she climbed behind the wheel. As he dropped the hood, Fauna started the engine. The old guy—who wasn't quite as old as he'd looked—pounded his fists on the hood and told her to get out.

Fauna flashed him her best smile, then dropped the gearshift into Reverse and jammed down on the accelerator. She executed a reverse J-turn, swinging the nose into position as she braked hard, gave it gas and braked hard again. She pulled onto the road, leaving dirt and gravel in her wake.

Perhaps she could find Blanski before it was too late.

MAMDUH NOKHTARI sat in his command vehicle on the edge
of the clearing and waited impatiently for his men to arrive.
The GIA leader had already checked his watch three times in
the past five minutes, and he was forcing himself not to look
again. He was definitely going insane with this entire project.
From the beginning, it seemed that nothing had gone right.

The American agent—or whatever he was—and the
French woman were interfering with their plans every step of
the way. Nokhtari was out of contact with Fuaz, so he had no
idea if everything was proceeding as planned. Moreover, there
had been no word from Ayman since he'd taken a team of men
and the Hip-E to snuff the Western infidels once and for all.

Now the sun was climbing higher into the sky by the moment, and there was still no sign of his men.

Most of all, though, Nokhtari knew he was aggravated because he missed Hasna. She kept him warm and comforted
and, although he would never have admitted it to anyone—
including her—he loved her deeply.

It was this waiting around that was driving him mad! Yes,
that was what it had to be. Nokhtari was a man of action and
a leader of the Algerian people's revolutionary movement. He
didn't have time to sit around in some forest waiting for people. Of course, the triggers were vital in the overall plan that
would eventually free his country from the oppression of the
Westerners. Moreover, it was under the behest of Osama bin
Laden that he continue to serve in his position. So that meant
he would do what he had to—whether or not he had a choice
was really irrelevant. He would do it for his people and because bin Laden told him to.

And before long he would be in Hasna's arms again, and
that was probably the best possible reason he could think of.

The steady din of an engine pricked his ears, and he sat up
in the stolen British Land Rover. He grabbed some field
glasses and looked toward the opposite wood line. There was
a clearing that separated the two vehicles. When the delivery
vehicle reached the edge of the woods, the driver was sup-

posed to flash his lights. The Land Rover could then drive along the edge of the woods and meet them on the opposite side of the clearing. This would minimize risk of detection by aircraft that might be spying from far above.

Another minute elapsed and Nokhtari could feel his heartbeat quicken. He was anticipating the moment of truth. The triggers were at last within their grasp. In less than seventy-two hours, the GIA-Djihad alliance would strike a debilitating blow against the warmongers of Algeria, and his people would at last know freedom.

The engine sounds suddenly faded away and a moment later the signal came.

"Let's go," Nokhtari ordered his driver as he reached out the window and ordered his troops on foot to follow.

The Land Rover rumbled slowly over the uneven ground at the edge of the forest. They took the route slowly and carefully, not wishing to damage their vehicle. They would need it to get out of this blasted forest and back to Nioro du Sahel where a plane waited to take them to the laboratory.

When they had reached the rendezvous point, the troops immediately began to unload the small metal boxes. They were still contained within their radioactive casings, although they contained no actual uranium. The U.S. government was at least smart enough not to transport weapons-grade plutonium together with the triggers. That would have been the ultimate steal for the GIA-Djihad.

However, the triggers would still serve their purpose well.

The man heading the delivery team hugged Nokhtari ceremoniously but quickly.

"You have done well," Nokhtari praised him. "I am most pleased."

"Thank you, sir," the man replied.

"Did you see Ayman in Kayes?" Nokhtari asked. "I have not heard from him."

The man looked surprised, then he frowned and swallowed hard. "You have not received word?"

"No."

"He was killed in action, sir."

"What?" Nokhtari roared. "I do not believe it! How could this be?" He grabbed a handful of the man's racing suit and demanded an immediate answer.

"We heard that the helicopter was destroyed. We assumed he was aboard."

"Never assume," Nokhtari said, releasing the man's shirt. "And the American? Was he killed in the process?"

"We are not sure," the man reported. "Our escort team went to find the Frenchman who is working for you."

"Dutré?" Nokhtari interjected. "What of him?"

"We don't know, sir," the man replied. "They never returned and we had to leave. You told us that delivering the triggers was our first mission."

"And you have done well," Nokhtari replied smoothly. "As soon as we have completed our transfer, return to Kayes. I want a full report on the status of your escort team and Ayman. Is that clear?"

"Yes, sir," the man snapped.

Before either man could say another word, the engine of the Nissan abruptly exploded in a ball of red-orange flame.

12

The Executioner was blitzing the enemy!

The high-velocity HE M-383 had arced gracefully through the air, and its quarter pound of RDX/TNT filling ignited within the high-pressure cartridge to explode on impact.

When the first round was still in flight, Bolan changed positions by running parallel to the wood line as he loaded a second grenade into the M-203. He reached his desired position, dropped to one knee and set the leaf sight for one hundred yards. The rifle bucked against his shoulder as he dropped the grenade into the middle of a group of GIA soldiers running into one another in search of cover. Several bodies were thrown in every direction from the explosion, effectively trimming the force from the Land Rover by almost half its complement.

Small-arms fire began to issue from several points around the rendezvous site, but they were only guessing. A majority of the shots landed far and wide of the soldier's actual position.

Bolan continued to make his way along the perimeter of brush and thickets. He needed to get closer to the main force and put them down before they escaped with the triggers. He was already counting himself fortunate to have even found the enemy, and he wanted to make good use of this before his luck ran out.

He stopped about twenty-five yards from the two vehicles

and knelt behind the thick trunk of a palm. All fire had ceased, and Bolan could detect movement in some areas as the terrorists attempted to secure better positions. They were probably waiting for the Executioner to slip up and reveal his position. Bolan knew autofire would definitely give it away, but a grenade placed in just the right point made it much tougher.

The soldier yanked one of the M-26 frags from his LBE and pulled the pin. He tossed the explosive side-handed, then pushed deeper into the woods. He would use the cover of the explosion to draw attention as he circled on their flank. The tactic was crude but effective. The grenade detonated just as the Executioner reached his first target.

Two GIA terrorists behind a thick stand of greenery ducked their heads when the M-26 blew. He raised his M-16 A-2 to his shoulder and triggered the weapon. The 5.56 mm NATO rounds hammered at the pair, ripping holes in their backs. Bolan continued toward the truck.

There was a slight dip in the terrain. The Executioner immediately dropped and crawled to the edge in time to see several of the terrorists running the trigger cases between the Nissan and the Land Rover. A tall, muscular man dressed in desert-stripe camouflage and a scarlet turban yelled at the men in Arabic. Bolan couldn't understand him, but the tone in his voice made it clear he was telling the men to put it in high gear and complete the transfer.

To attempt a close-quarters offensive was impractical. Bolan had tried to keep the triggers intact by simply immobilizing the Nissan with a 40 mm HE round on the engine. But now all bets were off, and he was left with no other choices. The soldier had prepared himself for any eventuality, including the thought he might have to destroy the triggers. It wasn't the preferred choice, but he was ready to do so if it meant keeping them from falling into the hands of the enemy.

Bolan reached into one of the hidden pockets in his blacksuit and removed the last Arges RP92 grenade. He chambered the shell as quietly as possible, closed the M-203's breech and lined his sights on the gaping back opening of the

Nissan. He had his choice between the Land Rover and the Nissan, which was already out of commission, but he didn't have a clear shot at the British-made utility vehicle.

He just couldn't risk a miss.

The Nissan was his choice, and it appeared that about half of the specially designed cases were still inside. Bolan took a deep breath, let half out and squeezed the trigger. The chug of the M-203 resounded through the woods even as the 40 mm explosive-incendiary hit the top of the cases. A red explosion engulfed the truck, lifting it off the ground and taking about four more terrorists with it.

There were shouts and what amounted to curses as the enemy troops returned fire. Bolan crawled backward in time to avoid a storm of autofire. Rounds plowed into the foliage around him, chopping off branches and twigs from the brush or shredding thick leaves. The sounds got closer as the GIA terrorists fired and advanced on his position.

Bolan beat a hasty retreat deeper into the woods. He would need to draw them away from the Land Rover, then double back and use his remaining grenade to put the truck out of commission. He paused several times to keep his bearings, dodging enemy fire as he vied for another flanking position.

The sound of a car engine approaching drew his attention from the task. He located the source of the sound through a small stand of thickets about thirty yards away. Sunlight reflected off the fire-red body of a sports car. Bolan quickly realized he wasn't too far from the course trail, and the gunfire had probably attracted the attention of another driver. He couldn't risk any more innocent, unwary bystanders to the merciless guns of the terrorists.

Bolan raced in the direction of the vehicle and burst onto the road just as the driver was climbing from the car. It was Calandre Fauna, and she appeared both angry and relieved when she spotted him.

"Just what—"

"Drive!" Bolan ordered as he jumped into the passenger side of the car.

She didn't argue but instead climbed behind the wheel and put the still running vehicle in gear. Two terrorists suddenly appeared ahead of her from the tree line as she floored the accelerator. Bolan yanked the Beretta from its holster and thumbed the selector to 3-round bursts. The subsonic cartridges barely coughed a report as the soldier leveled his weapon out the window and fired.

The first trio of rounds took one of the terrorists high, drilling holes in his chest. Blood sprayed from the wounds, and he danced a pirouette even as the Executioner was lining up on the second GIA gunman.

The remaining man was trying to track on the vehicle with his R4 as it raced past, but Bolan beat him to the punch. The soldier triggered his weapon again. Two rounds missed, but one of the 125-grain SJHP rounds caught the terrorist in the hip, spinning him away as the roadster roared on its way. The terrorist triggered his R4, and a score of rounds blew harmlessly into the air.

Bolan holstered his weapon and slammed his fist on the dash.

"What's wrong?" Fauna asked.

"I was in the middle of trying to stop them when you showed up," the Executioner growled. "They still have about half of those triggers."

"What about the other half?"

"I had to destroy them."

Bolan put his anger in check. He had a new problem to deal with now. Circumstances had worked against him this time around. A person couldn't win them all, and the Executioner knew it. He needed to forget his anger at Fauna and formulate an alternate plan of attack. He couldn't let the GIA get away—not when he was this close.

Fauna's expression suddenly changed from fear to concern. "You're bleeding, Blanski."

Bolan looked down and noticed the small, jagged furrow in his left forearm. One of the terrorist's rounds had to have caught him, and he hadn't noticed it in the rush of adrenaline. The wound looked superficial, but it was bleeding quite a bit.

The Executioner quickly pulled a thick field dressing from a first-aid pouch on his LBE and covered the wound.

"I'll be all right," he replied. He quickly studied the interior of the vehicle and asked, "Where did you get the wheels?"

"I stole them."

"What? From whom?"

She shrugged and tossed him a mischievous smile. "Some poor driver at the staging area."

"Well, we'd better lose them fast or we're going to have security forces all over us. Stop around the next curve and park this thing in the woods."

"But how will we—?"

"Just do it. The truck's not far away."

Fauna did as instructed and the pair went EVA. She struggled to keep up with Bolan's strides as he plunged deeper into the woods and headed for the Ram.

The French agent certainly had messed up his plans. He would have to check his maps when he returned to the truck to try to figure out where the GIA would take its prize. Six triggers still meant they could launch six missiles or detonate six bombs. And to Bolan's way of thinking, that was six too many.

Lesser men would have given up at this point. Yeah, they would have shrugged their shoulders in complacency and taken a long rest. Nobody could have blamed Bolan if he'd chosen to turn this problem over to authorities. Surely they could catch Nokhtari and his men and recover the triggers once they had located the terror group.

But Mack Bolan wasn't about to turn it over to someone else and risk the possibility of the GIA making a clean getaway.

This had been his mission from the start and would continue as such until it was completed. Whatever the GIA-Djihad had planned was far from over, and Bolan meant what he'd told Fauna and the Kateb in that first night of the race. He wouldn't rest until he had completely eradicated the terrorists and laid their bones to waste in the desert.

Which brought the Executioner to another problem. Jakom had mentioned early on that there were rumors of a base somewhere in the Niger desert. That was a big area, and Bolan couldn't possibly have covered all of it. Eventually, the triggers would probably end up there—if such a base even existed—but that would be quite a distance for this Mamduh Nokhtari to travel by ground.

That meant they were probably planning to take the triggers back to Nioro du Sahel and fly them out.

When they had reached the Ram, Fauna assisted the soldier with cleaning and dressing the bullet wound from a first-aid kit in the backpack. As she worked, she spared an occasionally haughty glance into his eyes.

"Why did you leave me?" she finally asked.

Bolan didn't reply, but instead concentrated on her work.

She stopped tying a bandage and repeated, "Why?" The tone in her voice was a bit more demanding now.

"I figured your part was done," the Executioner replied with shrug. "This is my fight now. There's no reason for you to risk yourself."

"Don't you think that's my decision?" she said, turning away from the icy blue gaze and continuing her work.

"Look, we don't have time to discuss it now," the Executioner snapped. "Let's put it aside and get to business. Okay?"

Bolan checked the maps while Fauna finished bandaging the wound, and as she tied the last knot he grunted with interest.

Fauna looked over his shoulder in the cab of the Ram and asked, "What is it?"

Bolan pointed to a complete layout of Nioro du Sahel. "You see this? This is an airstrip just outside of the city. Dutré said Nokhtari was planning to fly those triggers out. I'd lay odds that's where he plans to do it."

"Then we must get to Nioro before they do."

"No," Bolan said as he put the maps away and started the engine. He looked hard at her and added, "We have to keep them from ever arriving."

JAKOM AND Katzenelenbogen turned an area inside the large garage of the Amaury Sports Organization into a veritable base of operations.

A new computer, arranged by Brognola's connections, was set up in one corner. It was directly interfaced with Kurtzman's satellite communications network and a substation database at the Pentagon. There was also a telephone connection that would allow Katz to talk to the Stony Man team directly, if need be, and offered direct access to several international authorities, including Interpol and the French Security Forces assigned to the rally.

Katz sat in front of the terminal on a rolling stool and typed furiously at the keyboard. He didn't have the manual dexterity of Kurtzman or Price, but the former commander of the greatest team of warriors ever assembled knew a trick or two in the electronics department. A sheaf of papers from the briefcase he'd brought were scattered about the worktable that Jakom had converted to a makeshift desk.

Jakom sat near Katz and perused the documents. He would occasionally make a comment or mutter to himself as he studied the wealth of information Kurtzman's team had compiled on the Armed Islamic Group, Djihad and Osama bin Laden's Al-Qaida movement in general.

"There," Katz said with satisfaction, clapping his hands. "We've got ourselves up and running."

Jakom looked up from his work and frowned. "Now all we need to do is locate Blanski."

The phone on the wall buzzed for attention, and Jakom immediately rose to answer it. "Yes?" There was a short pause and then he said, "Yes, he is right here. Please hold."

Jakom gestured to Katz, and the veteran warrior quickly picked up an earpiece and microphone linked directly into the computer. "Go ahead."

"Yakov, it's Aaron," Kurtzman's voice resounded over the line. "We just got some information over the teletype. It seems that members of the French Security Forces just arrested a man by the name of Talbot Dutré in Kayes. He's a member of the DGSE, and he was apparently there to oversee security for the race."

"The name doesn't ring any bells," Katz replied. He looked over at Jakom, who was still listening, and the man shook his head. "My friend here is drawing a blank, as well."

"Well, mission control here has some information that might help. I'll let her fill in the details."

"Hi." Price's voice came through a moment later. "From what I've gathered by my connections at DGSE, Dutré was working with another agent, one Calandre Fauna. He claims that this woman was sent to spy on him, because DGSE authorities believed he might be working for the Armed Islamic Group."

"And the plot thickens," Katz replied with raised eyebrows.

"Oh, it gets thicker," Price quipped. "Upon questioning, Dutré claims he was innocent and that it was actually Fauna who was working for Nokhtari. He also states there was a man named Blanski with Fauna, who he understood was the one she was supposed to be watching."

"How did Dutré even know about Nokhtari?" Katz asked.

"That was our question. Nobody had ever mentioned his involvement in this thing up until now. There are a ton of GIA cells working outside the main force."

"Obviously, this Dutré is lying."

"Obviously," Price agreed. "But at least we have a better idea where to find Stri—" Price caught the slip. "Well, you know what to do from here."

"Yes," Katz said simply. "I'll get on it immediately."

"Thanks, Yakov. Oh, hold the line. The chief wants to speak with you."

Katz sighed but indicated he would hold. He gestured quietly at Jakom that he would prefer to have a little privacy. The line was secure from outside sources, but the Israeli soldier wanted to protect the Stony Man organization as much as possible. Jakom didn't take any offense. He nodded with a knowing smile and hung up the extension.

Brognola's bass voice boomed over the small earpiece. "I just got off the phone with the Man."

Katz grunted when he heard this announcement. He knew exactly who Brognola was referring to—the head of the most powerful nation on Earth. Katz couldn't exactly figure how the President had become involved, since this mission was one Bolan had selected as his own.

"He was on his way to the West Coast," Brognola continued in way of explanation. "Some kind of fund-raiser appearance. Anyway, I filled him in on a few details and told him we'd gotten involved with these stolen triggers. He's very concerned."

"No reason for him to be. Striker knows exactly what he's doing."

"I agree," Brognola said in a clipped tone. "And I also know that what he needs most right now is our support."

"What's the real story here?" Katz inquired. "Are we running out of time?"

"Basically, yes." There was a long silence between them before Brognola continued with, "If we don't have results one way or the other, he's going to get the military involved."

"That could create more problems than solutions."

"I can't argue with that," Brognola replied, "but I'm just passing along the message."

"Okay, I understand. I'll find him and let him know. Don't worry."

"I get paid to worry," the big Fed stated. "Good luck, Yakov, and watch your six."

"Check that. Out here."

When the connection was broken, Katz sat back, rubbed his eyes and let out a disgusted wheeze. With the President involved now, matters might only get worse.

How much was enough? Katz wondered. How much did it take before those in power would learn to rely on the Executioner? Hadn't he always come through, no matter how insurmountable the odds might seem?

Bolan wasn't concerned with his own welfare. Some might have considered that a stupid line to take, but in the Execu-

tioner's case Katz knew it was a sense of duty. Everything re-
volved around this rather simple principle. The warrior lived
by words like duty and honor. He didn't seek medals or hon-
orariums, and he wasn't looking for anyone to erect a statue
in his memory.

No, Bolan did what he did because it's what he had to do.
Katz had never known any man quite like the Executioner. He
was a unique breed, one of a kind, the only product of that particular mold. Sure, all of the men and women of the Stony Man
group ran a close second, and all of them were as valuable as
they were expendable. But it was Bolan's cause and Bolan's
work and Bolan's skill that they *all* wished to emulate.

"You do not look pleased."

Jakom's voice broke Katz's reverie.

"That wasn't good news," Katz said. "You heard that Blanski was last seen with this Calandre Fauna in Kayes. We'd better find them and quick."

"Then I can talk to some of my connections in Kayes."

Katz looked at Jakom and showed his old friend a grateful smile.

Jakom didn't say anything to the effect, but the expression
on his face told Yakov Katzenelenbogen that he knew something was very wrong.

"We are running out of time, aren't we?"

"Yes," Katz replied slowly. "And so is Mike Blanski."

13

"There they are!" Fauna exclaimed, pointing at the Land Rover visible through the windshield of the Ram.

"Check that," the Executioner replied.

Bolan gunned the engine and geared up into fourth, fighting the steering wheel as he worked to keep the Ram on the narrow road. Earlier, he'd removed the bed tarp and tailgate to improve the truck's aerodynamics. They were traveling along the east side of the Baoucle du Baoule, heading in the direction of the Badinko Forest. The enemy Land Rover was coming toward them, probably headed for the main road that ran from Kayes to Nioro du Sahel.

There were a couple of new additions to the group—a pair of dune buggies marked with Mali flags and each carrying four men. They were all attired in the tan-and-khaki uniforms of the French Security Forces, but Bolan wasn't fooled. The warrior knew they were GIA terrorists and the ploy was simple. The Land Rover could move under the protection of FSF assigned to protect equipment and such throughout the rally.

The appearance of these troops in the Republic of Mali wasn't a bit surprising. The country was still a French colony in some sense, although it had proclaimed itself a Sudanese Republic in 1958, only to join with Senegal a year later. French was the official language and the CFA franc the main unit of currency. Nomadic Berbers roamed the desert fringes, but few of the children in the country attended school and more than eighty percent of the population was Islamic.

Nonetheless, Bolan wasn't fooled by the GIA's attempted cover. He'd already identified his enemy.

Now, he meant to destroy them.

Bolan set the Ram on a collision course with the foremost dune buggy. It was time to play "chicken," and the Executioner was counting on the fact that the GIA troops preferred personal survival to death. As they sped on a direct collision course for the terrorists, the looks on the faces in the dune buggy changed from stout professionalism to surprise.

"Hang on!" Bolan ordered as he shifted into fifth gear.

The dune buggy swerved out of the way at the last second, crashing down the small ravine on the side of the road and coming to an abrupt stop. The Ram was headed directly toward the British-made utility truck. There was no way they could survive a direct collision with the bigger vehicle, but Bolan had no intention of allowing that to happen anyway.

The soldier powered around the Land Rover and threw the Ram into a slide. The back end of the heavy-duty Ram skewed around in time to swat the side of the rear dune buggy. The lightweight vehicle jarred its occupants, setting their teeth on edge as metal wrenched and bent under the sudden collision.

Bolan bailed from the truck with the Belgian-made FNC in his hand.

"Get behind the wheel!" he ordered Fauna.

She did as instructed while the Executioner jumped into the bed of the Ram. He swung the muzzle of his weapon in the direction of the groggy dune buggy crew, snap-aimed the FNC and squeezed the trigger.

A maelstrom of 5.56 mm slugs punched through the unwary group.

Bolan directed the muzzle in a corkscrew pattern, chopping the four terrorists to bits before they could resist. The frame of the buggy was splattered with blood as the Executioner decimated his enemy, leaving them no quarter to resist or escape.

The internal mechanism of the FNC finally landed on the last round, and the bolt locked to the rear.

Bolan wheeled, slapped in a fresh magazine and slammed his hand on the metal roof. "Head for the truck!"

Fauna immediately put the big vehicle in gear and lurched away from the site of Bolan's massacre, nearly dumping him out.

Bolan steadied his FNC on the hood of the Ram, keeping as much of himself behind the rear window as possible. There wasn't much he could do to avoid being gunned down, since the glass of the truck probably wouldn't deflect more than a couple of rounds. The point here was to keep the enemy off balance and on the defensive.

Fauna pushed the Ram onward, racing to keep up with the Land Rover. The 128-hp engine was only a V-8, much less powerful in comparison to Bolan's truck, but it could achieve road speeds in excess of seventy miles per hour. It had originally been designed for use by the British army units to tow their 105 mm guns and other similar field artillery, which gave it a considerable payload and a towing capacity of more than two thousand pounds.

Bolan leaned down to yell into the window so he could be heard. "Get up on the driver!"

Fauna pushed the Ram to its limit, crossing over to the left side and working to get Bolan even with the front compartment.

"No! No!" Bolan yelled. "The driver's side. On the right, Fauna!"

Fauna nodded, the expression on her face revealing she suddenly realized her mistake. This was a British-made vehicle, and that meant the driver was on the opposite side. Being French, she should have known better, since traffic laws were similar in her country to those of Britain. Obviously, she'd spent too much time around her American counterpart lately.

Bolan's frustrations only multiplied when Fauna tried to slam the truck into the Land Rover and nearly sent him flying out of the bed. She slowed at the last second, and then skirted immediately behind the Land Rover, having to decrease speed considerably to avoid a rear-end collision.

The sounds of automatic weapons fire suddenly reached his ears.

Bolan glanced behind him to see terrorists from the other dune buggy had somehow managed to get their vehicle out of the ditch. The two terrorists in the raised rear of the cross-country vehicle were standing on their seats and firing at him over the roll bars.

The Executioner knelt against the side of the truck to steady himself and returned fire. He could have timed an M-26 in an attempt to take out his pursuers, but it was the last one he had and he planned to use it on the Land Rover. He was also running short in the ammunition department, and that didn't help matters. The warrior took careful aim and squeezed off select bursts, flipping one terrorist back into his seat.

The race continued down the road, and Bolan was lining up his sights on the other GIA gunman when he was abruptly slammed against the truck cab.

The wind was knocked from his lungs as he dropped the FNC from the shock.

Stars danced in front of his eyes, and blackout threatened to overtake him.

The Executioner managed to maintain consciousness. He turned groggily to look through the back window and saw the Land Rover had braked suddenly. The driver was obviously skilled, maneuvering the Land Rover into a one-eighty turn and braking hard.

Fauna struggled to keep the Ram on course, but Bolan knew from the fishtailing that the back end was out of control. He could feel the truck losing ground as it skidded across the soft laterite, and the wood line rushed toward them. The collision was going to be unavoidable, and the Executioner did the only thing he could. He scooped up the FNC as he bailed off the back of the Ram.

Bolan hit the ground and shoulder rolled, coming to his feet with the muzzle of his weapon ahead of him. The Land Rover halted and he could see a hand protrude from the passenger side, waving for the dune buggy to stop. The passenger jerked a thumb in Bolan's general direction, snapped a quick order and then the Land Rover continued down the road.

The Executioner whirled as he heard the roar of an engine.

The truck slammed into a tall tree. The impact crushed the engine, sending the radiator back into the block. Above the sound of the crash, Bolan thought he could detect the explosive popping sound of an airbag. He rushed to the Ram and looked inside the cab, his heart thudding in his ears.

Fauna looked at him wearily and managed a weak smile. "Sorry."

"Forget it," Bolan muttered.

Blood was dripping down her face, produced by an ugly gash in her forehead. The approaching dune buggy reminded the Executioner it was no time for regrets. He opened the door and pulled Fauna from the truck as gently as he could manage, then coaxed her in the direction of the woods. He ordered her to find cover and turned to face his attackers.

He checked the action of the FNC. It looked as if the weapon was damaged and he had no time to risk it. The warrior looked up and watched the dune buggy draw nearer as he saw the Land Rover rapidly fading to a speck on the road.

As the enemy roared down on him, Bolan unsheathed the .44 Magnum Desert Eagle and leveled it at the attackers. He squeezed the trigger successively, carefully firing round after round. The 240-grain boattail slugs rocketed on a collision course at a muzzle velocity of 1,470 feet per second.

The first one knocked out of commission was the driver, but he was close enough that it had no effect on the dune buggy's course or speed. The lone gunman standing in back was the second one to buy it. The heavy-duty Magnum round crashed through his chin and blew off the better portion of his skull. The force of the round knocked him beneath the rear roll bar and sent him tumbling from the dune buggy.

Bolan had four rounds spent before he dived aside to avoid the metal-framed monster. The passenger attempted to wres-

tle the dune buggy under control and barely avoided a collision
with the truck before managing to bring the vehicle to a stop.

The Executioner was on his feet and moving toward it.

The remaining terrorist was struggling to get his weapon
out, but it was apparently pinned under the driver's body. The
GIA soldier finally stood up in his seat and vaulted over the
low-hanging roll bars. He landed outside the driver's side
with a knife in his hand and charged Bolan, screaming at the
top of his lungs.

The Executioner raised the Desert Eagle as the terrorist
leaped at him. The .44-caliber slug punched through the man's
chest and sent him flying backward. His body landed hard on
the ground and rolled several times before coming to a stop.

Bolan turned and walked back to where he'd seen Fauna
enter the woods. He found her lying prone behind a tree. He
quickly scooped up her unconscious form and carried her to
the dune buggy. He placed her in the passenger seat, then dis-
entangled the bodies of the terrorists from the machine. He
then secured his gear from the truck and tossed it in the back
seat before squeezing behind the wheel.

Bolan turned the key and the small but powerful engine
coughed twice before coming to life. The gas gauge read
nearly full, and all the other instruments indicated the dune
buggy was still in good running order.

For a moment, he turned to study Fauna. Her condition
worried him a little. She'd been through quite a bit in the
past thirty-six hours. Perhaps allowing her to stick around
hadn't been the best idea. Nevertheless, she'd done her best
to handle the Ram, and he couldn't blame her for that. She
wasn't the most experienced but she had guts, and sometimes guts were enough.

He didn't have time to take her back to Kayes and find
medical attention. She'd probably suffered a slight concussion, and he hoped she'd regain consciousness.

Bolan put the stick into gear and whipped the vehicle
around. He laid in a course of pursuit. The Land Rover was
still out there, and so far the Executioner's luck was holding.

He decided to stick with his theory about a rendezvous in Nioro du Sahel. Where they were headed with the triggers was now a complete mystery.

He let his photographic memory take control. The rally continued south to the Mali capital of Bamako. Bamako was at least 120 miles south of their present position. The Land Rover probably had the range to make it that far, but it didn't make much sense. It seemed like a wasted trip when there was a perfectly good airstrip in Nioro.

Unless something had caused them to change their plans.

Perhaps fate had smiled on the Executioner this time and he had one last reprieve. It wouldn't take him long to catch up to the Land Rover.

Something banged his arm, distracting him from the road. He slowed a little and looked down to see a console with a lid between the front seats. He lifted a latch in the rear and flipped the lid forward. He was surprised to find a cellular phone inside a canvas bag. The phone was plugged into an interior power source, and a signal meter on its face indicated it was fully charged and functional.

At least the GIA spared no expense.

Bolan pulled the receiver from the bag. He was probably taking a risk using the enemy's equipment, but he no longer had a choice. The dune buggy would get him only so far. It didn't have anywhere near the range or overall speed of the Land Rover. Not to mention that the warrior was running low on supplies and munitions.

As he punched in a special number, he realized it was time to call in the cavalry.

And he had a damned good idea of who would lead the charge.

THE EXTENSION JANGLED on the wall of the makeshift operations center.

Katz let it ring twice before he lifted the headset to his ear and punched the answering button on the computer terminal.

"Go ahead."

There was a long silence before the Executioner's voice greeted the Phoenix Force veteran. "Is this who I think it is?"

"You bet," Katz greeted him jovially.

"What are *you* doing there?" Bolan asked with surprise. "Forget it, there's no time. Are you up to snuff on what's happening?"

"If you're talking about this little joint venture between some very nasty boys, probably. I take it you're not secure?"

"Right," the warrior confirmed for him, "which means I don't have a lot of time. I've managed to eliminate about half of what I came here for, but the other half is on a truck headed out of here."

"What's the final destination?" Katz asked, immediately picking up on the Executioner's cues.

"I was thinking Nioro du Sahel, but obviously I was wrong."

"Actually, you were correct. Our French friends managed to head that off, thanks to your little adventure in Kayes."

"Somebody talked then?"

"Very loud," Katz replied with a grin.

Mack Bolan was anything but stupid. The triggers *had* been scheduled for delivery to a plane in Nioro du Sahel, but Dutré's capture and subsequent interrogation revealed this fact. French Security Forces and an American SF unit were sent to intercept the plane immediately. Now it appeared someone had gotten word to Nokhtari and the GIA leader was following an alternate plan. The only upside there was that the Executioner now realized what was going on, and he would trail the GIA terrorists until they reached their new destination.

"I'm a little heavy right now," Bolan continued, "but not too much. I also lost my wheels."

So he had a passenger who was injured, and the truck Jakom had given him was out of the picture. He was following Nokhtari, and if he was correct about Bamako he was probably on the rally route heading south. Katz checked his watch and realized that would put the Executioner in Bamako shortly before sunset.

"Do you think you can complete the run?"

"Doubtful. I've got some mechanical issues that need fixing. Would it be possible to get someone who can handle that?"

"I'll talk to our friend," Katz replied, hoping Bolan knew he meant Jakom, "and get it taken care of. Look for them at the staging point."

"Good enough. How are things at home?"

"Same as usual."

"Pass on my regards."

"Will do. Run a good race. You hear me?"

"Sure thing. Out here."

A click resounded in Katz's ear before the line went dead. The silence that followed was somehow dreaded and mournful. Katz knew he could do nothing for the Executioner. As he'd told Brognola, this was Bolan's game and he called the ball. The best thing any of them could do was rendering whatever support that the man requested.

The dice would come up where they landed.

Jakom hadn't returned from his trip for food, so Katz placed a call to the secure line at Stony Man.

It was answered immediately by Barbara Price. "Yes?"

"I just heard from Striker," Katz said immediately.

"Is he okay?"

"Yes." Katz heard the concern in her voice, but he didn't comment on it. "He's somewhere between Kayes and Bamako. He had to destroy half of the trigger shipment, but Nokhtari apparently still has the other half. I think he's convinced the GIA is going to try to fly them out of Bamako."

"We'll send our people there right away."

"No, I don't think that's wise," Katz countered. "As a matter of fact, I don't get the impression that's what he wants at all. For one thing, I think he has that French DGSE agent with him and she's wounded. She might need medical attention, but he couldn't risk taking her back to Kayes."

"All the more reason he probably needs our help."

"Well, he also asked if I could arrange to have a new vehicle and fresh weapons waiting for him in Bamako."

"But if we send reinforcements—"

"Then we could alert the GIA that we're onto them again," Katz cut in, "and Nokhtari will just find some other way to get the triggers out."

"Maybe you're right."

"Think about it this way," Katz pressed. "Whoever tipped the GIA to the raid in Nioro du Sahel is certainly going to be watching our every move. Striker seems convinced that Nokhtari doesn't know he's tailing them. I think he wants to use the element of surprise and take them out when they least expect it."

"And what if he's the one who gets surprised?" Price suggested. "We could have sent someone to help him and we didn't."

"I know what you're trying to get at," Katz replied quietly, "but this is his show. We need to back off and let him handle it."

"I don't know." The tone in her voice didn't sound convincing.

"Why don't you run it by Hal and see what he thinks?" Katz finally said after a long and uncomfortable moment. "In the meantime, I'll do what I can on this end and keep my ears open."

"Sounds good. Just keep us apprised."

"I will. And Barbara?"

"Yes?"

"Trust me on this one," Katz said. "I know I'm right."

"I know you're right, too, Yakov. Good luck."

Katz broke the connection and then stood and stretched. He had to get the ball rolling, but he couldn't do a damned thing until Jakom returned. His longtime friend and ally had all of the connections here. Katz supposed he could call back Stony Man and put them on this, but he was afraid they would go overboard and send a whole USMC regiment to help.

That was definitely something the Executioner could do without.

As long as Katz could make some sort of arrangements before the evening, Bolan would do his part. The only question that remained in Katz's mind was in regard to the GIA-Djihad alliance. He hadn't really been afforded the opportunity to alert Bolan to the sheer numbers that this new coalition implied. An entire army of Al-Qaida terrorists, secreted somewhere in the great African deserts, and probably in possession of nuclear arms.

Well, there was nothing he could do about it. If Bolan could stop Nokhtari and the GIA before they arranged delivery to whoever was on the receiving end—and Katz was certain it was Hassan Fuaz—there would be time to go after the GIA-Djihad later. Perhaps Brognola would even activate Phoenix Force for the job. It was certainly right up their alley. Well, all he could do right now was wait for Jakom to return.

And whisper a silent prayer for Bolan's success.

14

Djado Mountains, Niger

Hassan Fuaz slammed down the satellite phone, cracking the base and nearly incapacitating it in his anger.

Once again the nameless American agent had interfered with their plans, and delivery of the triggers by the evening would now be impossible. Nokhtari wouldn't arrive with their prize until tomorrow morning, and that was the very earliest he could expect them.

In the name of God, they were on a serious timetable. Bin Laden expected results, and he expected them quickly. They had less than forty-eight hours before they were scheduled to strike at Algiers with their doomsday weapon. The triggers were supposed to have arrived within a few hours, and now they were being transported by Nokhtari to Bamako.

Moreover, initial intelligence had it that this same Western infidel had destroyed a portion of the lot, and possibly even reduced the number of triggers by half. They could probably still implement their strategy, but there would be no margin for error or faulty electronics. If they had just found some way to purchase the triggers—maybe even construct some of their own as he'd suggested—they wouldn't be in this predicament.

Fuaz stormed from his quarters and walked down the hallway to the observation room. Qaseem had sent word earlier in the day that the first effects of the new biological agent were taking effect on their test subjects. They had dubbed the new smallpox concoction as GV Strain—God's Vengeance—and initial findings indicated the new weapon was a complete success.

The trio of sick-looking individuals encapsulated in the observation chamber would have probably attested to the effectiveness of the GV strain.

Wasim, the Algerian presidential adviser, already looked as if he might lose consciousness at any moment. The red tint that indicated he had a high fever was visible even beneath his dark skin. His eyes were sunken, and his breathing had already become somewhat labored.

But Wasim seemed to be doing slightly better than the man next to him. The traitorous mole who had entered the Djihad organization—who called himself Reshef—seemed unable to stop retching. His eyes and nose were red with the fever, as well. Fuaz postulated that he would die from the infection within twelve hours if the fever didn't first cook his brain.

And then there was Admiral Robert McKarroll. Fuaz had to admit that he looked considerably healthier than his counterparts, although he was definitely affected by the virus. Perhaps the many inoculations he received in military service meant he was slightly more resilient. Certainly, the admiral once had access to the finest medical doctors in the world. Yes, that had to be it.

McKarroll studied Fuaz with a blank stare, but there was just a flicker of hatred detectable behind those blue eyes. Fuaz was just a bit disappointed—he'd hoped to catch a glimpse of the vile American suffering more under the expert work of Dr. Hasna Qaseem. Nonetheless, he knew he should give it time. Maybe he would come back in a few hours and see how much further the disease had progressed in McKarroll.

Yes, that would be nice.

Fuaz made certain that McKarroll saw him laugh before he whirled and marched smartly from the room. Although he wouldn't have openly admitted it, Fuaz felt good getting away from there. While there was certainly no chance of contamination, the Djihad leader didn't want to test fate. If he did something to anger God, the most powerful one might wish to punish him the same way he was punishing the three men on the other side of that vacuum-sealed glass.

Fuaz didn't want to find out. He wasn't afraid of anything—man or machine—but the new GV strain frightened him. There was no punishment crueler than to be forced to contract the vicious smallpox virus and die a slow, horrible death. He would have to be careful not to show such squeamish and ridiculous fears around his men, and particularly not around Qaseem.

As a matter of fact, the sooner he was inoculated against GV Strain, the better he would feel.

As Fuaz reached the area just outside of his quarters, one of his lieutenants rushed up to his side.

"What is it, Tarik?" Fuaz demanded.

"We have received a new report from our people in Bamako," Tarik reported. "They have readied the plane, as requested, but they are concerned that Colonel Nokhtari might need reinforcements. They have requested we send additional men."

"Then do what you must," Fuaz replied. "Send a legion if you have to, but take care of this American. We have already lost precious time."

"A legion?" Tarik echoed thoughtlessly. "But, sir, that's a hundred troops. I—"

"Send however many men you think you will need, Tarik!"

"Yes, sir."

The soldier turned to leave but stopped to face Fuaz when the Djihad leader beckoned him. "Don't fail me, Tarik. I am not feeling very forgiving right now."

"Yes, sir!"

Fuaz turned away from the man with a shake of his head and entered the quarters. Perhaps some time with his concubines would dissuade him from his anger. Perhaps he could turn off his troubles for a time and enjoy the pleasures and ecstasies of his women. Most of all, he could turn his mind away from the American who had caused him so much trouble.

And if the opportunity ever presented itself, he would crush the life out of the meddling Western pig with his bare hands.

CALANDRE FAUNA awoke with a start.

Bolan looked sharply in her direction and felt a small weight lifted from his shoulders. She looked no worse for the wear, and at least she was conscious now. That meant he could worry less about her and concentrate more on the rough African terrain ahead.

Fauna sat up in the dune buggy and absently reached to the bandaged wound on her forehead. She touched the area and winced with pain, then squinted her eyes against the sun, which now stood high in the sky. The air was hot, arid as usual, and the sweat and dust clung to their sticky bodies. The Executioner was conditioned to ignore their less than favorable circumstances, but he could see it bothered his counterpart.

"What happened?" she finally asked him.

"You took a pretty good blow," Bolan told her. "Lost consciousness after I sent you for cover."

"The GIA?"

"They're a step ahead of us, and I'm keeping it that way until we reach Bamako."

"Bamako?" Fauna echoed, the disbelief evident in her voice. "What the hell is going on?"

"It seems your pal, Dutré, told the FSF about the airstrip outside of Nioro. Someone apparently tipped Nokhtari to this. I managed to contact my people, and they're sending me supplies and a new set of wheels. I figured I could track the GIA to wherever they're going."

"And how did you manage to do all of this?" Fauna queried. "Have I been out a couple of days or something?"

Bolan chuckled, taken aback by her snappy wit. He opened the console lid and showed her the cellular phone. "Our friends left us a little going-away present."

"That was sweet of them."

Bolan couldn't repress a full laugh this time. Perhaps that little conk on the head had toughened the French agent up a bit. Nonetheless, a couple of high-speed chases and a few bruises didn't make her a veteran. That status was shared by few people outside of the Executioner's world, and Bolan didn't want to become too secure.

Yeah, Calandre Fauna might have beauty and brains but she was no expert. However, she was going to have to pull her own weight. Bolan wasn't here on a baby-sitting mission, and if Fauna did bid him farewell along the way, then so be it. In some respects, the Executioner felt compelled to treat her more like an innocent bystander than a willing contender.

There was something soft and gentle about Fauna beneath that cool French exterior, and the warrior found himself reluctant to be too hard on her. Still, she knew the risks and she'd opted to accompany him anyway. For that he both admired her and considered her a fool.

"What did you have in mind for us next?" she asked.

"Much of it will depend on what *they* do," he replied, nodding at the road ahead to indicate their invisible quarry.

"What makes you think they'll try to fly the triggers out of Bamako?"

"It's the only thing that makes sense. There's nothing really between Kayes and there. Bafoulabé is to the west but it's too small. They'd attract all kinds of attention there."

"They might try for Kita," Fauna suggested.

"I considered that," Bolan replied dryly, "and it is a possibility. But I wouldn't hedge any bets on it. Bamako makes the most sense."

"Why?"

"It's crowded. More than half a million people live there, while the country is poor with little in the way of industry. The only reasonable place to fly a plane into or out of Mali airspace is Bamako."

"I see your point," Fauna finally said.

She fell silent and laid her head back against the highback headrest. It wasn't nearly as comfortable as the Ram, but she was probably still feeling the effects of her head injury. She was damned lucky to be alive, considering the seriousness of her accident. Maybe she was a good-luck charm for the Executioner.

Bolan quickly dismissed that idea. He'd probably been safer when she wasn't around. At least the mystery of who was trying to kill her was solved. With Dutré locked away in some nasty African jail while he awaited extradition back to France, Bolan could feel pretty secure in the thought that no one else would try to terminate his French ally. That left him to fight the GIA-Djihad problem.

And the Executioner wouldn't have had it any other way.

THE CITY OF Bamako was a beehive of activity—mostly hustle and bustle from the rally entrants and race crews who had been in and out throughout the course of the day. The actual bivouac that marked the end of the stage was at Bobo-Dioulasso in the country of Burkina Faso. Nonetheless, it wouldn't have been the Paris-Dakar-Cairo Rally if there wasn't a stop in Bamako.

Night was falling on the Mali capital, and there was still a considerable race ahead for most.

Bolan maneuvered the dune buggy through the side streets, careful to keep away from the heavily populated areas. The map indicated the small airport in Bamako was on the far side of the city, actually away from the general populace. That wasn't a bit surprising since it wasn't very large, and the air traffic into and out of the country was almost nothing. Aside from smaller planes and the occasional commercial jet, there probably was no air traffic.

Not that an oil sheikh or some royal sultan from a neighboring country didn't fly in now and again. Although Bamako was a city that generated most of its income from merchant sales to the Berbers and landholders of the Mali Republic, it did some trade with foreign countries, including the U.S. and most European countries. Industry wasn't really its strong point. Bamako thrived due to the sale of natural goods and tourism.

Bolan managed to slip into the secured staging area from the back way. The place wasn't really that secure, since most stops were only for thirty minutes to an hour. Some of the race crews probably wouldn't stop at all. Cheers were heard in the distance as those who decided to continue on through were encouraged by the throngs that lined the main thoroughfare.

The Executioner found a spot between two huge trucks and killed the engine. He turned in his seat to face Fauna, who was watching him with wide-eyed expectation.

"Now listen to me," he cautioned her. "Stay here. Don't go anywhere, don't do anything. Just wait here for me."

"Well, could I at least find a bathroom?" she countered.

"Yeah, but go straight there and straight back. No sight-seeing."

Bolan hated having to talk to Fauna as if she were a child, but he didn't have any choice. The woman was stubborn beyond control, and she didn't listen to a thing he said most of the time.

The warrior shed his LBE and pulled off the top half of his blacksuit before setting off in search of his contact. He knew whoever he was meeting would have been given a description. That was if Katz had managed to pull it off. Actually, he was bit surprised to have reached the grizzled Israeli, albeit comforted by the fact he had someone of that character backing him up.

No, there wasn't a thing to worry about. If Katz was behind it—or Stony Man—he knew he'd find his contact and get what he'd asked for.

Bolan walked along the fruit stands and stopped to purchase a couple of kumquats, a lamb stick and some bread. He realized he hadn't eaten since the stop at the oasis. The old toothless lady in native garb happily bagged the food for him. She was even happier when he paid her over ten American dollars, more than she probably could have earned in a whole week. She smiled and bowed, grabbing his hand and kissing his fingers.

The Executioner took back his hand, held up the food in a gesture of thanks, then continued along the stalls. He needed to look inconspicuous—just another entrant taking a break and doing a little window-shopping for the wife back home.

A shadow suddenly loomed above him as he reached the end of the stalls. The guy was big and ugly. Black eyes and a dark, scarred face studied Bolan with one of the meanest expressions he'd ever seen. Actually, he looked as if he wanted to wrap his hands around the warrior's throat and choke him to death. In the next moment, he tried.

Bolan stepped under the outstretched arms of the behemoth that lunged at him and planted a heel against the side of the man's knee. The human tower howled in pain, but the kick wasn't strong enough to take the leg out from under him. The Executioner was surprised he hadn't dropped the man, but then his many years of experience had taught him something.

Never try to take out an opponent bigger than you with one shot.

Especially when that opponent was carrying an equally big knife, as this one now was. Bolan reached for the Ka-bar fighting knife, then remembered he'd shed his LBE. He dropped the bag of food and lowered his center of balance, his hands in front of him.

The big monster charged again, but the Executioner was ready.

He dropped to one knee as the man slashed forward with the knife. Bolan grabbed the man's wrist and locked his arm in place. He jammed an elbow into the attacker's gut, and air rushed from the giant's lungs in a long wheeze. Bolan maintained his lock on the arm holding the knife, twisted into position and tossed the knife wielder over his shoulders.

The big Arab landed hard on his back, and more air escaped from his already ravaged lungs. The guy tried to suck in life-giving oxygen, but he didn't have the opportunity. Bolan rose, stomped on the guy's wrist, then drove his knee into the man's sternum to the unmistakable sound of ribs breaking.

Bolan retrieved the knife, shoving it into his belt, then

quickly picked up his bag and split under the scrutiny of a group of onlookers who had stopped to watch the fight. By the time the police had sorted it out, the Executioner planned to be long gone. He skirted the crowds and headed back toward the dune buggy.

"Mr. Blanski?" a voice to his right whispered.

Bolan stopped and dropped his hand onto the hilt of the knife. Shadows danced across one of the vehicles parked at the edge of the staging area. The solider realized he'd found his contact. At least, he hoped he had.

"Are you Mr. Blanski?" the man asked.

"Yeah," Bolan replied. "Who are you?"

"Ah," the guy said, ignoring Bolan as he stepped from the shadows. He was American—or at least Caucasian—and very short. The rolls of fat looked totally out of place beneath the fancy suit and silk tie that was loosely knotted.

"Ah, you are just as Mr. Jakom and Mr. Gray described you." He held out his hand and Bolan shook it. It was surprisingly dry. "You may call me Normal. If you'll follow me, I have the items you requested."

"Did you find me a car?" Bolan asked, fighting to stifle a smile. This guy appeared to be anything but normal.

Normal smiled. "If you'll just follow me, Mr. Blanski, we can go where things will be more private."

"Some reason we can't do this right here?" Bolan asked, raising his eyebrows as his eyes tracked the area for an unseen threat.

"I don't suppose, except that there's quite a bit of it. And I don't think I could park your vehicle in this small of a space."

Bolan nodded and gestured for Normal to lead.

He led the Executioner along the edge of the staging area for several minutes, skirting the backs of the vending stalls. In many respects, it reminded Bolan of the back side of a carnival. Just like the ones he'd played around as a kid back in Pittsfield. He couldn't recall the number of girlfriends he'd made out with under similar conditions, but he also knew it was a very long time ago.

Life had been much simpler as a kid—Bolan was puzzled that he remembered it now.

The two men finally reached the edge of the lot, and Normal continued across a small field that terminated at a small pond. The guy turned and walked along the edge of the pond until he reached a huge shed. A few turns of a combination lock and they were soon inside.

Normal closed the door and the place was in complete darkness. The Executioner cursed silently. He never should have allowed himself to get into a position where he could be ambushed. The lights came on and Bolan sighed with relief. In the center of the shed sat a brand-new M-998 High-Mobility Multipurpose Wheeled Vehicle.

The Hummer was a 4X4—a dream come true in this terrain. Under the hood was a 150-hp Detroit Diesel V-8 capable of a 2,500-pound payload on a sixty percent grade. The elevated air-ram in the hood told Bolan he was looking at a commercial model, which meant the engine had a turbocharger installed. It also sported an independent, double A-arm suspension with quad mounted coil springs and a front stabilizer bar.

Nice work, Katz, Bolan thought.

"In back," Normal announced, tapping the rear storage compartment, "I've equipped you with an MP-5 A-3, a case of M-26 frags, one M-72 A-2 LAW and five thousand rounds of 9 mm ammunition. There are also spare clips for a Beretta and a .44 Magnum Desert Eagle. Mr. Gray indicated that these were your preferred weapons."

"Mr. Gray was right," Bolan replied.

"If you'll not be requiring anything else," Normal said, "I must get back to my dinner."

Bolan nodded and Normal headed for the door. "I'll get the overhead door once the lights are off. Good luck, Mr. Blanski."

The soldier nodded, then walked to the Hummer. He climbed behind the wheel and started the ignition. The lights suddenly went out and the door began to rise ahead of him, exposing the twinkling lights of the city.

He would have just enough time to get back to the dune buggy and pick up Fauna before heading to the airstrip.

It was time for him to take the fight to the enemy.

15

The darkened airstrip stretched out straight and narrow before the Executioner like a knife edge.

Parked at one end of the runway was a desert-striped Mil Mi-6 Hook. It was marked with the red, white and black flag of the Egyptian air force. Its similarity to the Hip-E Bolan encountered in Kayes left little doubt it was Hassan Fuaz's Djihad forces. It was also possible the triggers were already aboard, since there was little activity around the helicopter.

Bolan viewed the perimeter through a set of NVD goggles he'd found stashed in the Hummer. He lay prone on a small ridge that afforded a view of the entire area. The lights of Bamako twinkled in the distance, and a hot wind blew across his back.

Calandre Fauna was positioned next to him. He passed the binoculars to her and pointed at the Hook.

"That's it?" she asked. "That's what they're flying the triggers out in?"

"Probably," Bolan assented.

"Are the triggers on board?"

"I don't know," he admitted quietly. "I was asking myself the same question. If they aren't, it would explain why the pilots are just sitting there. And if they are, then I'm left to wonder what they're waiting for."

"Wait a minute," Fauna said, swinging the NVD goggles to her right. "There's someone coming toward the chopper."

She passed the binoculars to him and pointed in the direction of headlights. The vehicle was moving at a pretty good speed, and when Bolan looked at it through magnification, he saw the familiar outlines of the British Land Rover through the green haze of the infrared enhancement.

"That's it," Bolan announced. "That's the vehicle the triggers were in."

He dropped the binoculars and doubled-timed to the Hummer. He pulled a wooden crate from the rear as Fauna sidled up next to him.

A quick inspection of its contents revealed that Normal had been mistaken. The crate actually contained a LAW 80, the UK's version of a disposable rocket launcher. Unlike its American predecessor, this particular weapon had a 94 mm warhead capable of penetrating tank armor. Bolan would have preferred an RPG, or possibly even an M-47 Dragon. Some kind of explosive device with multiple-round capability would have been better, given the fact he had no nighttime targeting system.

This time he only had one shot, and he would have to make it count.

"I'm going to get closer."

"Closer?" Fauna asked with disbelief.

He looked sharply at her. "Listen, destroying those triggers has become the priority. But I also think that chopper is headed back to wherever it came from. Maybe this desert base everyone keeps talking about."

"And what do you expect me to do," Fauna demanded, "while you go flitting about Africa in hopes of finding this base?"

"I want you to get back to Bamako." Bolan quickly wrote the number to Jakom's place. "Get in touch with a man at this number by the name of Mr. Gray. Tell him what's happened and what I'm planning. He'll know what to do."

"I want to go with you, Blanski," Fauna protested.

"No dice."

Bolan stopped packing additional clips into the pouches of

his LBE and pockets of his blacksuit and gripped her shoulders. "The best way you can help me is to do what I ask," he said gently. "Got it?"

"All right," she finally said, reaching up and pulling him fiercely to her. She planted a passionate kiss on him. When they had parted, with their lips only inches apart and her still gripping his hair, her voice was a choked whisper. "But don't go and get yourself killed, Mike. I still owe you for saving my life."

Bolan smiled, nodded once, then stuffed the last of the clips into his belt. When that was completed, he grabbed the LAW and sprinted off in the direction of the airstrip.

He quickly negotiated the rocky terrain and hit the bottom of the ridge running. He could already see that the Land Rover had stopped by the Mil Mi-6. The GIA terrorists were in the process of preparing to transfer the triggers into the rear-loading cargo area under the watchful eye of their leader and one of the pilots.

Bolan reached a point about seventy yards from the rendezvous site. The terrorists had left the lights of the Land Rover on, and that gave Bolan plenty of illumination while it still kept him completely invisible. Sometimes it was the tactical errors that allowed the Executioner to make it seem easier than it was. Nonetheless, he wasn't about to look a gift horse in the mouth.

He primed the LAW, knelt to steady his position and lifted the rocket launcher to his shoulder. He set his sight just above the Land Rover so that the warhead would strike the side of the truck. He didn't want to damage the chopper—the Hook helicopter was his ride out of here.

Taking a deep breath, he let it out as he squeezed the trigger. The LAW fired its five tracer rounds, ensuring Bolan was on target and allowing him to adjust his aim slightly. This added the effect of paralyzing the enemy for the split second it would take before the rocket deployed.

The warhead launched from the LAW and ran a straight course to the Land Rover. It exploded on impact, blowing the vehicle sky high and raining flaming pieces of molten metal on the confused terrorists. Secondary explosions ignited in the engine, and the Land Rover became an almost instantaneous heap of jagged, smoking junk.

Bolan rushed the GIA position before the terrorists could react. He hit the tarmac and raced toward the chopper, the MP-5 A-3 up and ready to meet resistance.

Two terrorists spotted the black-clad wraith rushing toward them and tried to bring their Skorpion machine pistols into play. Bolan cut them down with a sustained burst from the H&K submachine gun. The weapon spit 9 mm hollowpoints that perforated their heads and chests. Bolan was past them before their bodies hit the tarmac.

Another trio of terrorists lay near the flaming wreckage of the Land Rover, their bodies ripped open and seared by the explosion. Bolan swept the area with the muzzle of the subgun, but there was no further resistance.

The Executioner turned to inspect the chopper. It appeared to be in working order and unharmed by the destruction of the Land Rover. His assessment was confirmed when the rotors began to move and the engines on the powerful assault helicopter whined with ignition.

Bolan saw the cargo bed rising in the rear and rushed toward it as the chopper powered up. He rolled through the opening in time to see a tall, muscular Arab charge him from the front of the chopper. The Executioner saw he wore a scarlet turban—the man from the forest battle that he'd marked as the leader.

The soldier had time to shoot his attacker, but he wanted him alive. If he was dealing with a senior member of the Armed Islamic Group, he knew they might be able to lead him to the rumored stronghold. He would have to defeat this one hand to hand.

Bolan brought the muzzle of his MP-5 A-3 up and under the man's chin. The impact broke one of his opponent's teeth and knocked him backward. The Executioner stepped forward and reached for his wounded enemy, but the guy wasn't as injured as he appeared to be.

The Arab grabbed Bolan's wrist, twisted him outward and

swept his leg out from under him. The soldier landed on the hard metal floor of the chopper, his H&K flying from his hand. The Arab reached behind him and drew a knife. He slashed downward, but the Executioner caught the move in time, stopping the blade mere inches from his throat.

Bolan grabbed his attacker's knife arm and wrenched it at the wrist. He twisted his upper torso inward, arching his back and managing to wrap his leg around the Arab's locked arm. Bolan got to his knees, the weight and force of the move slamming his opponent headfirst to the ground. The Executioner was now kneeling next to the Arab terrorist, with the man's arm pinned between his legs. He pulled upward behind him and snapped the enemy's wrist.

The terrorist yelped with the pain and the knife clattered to the deck boards.

Bolan released his hold and unleathered the Beretta. He pressed the muzzle to the side of the terrorist's head before getting to his feet.

The vibrations increased as the helicopter lifted off the ground. The pilots obviously had no idea Bolan was aboard, and that would make things much easier. Once they had reached their destination, he'd let them in on his little secret. For the moment, he would see what information he could glean from his prisoner.

"Do you speak English?" he demanded, pressing the muzzle tighter against the man's temple.

"Yes," the Arab hissed.

"What's your name?"

"I am Colonel Mamduh Nokhtari," he replied. "Leader of the Armed Islamic Group and freedom fighter in the Al-Qaida army."

"You made a mistake starting this thing, Nokhtari," Bolan said. "I'm here to finish it."

Nokhtari laughed scornfully. "It is you who have made the mistake, Westerner. If you murder me, my people will avenge my memory. You have not stopped us. We were expecting this from you."

Bolan furrowed his eyebrows. "What are you saying?"

"Your precious triggers are not here. You did not destroy them." Nokhtari sat back on his heels, cradling his injured limb. "They are probably being delivered even as we speak."

Bolan could not believe what he was hearing. If Nokhtari was telling the truth, then they had somehow managed the transfer before they ever reached Bamako. The Land Rover had been nothing more than a decoy, and he'd fallen for it.

Damn! That meant he was headed right into the heart of the lion's den.

And there was a good chance that the forces of the GIA-Djihad would be expecting him.

YAKOV Katzenelenbogen stepped from the French SA 330 Puma helicopter and studied the scene in front of him.

At the airfield on the southern side of Nioro du Sahel was parked an old Russian-made Ilyushin cargo plane. It was the same plane originally intended by the Djihad to take possession of the triggers, but the FSF had put the nix on that. French army troops now had about twenty of the terrorists at bay. They were grouped together to one side while more FSF commandos thoroughly searched the plane.

Thanks to some quick work on the part of Stony Man, Katz had official sanctions in his role of "adviser"—his clearance came right from the Oval Office. U.S. interests were to be protected, as well, and with one phone call by the President of the U.S. to the Mali president, Katz was granted an opportunity to interrogate the prisoners. He needed some answers, including where he could find the GIA-Djihad base of operations.

Lemuel Jakom had stayed behind to hold the fort in case Bolan called in again. Katz was very concerned about the Executioner. According to initial reports, the CIA agent called Normal confirmed he'd delivered a vehicle and weapons to "Blanski," but since then there had been no word. Katz was certain that wherever the Executioner was, he was taking the fight to the enemy.

But there was only a small consolation in that thought.

Katz ambled stiffly over to one of the French security troops and inquired on where the commanding officer could be found. The soldier had to look around for a moment before pointing to a man standing near the rear of the Ilyushin. Katz nodded his thanks and immediately approached the FSF officer in charge.

"You're the commanding officer here?" Katz asked, slipping easily into French.

The man nodded. "Yes, sir, I am. And who are you?"

"My name is Mr. Gray. I am special envoy to the United States government, and assistant adviser for the National Security Council."

"And?" the man asked, raising his eyebrows.

He was tall and lean in his olive drab uniform, beret and black boots. A pistol belt encircled his waist and gold tabs adorned his epaulettes. The guy was an officer for the French paratroopers, one of France's special warfare units. That meant he was no idiot and Katz knew he'd have to treat the guy with some respect if he wanted any cooperation in return.

"Your superiors did not tell you I was coming?" Katz asked incredulously. He slapped the side of his head and said, "Why does this always happen to me? Sometimes these bureaucrats just can't seem to get it right."

The officer now looked sympathetic and a smile crossed his lips. He offered his hand and said, "I am Commander Gautier Auriville, Third French Paratrooper Regiment, assigned to security forces for the Paris-Dakar-Cairo Rally."

"Pleasure," Katz said, returning the man's smile. "Arrangements were supposed to be made for me to question the head of this organization. My people are very concerned for the safety of not only the rally entrants but the American interests here."

"I think I can arrange for that," Auriville replied.

The French paratrooper signaled to one of his men, and the guy double-timed over to where they stood. He snapped a smart salute, which Auriville returned quickly, then waited for his instructions.

"Lieutenant, this is Monsieur—" he paused to look at Katz, who repeated his name "—Monsieur Gray of the U.S. National Security Council. He wishes to speak with the man we identified as the leader of this band. Please have the prisoner brought to him at our command post. On the double!"

"Yes, sir!" the man replied, saluting again before doing a quick about-face and running for the group of prisoners.

Katz couldn't suppress a small grin, and he noticed Auriville's questioning gaze. "Your men are very passionate about their work, Commander. I am most impressed. You run a tight outfit here."

Auriville bowed, gratified by the comment. "Thank you, sir. You look as if you were once a military man yourself. Did you ever serve in the armed forces of your country?"

"Oh, yes," Katz murmured. "I served for a very long time."

"It shows," Auriville replied with a courteous nod. "Take all the time you need with their leader, Mr. Gray. I can assure you, it will be a very long time before any of these men ever see the light of day again."

"I'm sure," Katz replied easily, shaking the man's hand. "Thank you, Commander."

Auriville had his assistant escort Katz to their makeshift command post, a small outbuilding that stood by itself nearby. Katz lit a cigarette, but he didn't have to wait long. The guard suddenly appeared with a manacled prisoner in tow. The GIA terrorist didn't look extraordinary, especially not in his battered condition. It appeared that the French Security Forces had been a little tough on him.

The guard shoved the prisoner into a chair. Katz thanked the man and then indicated he could leave. The command post was otherwise deserted. Katz shook another cigarette from the pack and offered it to the Arab. The man took it between his lips and Katz lit it for him. When he appeared to soften some,

Katz switched as easily to the prisoner's language as he had from English to French.

"What is your name?" Katz asked quietly.

"I am Akim Marid, soldier in the Al-Qaida and a revolutionary for Islam. And that is all I will tell you."

"No, Marid," Katz replied coldly, "that is not all you will tell me."

Marid spit on the ground at Katz's feet, but the Israeli looked at the glob and shrugged indifferently.

"You're about to be hauled away by those French paratroopers out there. They're going to fly you back to France, lock you up and throw away the key."

"If that is God's will, or the cost of fighting for my people, then so be it."

"You ever been in a French prison, Marid?" Katz asked, keeping his tone as conversational as possible.

"No," came the murmured reply.

Katz took a drag of his cigarette, stubbed it out under his boot and then leaned very close to Marid. "You'll wish they had just saved themselves the trouble and hanged you after about one day there."

"I am not frightened of prison."

"No?" Katz sat up and smiled. "What about bin Laden. Are you afraid of bin Laden? Or Hassan Fuaz?"

Marid's expression paled some, and Katz knew he'd found his weak link.

"You talk brave now," Katz said, standing up and walking behind Marid. "But what makes you think that Fuaz or bin Laden himself won't be able to reach you in prison. They will assume you talked, even if you haven't."

"These are lies. All lies." Katz could hear the nervousness in Marid's voice.

"Fine," the Israeli commando replied. "They're all lies. I wonder what you'll think when they rescue you from the French. Will you be indebted to them? Probably not after they permanently maim you by poking out your eyes and cutting out your tongue because you failed in your mission."

Marid was sweating now.

Time to nail the lid on the coffin. "And what about your family? Do you really think they will allow them to live?"

"They would not harm my family!" Marid shouted.

"That's what you think," Katz goaded, yelling at him now to get his attention. "Fuaz kills his own kind, man! He guns down dozens of your people and calls it acceptable because he happened to kill a hundred Westerners or Europeans or Jews in the process! He blows up buses full of children because there might have been one or two Americans aboard!"

"I have never seen him kill our children," Marid insisted.

"Oh, no? Would you like me to list some of the things he's done? How about last month? The tour group in Tiaret."

Marid turned and looked at Katz with a horrified expression. "I am from Tiaret. Hassan had nothing to do with that!"

"No, but Colonel Mamduh Nokhtari did. And he did it under Fuaz's orders. Do you think Fuaz is going to allow anyone to trace the responsibility directly back to him? Don't be a fool."

"Hassan ordered this?" Marid echoed.

Katz nodded.

Marid looked away and said, "I do not believe you."

"It doesn't matter whether you believe me or not," Katz said. "I know the truth, and now that you know it you'll probably die for it. But there may still be a chance to save yourself."

"How?" Marid actually looked interested now.

"Tell me where your base is. We know there's a base somewhere in the Ténéré Desert. We also know it's only a matter of time before we find it. But if you tell me, I can arrange for you to remain here in Africa. We can cover your identity, and you can return to Algeria under the amnesty. You could escape with your family."

"They will kill me if I tell you this."

"They're going to kill you anyway," Katz reminded him.

"At least you will have a chance to escape. To go away some-where without them finding you. In a French prison, you're surely dead."

"I will tell you," Marid finally conceded. "But only if you will protect my family."

"I'm a man of my word," Katz replied. "I will do what I can to save your family."

Marid nodded and then gave Katz the coordinates. The Is-raeli veteran wrote it down to make sure there were no mis-takes, and he was completing his task when one of the SA 330 Puma pilots rushed through the front door.

"Monsieur Gray? There is a phone call for you on the chopper's ground link," the pilot said in English.

Katz nodded to the man, indicated to Marid that he would make the necessary arrangements, then left the guard shack. He really would do what he could for Marid. The guy wasn't any kind of real revolutionary. He was obviously just another one of Fuaz's stooges, a third hand who wore a uniform and toted a rifle and called it freedom fighting.

The very thought of such manipulation by Fuaz, bin Laden and the Al-Qaida movement angered Katz.

"Gray, here," he said, snatching up the phone in the chopper.

"Mr. Gray?" It was Jakom.

"Yes, what do you need?"

"There is a woman on the phone here. She said that she was told to call you at the request of our friend in Bamako. It seems that he has procured a chopper and he is headed in your direction. Presumably, he's searching for the same thing we are."

"Is she on the phone now?"

"Yes, I am here," came a woman's French voice. Katz knew he had to be talking with Calandre Fauna.

"Where are you?" Katz asked.

"I am in Bamako," she said. "I was asked to find you and pass on the message that your friend, and mine, has gone to search for the base. He destroyed the rest of the merchandise, and he's now preparing for a full assault by himself."

"He won't be alone, I can assure you," Katz said. "We know where he's going, and I'm about to make arrangements to assist him."

"Can you pick me up before you do?"

"Yes, it will not take us that long. Give me an hour and I'll be there."

"Hurry, Mr. Gray," Fauna pleaded. "We don't have much time left."

"I know," Katz replied grimly.

16

Mack Bolan could sense the Mil Mi-6 Hook chopper had begun its descent.

He had no idea what to expect, but he would rely on the ignorance of the pilots and hope his plan worked. The warrior now had Nokhtari bound, gagged and secured in a large cargo container. Throughout the almost two-hour trip, he'd discovered the large wood box contained tons of 7.62 mm NATO ammunition and 50-round box magazines for a pair of brand-new Galil ARs stored in a separate crate.

Several more crates contained a hundred Russian-made RGN hand grenades. From the looks of them, the Executioner surmised that Fuaz had probably stolen the munitions from the Russians, although an outright purchase wouldn't have been beyond the realm of possibility. Bolan knew very little about the RGN, but he was aware it contained an RDX/Wax filling and was designed to blow upon impact or after a three second time delay.

In either case, these weapons were a stroke of fortune and the soldier saw using them as a sort of poetic justice.

Bolan had taken advantage of the flight time to equip himself for war, and he was in the process of loading and storing the last clip when the chopper set down. A whine in the rotors signaled the pilots powering down the engines, and a few minutes later they emerged from the cockpit.

The Executioner had slung one of the Galils across his back and he directed the muzzle of the other one at the stunned pair.

"Who's in charge?" Bolan asked in his very limited Arabic.

"I am," replied the smallest of the pair.

"Strip. Both of you," he ordered them.

The two looked at one another uncertainly, but they quickly complied when Bolan waved the Galil at them for emphasis. Within a minute, the pair stood in the middle of the chopper stripped to nothing but ill-fitting boxer shorts.

Bolan nodded toward them to continue, but the men were hesitant. He stepped forward and raised the Galil to his shoulder, the muzzle set just a few yards from the leader's head. The message apparently became much clearer then, and the two men finished pulling off their boxers. Their expressions were quite humorous at that moment, standing there in their birthday suits, but Bolan knew it was no time for levity.

He waved them over to the fuselage and made them sit on top of Mamduh Nokhtari's veritable wood coffin. He had them reach up with opposing hands and grab a rail welded to the fuselage. He quickly tied their hands together with the heavy twine that had encircled the grenade boxes, then tied the opposing hands and feet.

They wouldn't be going anywhere soon.

With his task of neutralizing the chopper crew completed, Bolan lowered the rear ramp as he took a quick look out a starboard window. At first, nothing happened. They were in the middle of nowhere. There was no sign of movement visible—human or otherwise—in any direction.

But then the earth erupted and a hole appeared in the sand. Suddenly a group of six Djihad terrorists clad in the familiar desert camouflage and purple scarves scurried from the hole like a batch of cockroaches.

So that was it—their base of operations was buried!

The Executioner flipped the selector to center position, which allowed for full-auto fire. The Galil AR didn't have a 3-round-burst capability, but Bolan could forgive that. It was still a tough, reliable weapon and recognized as one of the most battle-worthy assault rifles in the world. There was no question the Israelis knew what they were doing when it came to the manufacture of firearms, and the Galil was no exception.

Bolan waited until the squad of men were close to the chopper, and then opened the side door. He quietly moved to the rear and around the fuselage while the unwary troops moved toward the door. The ruse worked and they were taken completely off guard.

The Executioner triggered the Galil in short, controlled bursts—and the 7.62 mm slugs took the two closest terrorists in their midsections, spraying their counterparts with blood. One of the rounds ricocheted off the chopper and caught a third Djihad gunman in the eye. The two that were gut-shot tumbled into each other before hitting the ground, and the third terrorist jumped away, dropping his rifle and holding his wounded face in his hands.

The one closest to the door was the most surprised, looking from Bolan to his naked comrades. He wasn't prepared for a firefight and so he was the next one to fall under the Executioner's deadly marksmanship.

Bolan fired one-handed at the remaining two terrorists, who now jumped to the sand and rolled away from the carnage. The warrior rushed toward the opening as he pulled a grenade from a slit pocket in his blacksuit and yanked the pin. Bolan let the grenade go as he reached the base entrance, dropping it closely midway between the two prone terrorists. There was no way for them to escape—the RGN exploded on impact and sent superheated fragments into tender flesh.

The Executioner descended the narrow steps and entered the confines of the base. He had absolutely no way of knowing where he was or the kind of numbers he might face, but there wasn't time to worry about that. He needed to find the triggers and destroy them, and he couldn't let anyone get in his way. Mack Bolan was now on a hellfire crusade to stop the Al-Qaida movement.

And he intended to win.

KATZENELENBOGEN WAS in direct contact with Stony Man as the French Puma helicopter set down on the airstrip outside of Bamako.

"We have the location of the Al-Qaida base," Katz told Brognola.

Despite the fact they were thousands of miles away, the specialized Comsat communications kept the lines of communications clear. Brognola's deep voice came back as crisp and vibrant as it would have if he'd been standing next to the combat veterans.

"Do we know what the troop strength is?"

"Unfortunately not," Katz replied. "The man I questioned said that they call the base Meccafatwa. Loosely translated, it means the City of Law."

"Pretty disgusting, considering there's nothing legal or just about it."

"Really. I'm landing in Bamako to meet up with the French DGSE agent who's been working with Striker. She says that he was planning to force the GIA pilots to take him there."

"How was he planning to manage that?" Brognola asked with a sigh.

"I have no idea," Katz replied grimly, "but knowing Striker, I'm sure he found a way."

"Do you think he might be at Meccafatwa?"

"I'd say the odds are pretty good."

"Okay, keep me posted. I'll notify the Man that we may have located those items we're searching for, and get clearance to involve the French authorities."

"I made pals with a man named Auriville. He's the commander of the French Security Forces assigned to the rally. He indicated he would lend whatever assistance we might need."

"I think under the circumstances," Brognola said, "that we should call on their troops to help."

"Okay," Katz said with little conviction, "but let's keep in mind that Striker might be inside. We don't want to risk blowing him to kingdom come."

"Understood. What are your plans?"

"I'm here strictly as an adviser," Katz replied. "As soon as I pick up this Calandre Fauna, I'm going to get back to Dakar and keep an eye on things from there."

"Good enough. Take care of yourself, old friend."

"Will do. Out here."

Katz disconnected the transmission and slid the door to the Puma aside. He looked around and quickly spotted an M-998 Hummer approaching the chopper at high speed.

The vehicle screamed to a halt ten yards from the LZ, and a lithe woman with dark brown hair emerged from the driver's compartment. She was dressed in teal stretch pants and a filthy midriff top. Her hair was mussed and a medical bandage was taped to her forehead. She approached the chopper cautiously with a nose-wrinkling smile. Luminous brown eyes studied Katz with a mixture of curiosity and apprehension.

"Are you Monsieur Gray?" she asked.

"Yes," Katz replied gently, returning her smile. "And you must be Agent Fauna?"

She nodded. "But you may call me Calee, Mr. Gray. There's no need for formalities."

"Hop aboard," Katz said, patting the seat of the Puma. "We're on a tight schedule."

Once she was secured in the back and the chopper had lifted off, Katz handed her a headset and switched them to a private frequency. There was no need to distract the pilots on the VOX, and this would allow them some freedom to speak directly.

"Has there been any word from Mike?" she asked.

Katz shook his head. "Nothing. I've talked with some people, some very important people, and we're going on the assumption he reached this base. We decided to send French paratroopers to help. The guy in charge is named Commander Auriville. Ring any bells?"

Fauna's eyes widened. "Yes, indeed. Gautier Auriville has an excellent reputation as a military officer. He will do everything he can to help you."

"That's good news."

"How may I be of assistance?"

"Well, my plan was to return to a little operations center I have set up in Dakar. If you want to, you could act as liaison for me." Katz frowned and scratched self-consciously at his three-day growth of whiskers. "I'm afraid my jurisdiction here is very limited."

"Can you get me back to that airfield in Nioro?" she asked.

"I'm certain that wouldn't be a problem."

"Fine," Fauna replied. She took a deep breath and sighed, and something misty and faraway appeared in her eyes. "I have quite a bit of pull where the French Security Forces are concerned. I will accompany Commander Auriville to this base."

"It could be dangerous, Calee," Katz warned.

When she spoke, the look behind her eyes became hard and Katz could barely hear her reply. "Not nearly as much as it is for Mike."

In that brief moment, Yakov Katzenelenbogen found a deeper respect for his newfound ally.

A TRIO OF GIA sentries never saw the Executioner toss the grenade.

The labyrinthine corridors of the underground base were poorly lit, and it was this fact that allowed Bolan to steal through many areas undetected. He'd reached a point in one of the corridors that dead-ended at a heavy door. It looked as if the thing operated with nothing more than a latch. There were no keypads visible and no evidence of an alarm system. Bolan suspected the triggers were behind the vaultlike door.

Either way, he would have to go through the troops to get there, and an RGN in midair was preferable to a firefight in the close confines of the base.

Bolan pulled the pin and counted off two seconds before lobbing the grenade in an underhand toss. He plugged his ears and waited. The RGN exploded in the center of the troops, dropping them instantly.

The Executioner rounded the corner and quickly inspected the destruction. Luckily, the door was still intact. The terrorists weren't. The combined effects of shrapnel and concussion had done quite a job on that crew. Flash burns had created silhouettes of the three figures on the walls, and some of the flesh was literally melted from their faces.

Bolan stepped past the grisly scene and reached the door. He tugged on the handle gently at first, then yanked when it didn't give.

He froze in the hallway with bated breath, listening for an alarm or a shout indicating the enemy was nearby. Only silence greeted his ears. The warrior pulled the door open and squeezed his muscular frame through the doorway. The interior was dark, cool and strongly smelled of gun oil. As Bolan's eyes adjusted to the gloom, he realized he was in an armory. Long shelves were stocked with hundreds of assault rifles, many of them AKMs, Galils and R4s.

The warrior couldn't see too far beyond the doorway but he sensed it was a big room and very deep. There were hundreds of weapons, maybe thousands. More than enough to equip a small army. Bolan knew he wouldn't find the triggers here, but his discovery went a long way to showing just how large a force the GIA-Djihad had amassed.

Bolan left the armory and continued back in the direction he'd come. He'd used his knife to mark the walls so that he wouldn't lose his way inside the huge confines. Thus far, he hadn't run into anywhere near the resistance he'd expected. Maybe he was too late. Perhaps the terrorists had already left the area, triggers in their possession, and were now headed for whatever operation they had planned.

A moment passed and the Executioner suddenly forgot about that as he went down another hallway and quickly found himself in an anteroom. He noticed a desk with a chair. One end of the room was decorated with a bed, and long satin pieces and beads hung from the ceiling. He proceeded cautiously through a door and found a toilet and large tiled bathing area.

They appeared to be the quarters of a king, and Bolan quickly guessed they belonged to either Nokhtari or Fuaz.

At the sound of movement behind him, Bolan turned to meet the threat, the muzzle of the Galil up and ready for action.

A group of six Djihad terrorists burst through the doorway and fanned out, bringing R4s and Skorpions into the fray. Bolan triggered the Galil, directing the barrel in an S-pattern as he dived to the ground. Two terrorists took the 7.62 mm flesh-shredders in the chest. One was thrown backward into the wall, and the other dropped his weapon into the tile tub before following it headfirst.

Another gunman leveled his Skorpion machine pistol and pulled the trigger. The weapon chattered in his hands as .32 ACP-compatible slugs burned a furrow in the tile near Bolan's face. Chunks of the porcelain showered the Executioner, and one of them cut a jagged notch in his shoulder.

Blood began to run from the wound and into the bath as Bolan propped himself on his elbows and triggered the Galil in a sustained burst. The heavy-caliber ammo drilled through the terrorist's belly and blew pieces of vital organs out his back.

The Executioner rolled away from his position and regained his feet, nearly slipping on the slick tile. He quickly noticed that the light in the room was coming from candle holders on the wall. He maneuvered toward the door as he aimed the Galil in the direction of the brass plates and fired controlled bursts. The rounds landed on target and immersed the room in sudden darkness.

Bolan crouched as the remaining terrorists opened fire. He could hear the rounds zing above his head, rushing past like angry hornets and some of them even grazing his blacksuit. The Executioner whipped out a grenade, yanked the pin and tossed it overhand toward the bomb overhand toward the far wall. He had a second one in hand before the first one barely made contact.

A blast ripped through the area, blowing chunks of reinforced concrete from the wall even as Bolan lobbed the second one. In the wake of the first blast, the second one seemed even more powerful and deafening. Bolan rushed to the door and left the anteroom. He sprinted down the corridor bound for any place other than there.

The warrior rounded a bend and practically bumped into two guards—they had probably been left by the bath team on the off chance Bolan escaped. They were too close for a gun battle, and the Executioner seized the advantage. He drew his combat knife with lightning speed and caught the first gunman in the liver. He grabbed the terrorist's throat while he was still upright and pushed him into the second Djihad terrorist trying to free his weapon for a clear shot.

Bolan brought the Beretta into action, whipping the pistol from its holster and sighting across the shoulder of the first terrorist. The muzzle stopped three inches from the second gunman's face. There was a brief pause as the man sucked in a breath of surprise, and then the Executioner stroked the trigger. The 9 mm Parabellum round chugged through the terrorist's cheekbone and tore half of his face away upon exit.

Both corpses hit the floor simultaneously in a heap.

Bolan withdrew his knife and put it in its sheath without pausing to clean it. He picked up the Galil he'd dropped, ejected the magazine and inserted a new one on the run. He continued through the hallways, searching for any areas that weren't marked.

Obviously, the base occupants had somehow been alerted to his presence. He was still a bit surprised that the resistance wasn't as great as he'd expected. Yeah, something was definitely wrong here. He wondered if Nokhtari hadn't duped him as he traversed the maze of corridors.

Bolan reached another turn and stopped to listen. He crouched in the shadows and allowed a moment to catch his breath. Thus far, his search for the triggers had been fruitless. The numbers began to tick off and he considered his options. If the triggers weren't stashed somewhere inside this base, then he was wasting his time. The most frustrating thing about it was that he didn't have a clue where to look next. He'd covered practically every nook and cranny, and still nothing.

The Executioner reached a decision and doubled back. He

began to consider his alternatives—it started with Mamduh Nokhtari. He would have to find a way to get Nokhtari talking. The GIA leader hadn't put up any resistance when Bolan threatened to come to the base. Maybe the triggers were still somewhere in Bamako. Maybe Nokhtari had purposely led him here in the hopes that the resistance at this base would overwhelm him. Nokhtari was obviously ignorant of the soldier's talents.

As was the squad of ten GIA terrorists rushing toward him.

The Executioner pulled an RGN, rolled it down the hallway and hit the dirt as the pair in front opened up with R4s. The explosion ripped through the corridor like a nuclear bomb, lifting several of the terrorists off their feet and sending them into their comrades. Another man staggered away from the group, blood trickling from his ears.

Bolan began firing controlled bursts, dropping one GIA gunman after another before they could recover from the force of the blast.

Three of them managed to lay down a steady stream of fire as they backed away.

The Executioner got to one knee and snap-aimed the Galil. He triggered a burst that caught one of the terrorists in the shoulder, spinning the man away as the rounds from his weapon struck the ceiling and ricocheted in every direction. One of those rounds barely missed Bolan, chewing up the concrete near his feet. Stone shards zipped upward and slashed the warrior's shin.

Bolan bit back the pain and continued to fire on the remaining pair.

The sound of autofire reverberated like ceaseless thunder in the narrow corridors. A staccato of fresh bursts from different weapons suddenly competed for attention in the cacophony of reports. Bolan stopped firing and watched with surprise as the enemy troops suddenly danced in place and were then thrown forward by some unseen force.

Bolan kept the stock of the Galil pressed to his cheek as he waited for some of the smoke to clear. The heavy smells of rock dust, sand and gun powder permeated the gloom ahead.

Several seconds elapsed...

Five...

Ten...

The Executioner waited, holding his breath and preparing to engage anyone or anything the enemy threw at him. He'd walked into this damned hive of terror and he had every intention of walking out. Bolan would not be cut down senselessly by the GIA-Djihad terror machine. There were too many lives at stake—he had a duty to save those lives.

It wouldn't end here.

The sounds of several pairs of feet shuffling along the corridor got louder.

As the thick smoke dissipated, Bolan could make out a small petite shape beyond it, surrounded by men who looked as if they were in uniform. The shape was familiar, and Bolan immediately recognized those lines as they emerged through the haze.

"Mike?" called Calandre Fauna's voice.

Bolan stood. "It's me."

Fauna rushed to him and threw her arms around him.

Bolan let her—she was just glad to see him alive and he could understand that. Truth be told, he was pretty happy to be alive himself. She continued to clutch him, threatening to crush the very breath from his lungs. The dust was settling now, and Bolan could clearly make out Fauna's escorts.

A tall man in the green uniform of the French paratroopers walked up to them.

"We are glad to see you alive, Monsieur Blanski," the man said pleasantly as Bolan separated from Fauna.

The two men shook hands.

"Thanks," Bolan replied.

"Mike," Fauna interjected, "this is Commander Gautier Auriville, chief operations officer for the French Security Forces."

"It is a pleasure to meet you, sir," Auriville said. "Mademoiselle Fauna speaks highly of you."

Bolan looked at Fauna and saw her blush. "I'll bet."

"The triggers are destroyed, yes?" Fauna asked.

Bolan shook his head tiredly. "No. They pulled a switch on us somewhere. I've got Nokhtari, though."

"Colonel Mamduh Nokhtari?" Auriville asked with disbelief in his voice. "The famed leader of the Armed Islamic Group?"

"Yeah."

"This man is wanted in my country for many crimes," Auriville said. "I must take him back to France to answer for the murders he's committed."

"He is correct, Mike," Fauna added. "This was one of my primary missions. I know that Nokhtari has committed atrocities against Americans, as well, but he has murdered our people, too. We want him badly."

"You can have him," Bolan replied coolly, heading in the direction of the exit. "But first I want some answers."

17

Mack Bolan stormed into the Hook chopper and found his captive pilots dressing under the armed scrutiny of a half dozen of Auriville's men. He roughly shoved the pair aside and opened the crate.

Nokhtari's bound and gagged form lay in a pool of sweat. The Executioner looked into the hate-filled eyes of his prisoner a moment, then yanked the GIA terror leader out of the crate. Bolan snatched the gag from Nokhtari's mouth and pinned him against the wall of the chopper. He pressed the muzzle of the Beretta to his head and smiled coldly.

"Before I turn you over to these nice men here," Bolan growled, "I want some answers. Where are the triggers?"

"You fool!" Nokhtari shouted with a sneer. "It is too late. You cannot stop the Al-Qaida movement. Why don't you just admit that you have lost and accept your defeat with honor?"

"Why don't you save the speeches?" Bolan replied. "I don't have time for your games, Nokhtari. Talk now or I'm going to bury a bullet in your brain."

"You will learn nothing!" Nokhtari spit, then he fell silent.

Auriville and Fauna had now joined Bolan. They watched with a mixture of interest and apprehension as the Executioner interrogated the prisoner. He was a prized possession. Bolan knew the French had long desired to apprehend Nokhtari and bring him to justice. He knew he shouldn't kill the GIA leader, but his mission took precedence. Fear of death was the most tried-and-true method of soliciting answers.

Bolan grabbed Nokhtari by the back of the neck, pushing him to the door.

"Wait here," he ordered Fauna and Auriville.

The two pilots were also watching, the fear evident in their expressions. It was obvious they were distressed over the uncertain fate of their leader.

Bolan hauled Nokhtari out the door and walked a distance from the chopper, ensuring he was only partially visible through the windows. He forced Nokhtari to his knees and pointed the weapon at the back of his head.

"Last chance," Bolan warned. "Where are the triggers?"

"Fuck you, American."

Bolan landed a blow with the pistol butt against the back of Nokhtari's skull. The man landed prone in the sand. The Executioner then held his pistol a few inches from the terrorist's head and squeezed the trigger twice.

The Beretta barked in the quiet desert air.

The Executioner stormed back to the chopper, gathering a myriad of odd looks from the FSF soldiers gathered outside the Hook. He ignored them, concentrating on the task ahead as he crossed the threshold.

One look at the two pilots was enough to tell Bolan it had worked. They figured that with their leader dead, they would be next. They now seemed quite anxious to spare their own lives. Devotion to duty only went so far. These were just hired hands in the Al-Qaida movement—they weren't terrorists of the same caliber as the field troops.

He walked up to the pilot and put the warm muzzle against his head. "Fauna, do you speak Arabic?"

"Yes," she said shakily.

"Ask him where the triggers are."

Fauna began to open her mouth, but Auriville cut in before she could speak another word. "You have just killed our prisoner, Monsieur Blanski. Why should we now cooperate with you?"

Bolan lent a very hard look at Auriville and frowned. "Trust me. I know what I'm doing."

Bolan nodded to Fauna and she asked the question.

"He is not sure, Mike," she relayed. "He was ordered to fly an escort team to Bamako under the orders of Hassan Fuaz."

"For what purpose?" Bolan countered.

Fauna translated, "The troops were apparently ordered to intercept the triggers and take them out by another route. These were reinforcements requested by Nokhtari."

"Were they supposed to wait for them?"

"No," Fauna replied, "they were told to drop off Fuaz's soldiers and stand by until Nokhtari arrived. Then they were ordered to fly back here and wait for further instructions."

"Where is Fuaz?"

Fauna asked the question and listened for the answer. "He is at the lab, where they picked up the troops originally."

"The lab?" the Executioner echoed.

"That's what he said," Fauna replied.

"Where is this place?"

"It is in the Ténéré Desert, built into a cavern at the base of the Djado Mountains."

"That is about four hundred kilometers northeast of here," Auriville cut in quickly. "Near Seguédine."

"Fine." The Executioner turned to Auriville. "Commander, I need one of your men to help me pilot this thing. One who speaks English, if possible."

"You wish for cooperation after what you did?" Auriville asked with disbelief.

Bolan chuckled. "Oh, you can take Nokhtari to France now. He served his purpose."

Auriville looked at Bolan with disgust and anger. "What good is he to me? You have killed him. My superiors do not wish to imprison his dead body!"

"He's not dead," Bolan announced sharply. "I fired next to his head. He's unconscious but alive. So take him."

"Why this deception, Mike?" Fauna asked, her voice taking on its own angry tone.

"Because I didn't have time to explain it," he replied, "just as I don't have time now. I need to get to this base and stop Fuaz from whatever he's planning to do."

Auriville began to laugh loudly. "You really had us fooled, Blanski. I must commend you for your ingenuity."

"No problem," Bolan said easily. "Now, how about that pilot?"

"It will be my pleasure."

HASSAN FUAZ WATCHED with satisfaction as the two guinea pigs suffered.

He felt nothing but hatred for the men rotting before him—and nothing but pride that the GV strain was working. Wasim was probably taking his last breaths, and McKarroll was deteriorating at a much faster rate now. They had taken Reshef's body out and incinerated it an hour ago.

Yes, the enemies of Islam would never know what hit them.

He had to admit that Hasna Qaseem had really outdone herself this time. Those many years of education in the finer schools had paid off, and the Al-Qaida movement was about to strike a blow for the Islamic world that wouldn't soon be forgotten. Thousands, even millions, would die under the onslaught of the virus. And scientists around the world would be stumped by this new outbreak of smallpox.

After infecting the cramped cities and rural sprawls of Algeria, Fuaz could then move on to other more influential and important targets. Other major African cities would topple, and bin Laden would establish a new order. Once they had thoroughly spread the virus, they could more or less take the rest by attrition. Billions of dollars would be spent to obtain the vaccine. But only after Al-Qaida possessed the entire African continent.

It would be a slaughter to make the Jewish genocide by Adolf Hitler seem like child's play.

The appearance of his chief lieutenant, Tarik, incensed Fuaz. It always seemed that this man was showing up when he was least wanted. It was a minor irritation but one that Hassan Fuaz absolutely despised. Couldn't the leader of one of the greatest jihad movements in existence have a little peace and quiet once in a while? Tarik was always pestering him with silly, mundane matters that could have easily been handled by others. Fuaz would normally have grown used to it, but there was just something about Tarik that he didn't like.

Fuaz certainly wished that Nokhtari had returned.

"Sir, I am sorry to disturb you," Tarik said.

"Aren't you always?" Fuaz snarled, rising from his seat in the observation chamber and leaving the remaining pair to suffer and die.

"Y-yes, sir, but it's very important."

"Isn't it always?" Fuaz snapped. "What is so pressing that it could not wait?"

"Ayman is here to see you, sir," Tarik said hurriedly. "He says he brings bad news regarding Colonel Nokhtari."

"Something has happened to Mamduh?"

"I do not know, sir," Tarik replied sheepishly. "He refuses to talk to anyone but you."

"Send him to my quarters. Immediately!"

"Yes, sir."

Tarik rushed off and Fuaz proceeded to the meeting place. He dismissed his wives and concubines rather brusquely, a thousand questions going through his mind. He hoped that Nokhtari was all right. His troops had intercepted the triggers about an hour north of Bamako, and delivered them to another Mil Mi-8 waiting nearby. The thought had originally been to send the troops to destroy the American, but it had been Nokhtari's idea to lead the meddling Westerner into a trap.

Now Ayman—who was believed to be dead—had come to the Djado base and yet there was no word from his master. With Ayman here and the triggers, albeit only half of them, now safely in their possession, that left Nokhtari as the only missing link.

They were behind schedule—this also troubled the Djihad leader. But Qaseem had assured him they could make up for lost time, and still introduce the first doomsday bomb on time. Everything would be all right and Fuaz calmed his nerves. He would deal with any problems one at a time. There was no point in letting this upset him before he had all of the information.

A heavy knock sounded at the door.

"Enter!" Fuaz called.

Ayman stepped through the doorway and he looked like hell. His eyes were bloodshot, there was a deep cut above his right eyebrow and his right wrist was bandaged. He wore a thin T-shirt and Fuaz noticed the thick padding beneath it that indicated his ribs were taped. Evidence of a burn was just barely noticeable on the upper part of his chest.

"Ayman, my brother," Fuaz said, walking forward and hugging the big man.

Ayman appeared a bit taken aback, as if he were surprised to have Fuaz treating him so well. The Djihad leader wasn't usually so amiable. Fuaz held a secret disapproval for many Algerians—even those of the Al-Qaida movement—because it seemed to him that they were less than pure.

Then again, what soldier for the jihad really was pure?

Perhaps none, but Fuaz couldn't help his feelings. These were his Islamic brothers and comrades, true, but they weren't Egyptian. Not that it really mattered, for they were all Arab men in the service of Osama bin Laden. Fuaz had learned to look past some of his prejudices and nuances in the interest of a greater cause. A cause that would soon see victory against its most hated enemies.

"Tarik tells me you bring news of Colonel Nokhtari?" Fuaz inquired, referring to Mamduh by his official title. It was important to keep subordinates mindful of their positions.

"Yes, Master Fuaz," the big Algerian replied with a bow. "He has been captured by French Security Forces. He was overpowered by the American."

For a moment or two, Fuaz wasn't sure of what he'd just heard. "You say he was captured. Not killed?"

"Yes, sir," Ayman replied, his eyes growing wide. "I have no reason to lie. You may test my loyalty if you wish."

"No, Ayman, that won't be necessary," Fuaz said quietly. "How did it happen?"

"His plan to snare the American failed. While the American took the bait, he managed to eliminate our men and somehow coerced them to take him to Meccafatwa."

"Our men there were not able to oppose him?"

Ayman lowered his head. "That is the other news I bring, and I'm afraid it is not good, either."

"Continue," Fuaz said, even as he felt the constriction in his throat.

"Meccafatwa was destroyed. I am told that many were killed in action." Ayman waited a minute to give his statement time to sink in.

Fuaz didn't say anything immediately, but just looked at Ayman in silence. He could feel the anger boiling in his stomach and taste the rage rise into his mouth like bile.

There was no question that the American would now be much more intimate with the GIA-Djihad movement. Perhaps he might not get any of the detainees that survived the assault on Meccafatwa to talk today, but they would break eventually. French prisons were infamous for being hard on those who occupied spaces within their walls. Most of them would not survive more than five or ten years. Someone within his organization would talk much sooner, though. Fuaz had absolutely no illusions about that. Men had their breaking points, and Fuaz knew he could not expect every man to resist.

"Where is Colonel Nokhtari now?" Fuaz finally asked.

"I do not know," Ayman replied, "but I can talk with people I have met and they could probably have an answer to that question in a few hours."

"If he's alive and in jail, then we must find him. At any cost."

"Understood, sir."

"You look like you have been through God's fire, Ayman," Fuaz noted. "Are you able to go on or do you require some rest?"

"I will be okay, sir," Ayman said, stiffening some and trying to hide his pain.

Fuaz smiled. "He could not destroy the great Ayman, eh?"

"No, sir. He defeated me once in a hand-to-hand contest in Bamako, but I was not at my best after barely escaping from the chopper explosion. This man, he is extremely well trained, sir. He must be destroyed or he will surely interfere with our plans."

"I am not afraid of this man, Ayman."

"With due respect, sir," the huge Algerian said as he rubbed his wrist, "perhaps you should be."

"I'VE JUST RECEIVED word, Hal," Yakov Katzenelenbogen announced.

"What's the situation?" the Stony Man chief inquired.

"French authorities now have Nokhtari in custody, and Striker is on his way to some kind of laboratory. It's a cavern in the Djado mountains. Their base in the desert has also been destroyed, and Auriville's paratroopers mopped up any pockets of resistance."

"You mean there are two bases?"

"Well, sort of," Katz said. "Meccafatwa turned out to be a stronghold for housing troops, but that's not the only place the GIA-Djihad movement is operating. Striker realized he'd been duped when he discovered that they managed to dump the triggers with another team. Now he's convinced they've been taken to this mountain laboratory, and he's going there to finish the job."

"What about Hassan Fuaz?"

"Fuaz is apparently the mastermind behind all of this," Katz replied evenly. "It's no secret he's acted as one of bin Laden's cronies for years. He's dangerous and powerful, but he's also just a puppet paying lip service to the Al-Qaida movement."

"What kind of laboratory is this?"

"We're not sure but Striker seems convinced they'll use the triggers in chemical weapons."

"Yes," Brognola interjected, "a nuclear threat does seem unlikely under the circumstances. Any thoughts as to what they might be using?"

"No, but then I'm afraid to guess."

"Yeah, I don't blame you." Brognola sighed and added, "Well, whatever it is, I'm sure it's meant to create as much of a statement as possible."

"Do you still have Phoenix on alert?"

"On alert, hell," Brognola replied, "they're on their way here. Why?"

"Well, we have to be ready for any eventuality. Fuaz isn't that bright, but he's managed to evade capture this long. He does cover his tracks well. If he gets away from Striker, or worse..."

Katz let his voice trail off and the moment of silence told him Brognola got the meaning.

"They'll be ready if I need to send them in," Brognola replied. "The Man wants to try to handle this quickly and quietly. The less people involved, the easier that is."

"Quickly and quietly?" Katz couldn't help let out a chuckle. "He should know better. I imagine the GIA-Djihad will end in anything but quiet."

MACK BOLAN WAS about to make some noise.

The Djihad pilots had told him that the only way to get into the mountain laboratory was by coded access. Bolan could have just ordered an air strike to pound the side of the Djado mountains, but that wouldn't have guaranteed the end of the GIA and their Da'awa wal Djihad allies. This was going to require a surgical strike, plain and simple.

It was time to put an end to the terror machine.

Bolan had equipped himself with fresh magazines for the two Galils. A half-dozen RGN grenades dangled from his LBE, and the combat knife was secured in its sheath. Eight 50-round box magazines were scattered among four pouches along the web belt, and the Desert Eagle and Beretta were in their respective places, as well. Bolan had also acquired several blocks of plastic explosive from the FSF demolitions team.

Inside the Mil Mi-6, Bolan had located what looked like plans to the mountain stronghold, although it barely qualified for that title. As a matter of fact, aside from the coded access there didn't appear to be any other security measures. However, Bolan knew there would be substantial resistance both inside and out. Only the fact they had the markings of the enemy did they have a chance to set the thing down before someone blasted them from the sky.

They were marked as enemy, too.

Bolan had acquired the scarlet turban worn by Nokhtari, and it was probably a trademark. The Executioner had never seen any other member of the GIA or Djihad forces wearing such a headdress. He had also attired himself in desert-stripe fatigues, and with a dust mask on his face he was certain he could pass muster at a distance.

The main force was in preparation for training. While the two pilots hadn't been privy to all of the GIA-Djihad plans, they had seen troops training in NBC protective gear. That confirmed Bolan's suspicions that Fuaz intended to use some kind of chemical weapon. The Executioner would have to be careful that he didn't get into whatever nasty surprises Fuaz was cooking up. Bleeding from every orifice or having his skin peel off weren't the most appealing of propositions. He'd faced it before and survived, but would prefer not to again.

Bolan finished his work and then squeezed himself into the copilot's seat as the French pilot easily moved the Hook through its motions. The warrior donned a headset and stared out at the barren expanse. In the hazy distance of blowing sand, he could barely discern the peaks of mountains.

"What's our ETA?" Bolan asked.

"Approximately one-eight minutes, sir," the pilot replied.

His name was Clovis Du Perrin. According to Auriville, he was a crack pilot and an invaluable soldier. The guy reminded Bolan of Jack Grimaldi in some respects, and although he was grateful for any help at all, he wished he had Stony Man's ace flyer with him right at that moment.

The Executioner had no idea what kind of experience Du Perrin had, and even less of an idea if the guy would crack under fire. Bolan planned to maintain radio contact with him, since the Hook was his only ride out of the middle of the desert. The Ténéré was unforgiving. Sure, there were towns nearby, but Bolan doubted—given the fear about terrorism in Africa— that he could have solicited help in the event he was stranded.

"You'll need to maintain radio contact," Bolan reminded Du Perrin, "but don't break silence unless I do."

"I understand what to do, sir," Du Perrin replied. The guy was always smiling and Bolan wondered if he weren't happy just to get a little action. Many pilots were a bit crazy anyway, so there wasn't any reason for Du Perrin to be different. Some unknown mechanism made these kind of men edgy and restless. Just like David McCarter, they craved action and thrived on the adrenaline rush that came from combat.

Bolan had no such aspirations. He was a soldier first and foremost because that's what he knew how to do best. The Executioner couldn't imagine life any other way. He didn't do it for glory or adventure. He did it because it's what came naturally to him.

"As we get closer," Du Perrin announced, "you know they will attempt to contact us."

"Probably. The pilots didn't mention this, either. I was going to ask, but I figured they'd just lie and say you didn't have to call in."

"Then there is the chance they might shoot us out of the sky, yes?"

"Maybe. We're just going to have to take that chance."

Bolan looked at the map again. "There's a landing pad about three hundred yards from a large rock they call the gateway, or something like that. If we go straight there and land, we're less likely to draw fire. I'm hoping they're expecting Nokhtari and we'll be greeted with open arms."

"How do you plan to get inside?"

"If I can't do it the easy way, then I'll blow a nice big hole in the door."

"You like to make an entrance, *oui?*"

"Not unless it's absolutely necessary," Bolan replied grimly.

The next few minutes of silence was abruptly broken by a burst of static followed by a voice coming through their headsets. It sounded like Arabic, and Bolan only caught parts of it. He turned and looked at Du Perrin with a serious expression.

"Can you understand them?"

"Yes, of course," Du Perrin replied. "It is the Djihad. They are asking for our clearance code."

"Yeah," Bolan muttered, "it figures."

18

"What do you want me to do?" Du Perrin asked.

"Key the radio but don't say anything," Bolan ordered quickly. "There's a pretty good chance these choppers are also equipped with identifiers. Let them think we're having radio trouble."

"Yes, sir," Du Perrin snapped dutifully.

The French paratrooper pilot did as instructed, keying the transmission button for a few seconds, then releasing it. After about four or five times, he stopped and the pair waited. Again, there was a request for a code clearance and the threat of destruction if they didn't comply. Du Perrin looked at Bolan, who nodded, and repeated the process of keying the radio.

The voice came back again, this time with alternative instructions.

"What did they say?"

"They are saying that we're transmitting, but they're not hearing. They said they have our identifier code and confirmed we are one of theirs. They are welcoming us home." Du Perrin looked up at the Executioner and grinned. "It worked."

"Key it again for good measure, then end transmission," Bolan said.

Du Perrin did as instructed, then proceeded to the coordinates on the landing pad. He slowed the Hook considerably to avoid flying over the small landing zone. He had to make it appear that he knew exactly where he was and what he was doing. As if he'd done it a thousand times before. Bolan kept quiet and let the man do it.

Within minutes, he'd set the chopper on the helipad.

"Now what do we do, *monsieur?*" the pilot asked as he set the engine to idle.

"You wait here for my signal," Bolan said, climbing from the seat. "I'm going to take care of business."

"SIR," TARIK SAID, rushing to catch up with Fuaz in a hallway.

The Djihad leader was now dressed in full combat gear and preparing to supervise his men in their operation drills. He would be inoculated against the virus, so he saw little need to dress himself down in the heavy NBC suits. The other men wouldn't be inoculated until it could be produced in mass quantity, so only the command staff and senior officers would receive their inoculations before the operation began.

"The chopper you sent to Bamako has returned," Tarik continued. "We believe Colonel Nokhtari is aboard."

"What?" Fuaz thundered. "How can this be? Ayman told me that Mamduh had been captured by French special forces."

"I do not know, sir, but Colonel Nokhtari's chopper is here and our initial scout crews are certain they saw him seated inside."

"Send an escort out to meet him," Fuaz ordered. "I will go and greet him personally at the door. And find me Ayman. I want him to be present for this."

"Yes, sir."

BOLAN STEPPED OFF the rear boarding ramp and tensed his muscles.

A squad of armed Djihad soldiers in full battle gear was marching out to meet him. At least they weren't members of the GIA, which lessened the likelihood of immediate recognition.

Bolan had tried such ruses before on many occasions. He called it role camouflage—the ability to make your enemies see what they were expecting to see. There were some things the Executioner could be thankful for, like the fact that he and Nokhtari were approximately the same height and weight. Bolan's shoulders were a bit broader, but he'd covered some of that with the crossed bandoliers Nokhtari was apparently known for wearing.

The warrior stepped forward—the Galil dangling muzzle down under his right arm—and returned the short bow by the apparent leader of the group. The Djihad terrorist spoke something in Arabic, and Bolan assumed it was probably a greeting. He nodded, then waved toward the lone tall rock that he knew marked the entrance to the lab. The gesture was clear and the man nodded and immediately ordered his troops to escort their guest to the door.

Bolan fell into step between the soldiers, trying to gauge their reactions. If something went awry in his penetration of the lab, he would have to shoot his way out in a big hurry.

The group moved past the shadows of the gateway and reached a sliding door. An electronic keypad with card-coded entry extended from the rock itself. It was an impressive setup. Bolan let his eyes rove over the pad as the leader stepped forward, swiped a card that dangled from a thin chain around his neck and punched in a series of seven numbers. The Executioner committed the numbers to memory and marked the leader for eventual termination. At some point, he might need the code key.

The door slid aside and the group started to enter, Bolan moving with them. They were perhaps five yards inside the laboratory when an older man rounded the corner accompanied by two others. The guy was dressed like the other troops, but he carried only a side arm. He walked with the pomp and arrogance of a man in command, and Bolan surmised he was looking at none other than Hassan Fuaz.

The second man was smaller, wearing a purple scarf and carrying an AKM. Bolan didn't recognize him, either. But there was no mistaking the third man. The hulking form immediately set off alarms, and the Executioner knew that it would only take seconds before the game was up. The third man was the same one he'd fought at the bazaar in Bamako.

"Mamduh—" Fuaz began, but he cut his words short because his jaw dropped open and his eyes grew wide.

Bolan swung the muzzle of the Galil into play and opened fire. The three terrorists in front of him died instantly under the 7.62 mm onslaught. The rest tried to fan out, but there was no cover in the narrow hall.

The Executioner whirled and cut down the rest of his escort while Fuaz and his men dived behind opposing walls where the hallway branched off. He raked the area with autofire. Two of the men tried to escape through the door but it had already started closing, and they couldn't reverse it in time. The pair was chopped to ribbons by the hail of rounds Bolan fired at them.

The warrior turned as he palmed an RGN. He backed up to the door, tossed the hand grenade and plugged his ears. He could hear shouts of distress as the grenade exploded, delivering fragments in every direction as the RDX/Wax filling exploded on impact.

Bolan could hear a scream, and he sprinted down the corridor and rounded a turn. The smaller terrorist who had been with Fuaz was lying in a puddle of blood. Fragments of bone protruded from his thighs and chest. The guy's screams died as he began to choke on his own blood. The Executioner sent a mercy round into his head and moved on.

Fuaz and his behemoth of an escort had disappeared. Alarm Klaxons began to resound throughout the lab, alerting its defenders there was an intruder that needed dealing with. Unknown to the terrorists, this was no ordinary intruder.

It was the Executioner, and he was on a search-and-destroy mission.

HASSAN FUAZ and Ayman burst into the lab just as the alarms began to ring.

"What is going on, Hassan?" Qaseem asked.

"We have a security breach," Fuaz told her. "Nothing we

cannot handle. Continue with your work here. Lock this door and don't let anyone in or out but me. Do you understand?"

"If there is any threat at all, we need to store the virus in a safe place."

"You need to do what I tell you!" Fuaz bellowed, feeling the blood rush to his face and his breath quicken. "This is my arena, Doctor. I will handle this!"

Qaseem looked surprised, but Fuaz didn't give her the opportunity to respond. He turned, left the room and called orders to Ayman lumbering behind him.

"Get our troops on maneuvers over to the rally site. We're going to get the first bomb on board the plane and get out of here as soon as possible. Tell internal security to keep this American busy until we can take off."

"Yes, sir. But what about Colonel Nokhtari, Master Fuaz?"

"Colonel Nokhtari is dead, Ayman!" Fuaz snarled. More calmly, he added, "At least he's as good as dead if we cannot finish our mission. Perhaps this operation will be doubly effective. We could threaten to use the bomb if the French did not arrange his immediate release, and then we could use it anyway once he had safely returned."

"You would do this for Colonel Nokhtari?"

"I would do it for any one of you, Ayman," Fuaz lied. "But for now, you must obey my every order. The success of our organization and of Al-Qaida depends upon it."

"It will be as you wish, Master Fuaz," Ayman replied with a bow.

The two men continued onward toward Fuaz's destination.

BOLAN STALKED the hallways like a machine. He would find the triggers and Fuaz, and he would deal with them both in very similar fashion. He would resist anything in his path, and that included the six terrorists who had set up firing positions in small alcoves in the corridor ahead.

The Executioner found his own cover in an alcove and returned their autofire while he primed a grenade. The RGNs were unmistakably effective in places such as this.

The ceilings in the lab complex weren't nearly as low as the bunkerlike base in Meccafatwa, but the hallways were still narrow. That meant the enemy had no effective way of amassing any kind of insurmountable force against Bolan at any one given time.

The Executioner liked that idea and was going to use it as his best weapon. He threw the grenade down the hall. It bounced twice but didn't explode. The effect was pretty much the same, however, as the Djihad terrorists saw it land and practically scrambled over one another to escape the deadly blast.

One of the last men had to have realized that he shouldn't have made it because he stopped running and turned to look at the grenade. Bolan had already broken his cover and was moving forward. The terrorist smiled as he raised his AKM and began to advance on the Bolan. The Executioner dived to the floor. His opponent opened up and burned the air above his head with 7.62 mm rounds. Bolan raised the Galil and fired his weapon, chopping the terrorist off at the ankles. The man fell to the ground, screaming as his comrades rushed to assist him.

Bolan triggered another low burst, and the terrorists got close to helping their comrade when the grenade exploded. The Executioner was as surprised as his enemy. One of the stray rounds had to have struck the grenade and caused it to detonate. In either case, the explosion had wounded some and stunned others enough for Bolan to take the advantage.

The Executioner cut the group down, finishing those who had survived the blast.

Bolan reached the end of the hallway and noted a door. He pressed his ear to it and heard nothing beyond. He could have been walking into an ambush, but he didn't have time to worry about that now. There were lives at stake and he needed to stop the GIA-Djihad group before those lives were lost.

The soldier pushed through the door and stepped inside. The room was empty, except for a few chairs. But it was the area beyond the hermetically sealed plate glass that tormented Bolan. The scene almost reminded him of his days against the Mob when he would discover "turkeys"—those vestiges of human waste that spoke volumes on what kind of horrors man could inflict on his fellow human beings.

Two men were secured to chairs. Droplets of sweat poured from their faces, and their skin was the color of ivory. Sunken eyes that were bleeding looked at the Executioner, and there appeared to be almost a plea of help in one of those. This man was immediately recognizable because Bolan had seen enough pictures of him in his time.

It was Admiral Robert McKarroll, U.S.N.

Bolan didn't see a door in the observation room, so he doubled back and checked an adjoining corridor. He quickly found another door set in the wall at a dead end. Bolan tried to open it but it was locked. The Executioner put his weight against it and kicked at the lock. The door held firmly.

Well, there was more than one way to fix that problem.

Keeping his back to the wall so he could watch the opposite end of the hallway, the soldier reached into his demo pouch and retrieved a block of C-4. He pulled a chunk of it away, rolled it to golf-ball size and then flattened it against the lock mechanism.

He then molded an edge for the electronic blasting cap, wired the device and blew the door.

Chunks of dust and wooden shards flew in every direction as it gave under the pressure of the powerful explosive. Most of it was completely ripped from the hinges, but the Executioner was hardly worried about that. It had its desired effect. Bolan came through the door and found himself in some sort of anteroom. The backs of McKarroll and the other man were now visible through a one-way viewing area.

A door set in the side led into the chamber and Bolan walked toward it.

He had to get McKarroll out of there and get him—and his counterpart—medical attention soon. It looked as if they had drugged and beaten the pair half to death.

Bolan reached the door and put his hand on the handle.

He stopped himself at the last second and decided to check the door.

A brief inspection didn't reveal any hidden wires or booby traps.

Satisfied he'd covered all his bases, Bolan opened the door and stepped inside.

CAPTAIN CLOVIS Du Perrin realized there was a problem when alarms began to resound throughout the complex. Men scurried from seemingly out of nowhere and all began rushing in the same direction. They weren't headed into the laboratory—not where Blanski had gone.

No, these men were running right past the natural monolith that marked the entrance and continuing on to something else. Du Perrin didn't know what that something else was and he was betting Blanski didn't know, either. Nobody had even noticed him sitting there inside the chopper. He'd kept to himself and the Djihad terrorists had done the same.

Now it was time to look into this new little development.

Du Perrin fired up the chopper's rotor and started the engines. He donned his headset and waited for his instruments to read nominal before lifting off the ground. He swung the chopper around in a circle and then lifted higher and higher until he was afforded an unlimited view of the immediate area.

Hidden beneath a massive desert netting was some sort of plane. Du Perrin would have completely missed it had it not been for the heat signatures on the infrared scanners. There was absolutely no question about it—the GIA-Djihad alliance had something in store for someone, and it involved a weapon of mass destruction.

The thing that frustrated Du Perrin the most was that he couldn't do a damned thing about it. He had no armament on the Mil Mi-6—not even so much as a coaxial machine gun. There was really nothing he could do to stop them if they wanted to take off, short of crashing his chopper into them. And that probably wouldn't have made Monsieur Blanski happy.

Du Perrin could do little more than keep an eye on them.

"ADMIRAL?" The Executioner shook the Navy officer. "Admiral McKarroll, can you hear me?"

"Y-yes..." McKarroll said, his blank eyes looking back at Bolan like a death stare. "You m-must go fr-from..." McKarroll had a coughing fit.

"I'm going to get you out of here, Admiral," Bolan consoled him.

"No, you must not—must not take me from... Just leave me."

Bolan was puzzled now. The Navy man was obviously delirious—but upon a closer inspection the Executioner hadn't really noticed a mark on him. It wasn't as if they had beat him or tortured him. No burns, no open wounds—the man was just plain sick. Almost as if he'd contracted some sort of disease.

"You can-cannot take me," McKarroll insisted.

"If I don't take you out of here, you'll die," Bolan argued.

"I'm going to die anyway." The poor guy was suffering, but he worked hard to get the words out. "They have invented a new—a new virus. Smallpox. You must stop them. Find the doctor...the woman doctor. She has the vaccine and the—the toxin. Don't let it leave here. Please don't let..."

And with that, Admiral Robert J. McKarroll, United States Navy, took his final breath.

The Executioner quickly checked the other man for a pulse—there wasn't one.

Bolan felt rage boil in his gut. So that was it! They were planning to use a new biological weapon against their enemies. A new strain of the smallpox virus that probably killed within days instead of weeks or months. Such a weapon spelled doom for anybody who opposed the GIA-Djihad. That still didn't give the Executioner a motive, but at that point it no longer mattered.

Bolan marched purposefully from the room and headed back the way he'd come.

The radio on his belt squawked for attention. "French Bird to Striker, French Bird to Striker."

Why the hell was Du Perrin breaking radio silence? They couldn't take a chance of their transmissions being monitored. He'd ordered the guy not to call unless it was a matter of life and death, so Bolan could only assume the guy was intelligent enough to decipher what that meant.

"This is Striker, go ahead, French Bird."

"I am observing a plane, a large carrier on the north side of the lab. It is hidden, but I think there may be access to it from the laboratory. It's powering up its engines. I think they accelerated their schedule. I have no way of stopping them. Over."

"You said it's on the north side?" Bolan reiterated, jogging in that direction.

"Affirmative."

"I'm on my way."

So they were planning to move things up a bit. Well, there was a pretty good chance at least one of their new weapons was aboard. So he was going to have to stop the plane anyway. So many things to do and so little time remaining.

Now his mission was twofold. Not only did he have to locate this plane and destroy it, but he also still had to deal with Fuaz. Add to that the fact he would now need to find this woman scientist. If she had a vaccine, it was all the more important.

Not only because it would save countless lives.

But also because Mack Bolan knew he'd just been exposed to one of the most deadly viruses on Earth.

19

It didn't take the Executioner long to find the hallway where he'd first made entry into the laboratory. The bodies of the Djihad terrorists he'd gunned down were still lying there in awkward positions, the blood now black and dried on their uniforms.

Bolan continued down the side hallway and turned in a northerly direction, determined to find the plane Du Perrin had spotted. He would have to neutralize any resistance, as well as destroy the thing somehow. The remaining C-4 plastique he carried would provide that answer.

The hallway curved at one point. Bolan pressed his back to the wall and proceeded more slowly, the Galil held at the ready. There was no question in the warrior's mind that they would have the plane well guarded.

But Bolan also had the terrorists at a disadvantage. They had been training all night and were probably tired. It had been nearing dawn when Bolan and Du Perrin had flown into the complex. The Executioner hadn't had any sleep in over twenty-four hours, either, but he had become accustomed to twice that long on his feet without food or rest. It was unlikely his enemy was used to that sort of thing; the terrorists were probably hungry, tired and weakened from their training.

The hallway terminated at a door, and Bolan crossed over to it in a crouch. He knelt and put his ear to the door. He could detect men's voices on the other side and hear sounds of equipment being moved. There was a hurried pace about the noises, and the Executioner knew he was running out of time.

Bolan slung his Galil over his arm and pulled two RGNs from his web gear. He yanked the pins, clutched one bomb in each hand and opened the push-latch mechanism on the door with his forearm as quietly as he could manage. Two guards stood a few yards from the door, their backs to him. They didn't hear him over the sound of the activity ahead.

A large, unmarked attack plane was parked at the base of a runway. The runway ran out toward the desert and disappeared into the sand—probably coated with a thin film to keep it concealed—and a huge camouflage netting was erected overhead to conceal the bird. About twenty or thirty men were quickly loading crates into the rear.

Beneath the underbelly, the tail fins of two giant warheads were visible. A pair of Djihad soldiers guarded the weapons while scientists in white suits worked feverishly on the missiles. At the rear of the fuselage was a blue dot, surrounded by a white stripe, then a red stripe. Those were the colors of the French flag, and Bolan wondered if this particular plane had been delivered courtesy of Talbot Dutré.

The Executioner wished he could identify the aircraft. It had obviously been stolen from the French air force, but he couldn't be sure what type of machine it was. The pilot's area did seat two, and the shape was a fixed geometry type with a large delta wing, much like the 117-A Nighthawk. It also had a single engine at its rear that looked as if it could generate some significant power.

Bolan knew he'd have to go for the engine. If he took out the wings, they wouldn't be able to take off. But if the virus was in the warheads, he risked infecting the whole damned lot of them—that was something he didn't need on his conscience. So the engine was his target, and he just hoped he didn't ignite the fuselage in the process and blow them all to kingdom come.

Bolan rolled the two grenades gently past the guards and stepped back through the door. He counted to three, and the blasts suddenly reverberated down the hallway. Screams mingled with shouts of surprise died off as the Executioner jumped through the doorway and brought the Galil into play. The soldier began to systematically eradicate the opposition with controlled bursts from the Israeli-made assault rifle.

Two terrorists tried to flank Bolan, but he was ready for such a maneuver. His first burst took one of the Djihad gunmen high in the chest. The 7.62 mm NATO rounds punched quarter-sized holes through the terrorist's sternum and blew tennis-ball sized chunks out his back. A similar fate met his counterpart, but several of the rounds perforated his liver and stomach.

Both men were dead before they hit the ground.

Bolan concentrated his attacks on the clusters of troops rather than on individuals. Many of them were obviously unprepared for the firestorm the Executioner was generating. The heavy-caliber bullets drilled through legs, bellies, chests and heads. Body after body fell under the onslaught, and other than scattered return fire audible as Bolan changed clips, there was little evidence of resistance.

Those that didn't die abandoned the fray or jumped behind rocks and used them as cover. Bolan slowly advanced across the gap and soon reached the plane. The two terrorists who had been guarding the bombs jumped from behind cover and fired at Bolan. The rounds from their Skorpion 61 machine pistols chewed up the earth around the soldier. He dived away from the autofire and took up a position behind a large boulder. The pair of terrorists fired and moved in leapfrog pattern, attempting to overrun his position.

Bolan had an idea. He yanked one of the RGN grenades from his LBE, armed it and tossed the bomb in their direction. The terrorists saw it land and turned to find cover. They were too close to the rear of the plane, which left them in the open without any shielding. As they turned to run, Bolan popped up from behind the boulder, raised the Galil to his shoulder and fired.

The first terrorist's head erupted under the impact of three of the NATO rounds. The headless corpse continued forward, arms flailing as it toppled forward and twitched.

The second terrorist nearly escaped, but Bolan managed to land a shot in the leg at the last moment. The man dropped his weapon and screamed before collapsing to ground. He grasped his leg and tried to drag himself behind a boulder. Bolan broke cover and rushed forward, triggering his weapon to finish the job. The rounds chewed up flesh in the guy's back, and the terrorist died only a yard or two from his cover.

The Executioner returned to the plane. Others behind cover tried to shoot him, but they couldn't get close enough without risking damage to the aircraft. They were probably under strict orders to see that the plane wasn't damaged.

Bolan ignored the rounds striking the ground near him and retrieved the last of the C-4 from his demo bag. He produced a blasting cap, molded the sticks around it and placed the powerful plastique on the inside frame of the heavy steel and aluminum alloy of the tail pipe. Just below the French marking, Bolan noted stenciling that read: Armée de l'Air.

So he had been correct—it was a French air force plane.

Bolan turned in time to see that the two scientists had broken cover and were rushing for the door. He sprinted toward them in pursuit as he keyed the electronic detonator. The C-4 ignited under its heat and pressure blasting cap. A mammoth explosion rocked the compound as the blast ripped apart the exhaust port and melted parts of the tailpipe to the fuselage.

The Executioner burst through the door before it had completely closed behind the scientists. He chased them down the hall, slowly closing the distance between them. They rounded a corner, and he increased his stride to overtake them.

Bolan took the corner and stopped himself short.

The scientists rushed past two of the men that Bolan had been looking for. Hassan Fuaz stepped behind his hulking bodyguard. The bigger man did nothing to hide the murder and hatred in his eyes. There was no question he planned to destroy the Executioner this time, and the smirk of satisfaction on Fuaz's face told it all. The Djihad leader planned to watch the show with pleasure.

"I do not know who you are, American infidel," Fuaz said in flawless English. "Moreover, I do not care. But I mean to see you dead as my last great act for Al-Qaida."

"Is that right?" Bolan deadpanned.

"I am now going to let Ayman here tear you apart," he continued. "I would do it myself, but I have no wish to dirty my hands on an unclean Westerner. Ayman, however, has no such inhibitions."

The man called Ayman growled as he stepped forward.

Bolan threw a warning look in the giant terrorist's direction, but the insanity behind those dark eyes said he didn't care to heed it. Ayman closed the gap in three strides, reaching out for Bolan's throat.

The Executioner raised the Galil and fired.

The rounds tore through Ayman's belly, nearly eviscerating him. Chunks of intestine erupted from his back. The huge Algerian looked down at his stomach, his hands going there as blood and water poured between his fingers. He looked back at Bolan with shock, and the Executioner fired a 3-round burst to his head before the bolt locked back on an empty chamber. Ayman's body toppled, and Bolan had to sidestep to avoid being pinned under the giant corpse.

Ayman hit the ground with a thud.

"This is how you fight?" Fuaz demanded. "By shooting an unarmed man?"

"You're armed," Bolan snapped as he dropped the Galil. "Go for it."

A dark hue filled Fuaz's features as he clawed for his side arm.

Bolan had an RGN out and primed before Fuaz had cleared the weapon from its holster. He tossed the grenade at the mogul of terrorism. "Catch!"

The soldier hit the floor as the grenade hit Fuaz's chest. The impact fuse ignited and the hand bomb exploded instantly. The RDX/Wax filling blew Fuaz apart, sending limbs and flesh in every direction. Bits of seared human meat and blood rained onto Bolan's back.

The radio on the warrior's belt signaled for attention.

"French Bird to Striker."

"Go," Bolan said after keying the mike.

"I hate to tell you this, *monsieur,*" Du Perrin said with a cracked voice, "but the Nigerois air force is on its way. The pilots have orders to bomb that fortress. You must get out now."

"What?" Bolan asked in disbelief. "Well, tell them to abort. I haven't completed my mission."

"I have tried to explain this, but they do not listen. They have their orders and they plan to carry them out. They were also instructed to shoot down any aircraft attempting to stop them."

"Are you back on the airstrip?"

"No, I am still circling. It appears you have destroyed the plane."

"Yeah. How long before the Nigerois arrive?"

"Approximately twelve, that's one-two, minutes."

"Put down on the pad and wait for me."

The soldier rose and observed the carnage before him.

There was very little left of Hassan Fuaz. His reign of terror and murder had come to an end. Thousands had died by his hands—or at the hands of his followers—and the Executioner had managed to avert the death of perhaps many more. With that part accomplished, he was only left with one other item of unfinished business.

Bolan drew the Desert Eagle and stormed the hallway in the direction the scientists had run. He reached a thin metal door and tried to open it, but the latch wouldn't budge. Bolan aimed the gaping muzzle a few inches from the lock, turned his head and squeezed the trigger twice. The .44 Magnum rounds punched through the lock as if it were sheet metal.

He kicked in the door and entered the room beyond, tracking the area with the Desert Eagle. It was well lit with white walls and cubicles divided by metal panels. One section was completely open, and a row of computer terminals lined one wall below a glass observation case. Beyond that case was a blue-green liquid inside a thick glass container.

The room was empty of human life with the exception of a petite, dark-haired woman in a lab suit and a camouflage-clad terrorist toting an R4. The Djihad gunman whirled at Bolan's entrance and swung the muzzle of the R4 in the soldier's direction but the Executioner already had target acquisition.

Bolan squeezed the trigger.

The big Israeli-made pistol boomed a thunderous report. It exploded in the ears of Bolan with the same finality that the bullet hit the terrorist in the chest. The 240-grain slug slammed through the gunman's chest and blew out the lower section of his heart. The man's weapon flew from his fingers, clattering to the feet of the woman as his body sailed half the distance between where they stood and the far wall. He crashed into a tabletop cluttered with various instruments. The table collapsed beneath his weight, and his body, along with the expensive electronics, crashed to the polished floor.

"Don't try it," Bolan ordered, turning the Desert Eagle in the woman's direction when she reached for the weapon.

She tried anyway, but Bolan had expected such a move. He took steady aim and fired, the round striking the R4 and sending it to skitter across the floor. The woman stood slowly and stared daggers at Bolan, but the warrior ignored her unveiled threat.

"The vaccine to the virus," Bolan said simply. "I want it."

The woman smiled. "There is no vaccine. And no way to reverse the effects of my creation."

"Well, that's too bad," Bolan replied, letting the Desert Eagle fall to his side. "Because that means we've both been exposed, then."

"What are you talking about?" she asked, apprehension evident in her eyes.

"I've been exposed to your 'creation,' as you call it," the Executioner announced. "And now you have, too. So I guess we both die here."

"Foolish American! What makes you think I cannot find a cure. I invented the GV strain."

"Because you're never going to get the chance."

"And why not?"

Bolan made a show of looking at his watch before replying, "In about eight minutes, the Nigerois air force is going to blow this place to kingdom come. Neither of us is leaving." He gestured toward the glass vial. "Is that what you planned to poison the world with?"

She looked over at it, and a haughty mask filled her expression. "Yes. That is God's Vengeance."

"Well, it won't leave here, either. The three of us will be buried beneath the rubble. Your virus will die, and its secrets will die with you."

"You cannot stop me!" the woman said with an incredulous tone.

Bolan pointed the Desert Eagle at her. "Watch me."

"If you do not let me go, we shall perish here. The virus—"

"The virus has to have a host," Bolan countered. "Besides you, I'm the only one left alive who's been exposed. I have no intention of letting anyone else become infected. If that means I die, then that's what it means."

"I have a suggestion. I wish to make an offer for amnesty."

"For what?" Bolan asked. "You have nothing to trade."

"I am Dr. Hasna Qaseem," she said. "I used to work for the World Health Organization, but I became a servant of Osama bin Laden and the Al-Qaida movement. They fooled me into believing I was working to help the Islamic peoples.

"But as time went by, I began to have second thoughts. Then members of my family died in Libya, victims of an attack by the Da'awa wal Djihad. Good people that Hassan simply dismissed as 'acceptable losses.' I created the virus in hopes of exacting my revenge against Hassan for ordering the attack. But I could not guarantee my safety if he decided to turn on me. So I generated a vaccine against the GV strain. It was my only bargaining tool if Hassan ever decided I'd become expendable."

"That's a good story," the soldier replied coolly, "but you just told me there was no vaccine."

She nodded and gestured toward a locked refrigerator at the far end of the room.

Bolan waved the pistol in that direction.

Qaseem proceeded to the cooler and pulled a small gray lock box from a shelf. She took a key attached to a chain around her neck and opened the box. Bolan stepped forward and looked inside. There was a glass vial, about the size of a test tube, with maybe eight ounces of milky liquid inside.

"That's it?"

"It is very unstable and must be chilled to maintain its efficacy. But it will work against God's Vengeance. You must believe me."

"Have you inoculated yourself?" Bolan inquired.

"Yes."

"How do I know I can trust you?" the Executioner challenged her.

"I never wanted to use God's Vengeance against the Algerian people," Qaseem replied. "I was in love with Mamduh Nokhtari, leader of the GIA. He impressed me with his strength and his dedication. I thought that perhaps I could convince him not to use the missiles against our people. He agreed that he didn't wish to see any more Algerians die, regardless of how many of our enemies might suffer."

"You killed innocent men," Bolan stated. "You let innocent men die to prove your virus was lethal. You will have to pay for that."

"I realize this. But I also did it so that millions could live. I had to convince Fuaz that he could trust me. I never planned to load the chemical onto the missiles. I had a fake batch that I switched with the real strain. Later, Mamduh and I agreed to come up with some reasonable explanation why nobody was infected. To delay until we could escape."

"Nokhtari's going to prison," Bolan said, snatching her by the wrist. "As are you. Now grab the vaccine and let's go."

The two rushed from the lab and sprinted down the hallway. The radio on Bolan's belt again called for his attention.

"Go," Bolan said into the headset.

"French Bird to Striker, you have three minutes. Hurry, *monsieur*."

"I'm on my way. Just sit tight."

The pair rushed from the fortress, heading for the Hook chopper. They climbed aboard just in time to hear the first sounds of approaching fighters. Bolan pushed Qaseem into a nearby seat and strapped her in.

"Hold on tight to that box, Doctor," Bolan urged her with a frosty smile. "You and I have an appointment later."

The Executioner picked up the microphone in the back as he punched the button to raise the rear cargo ramp. He ordered Du Perrin to take off, then strapped himself into another seat directly across from Qaseem. The woman's eyes met his, and something unspoken passed between them.

It was quite a story she'd told him.

The Hook lifted off the ground, and Du Perrin swung it away from the complex, headed due south to avoid the fighters high overhead. They would destroy the base and bury the GIA-Djihad alliance in the rubble. There would be other factions that would unite under bin Laden's call for Islam to continue fighting.

Bolan turned to look out the window and watch as the first wave of SEPECAT Jaguar International strike aircraft moved overhead and dropped their payload of high-explosive bombs. Flame and massive explosions erupted as the ordnance struck the rocky mountainside, blowing huge boulders from the cliff walls and burying the lab beneath tons of rubble. Even as the first squadron lifted up and away from the destruction, a second wave was not too far behind.

This part of the jihad Al-Qaida movement was dead.

And Mack Bolan was damned glad to have survived.

Epilogue

End Stage—Cairo, Egypt

The crowd roared as the first car crossed the finish line. It was a modified Peugeot. The fact it was driven by a French-Algerian racer named Damien abd-Abdul Kareef seemed to make the ending of the race fitting to the observer.

The Executioner smiled as he watched from the balcony of his hotel room. Twelve days had elapsed since the destruction of the GIA-Djihad base in the Ténéré Desert. The Algerian populace—as well as all of Africa—was safe from the terror threat. Mamduh Nokhtari was now back in France, as was Hasna Qaseem, and things had quieted somewhat with the race drawing to a close.

A knock at the door reached his ears.

Bolan pulled the Beretta from where it was concealed at the small of his back and moved over to stand against the wall. He pulled the hammer back and waited for another knock.

"Yeah?"

"It is me," came a familiar voice. "I have brought a friend."

Bolan nodded, put his pistol away and opened the door to admit Yakov Katzenelenbogen and Harold Brognola.

"Welcome to my humble abode," Bolan quipped.

The two men took a moment to study the spacious apartment. It was decorated with rare art pieces and fine curtains. The rooms were huge, and the entire décor was fit for an emperor. Mack Bolan wouldn't normally have surrounded himself with such lavish accommodations, but he was enjoying the suite, courtesy of a few connections from the French government.

"Humble?" Brognola said with a snort. "This place makes a penthouse suite at the Waldorf look puny."

"Uh-huh," Katz agreed.

"Have a seat," Bolan offered as he closed the door. "Want some coffee?"

Both men declined and Bolan poured himself a cup.

Katz lit a cigarette after they were seated and the three men exchanged glances. "Any more word from Calee Fauna?"

"Nothing," Bolan said. "I imagine she's got her hands full. I don't think I'll probably see her again."

"The Man asked me to pass on his personal thanks," Brognola interjected. "He's well aware of what you risked, Striker. We're all aware. You've, uh, been feeling okay, right?"

"Fine, Hal," Bolan replied quickly. "I feel fine."

"Good."

Katz cleared his throat. "Dr. Qaseem has been moved to a secure site for the time being. It looks like the French government might put her talents to good use."

"She's an intelligent woman," Brognola added.

"And also a very dangerous one," Bolan reminded them. "She belongs in prison until she's too old to threaten anybody else."

"Unfortunately, that won't be our decision," Brognola said. "Perhaps she can redeem herself for what she did. It's not un-heard-of for people to turn themselves around and work for the betterment of society. Look at people like Jack Grimaldi if you don't believe me."

"I believe you," Bolan replied quietly. "I just hope she doesn't blow her chance."

"So do we," Katz said.

"Hey, Yakov, that reminds me," Bolan replied. "Thanks for your help back there. I'm not sure I could've have pulled that off without you."

"Don't mention it, Striker. It's always my pleasure. To tell you the truth, I haven't had that much excitement in a while now."

"Just like old times, huh?"

"Sure was."

The Executioner turned his attention to Brognola. "So what brings you here, Hal? You didn't come all this way just to see how I was feeling."

"Why not?"

"Because they invented this thing called a telephone," Bolan shot back good-naturedly. "So what really brings you here?"

"Well..." Brognola hesitated, looked at Katz, who nodded, and then turned his attention back to the warrior. "The President has asked me to make the offer once more. We'd like you to come back to the Stony Man program. Full-time, so to speak. The Man wants bygones to be bygones."

"We've talked about this before, Hal," Bolan replied gently but firmly. "You know the answer, and it hasn't changed. But tell him I appreciate his determination."

"I told him what you'd say, but I was ordered to come here and ask, man to man."

"I figured," the Executioner said. "But he has to understand that I'm most effective doing the job my way, on my terms. I can't always play by the rules because the enemy doesn't. You know that."

"Yes, I do."

"But I can tell you this," Mack Bolan continued. "If you ever need me, I'll be there."

DEATH LANDS®

**brings you a brand-new
look in June 2002!
Different look...
same exciting adventures!**

Salvation Road

Beneath the brutal sun of the nuke-ravaged southwest, the Texas desert burns red-hot and merciless, commanding agony and untold riches to those greedy and mad enough to mine the slick black crude that lies beneath the scorched earth. When a Gateway jump puts Ryan and the others deep in the hell of Texas, they have no choice but to work for a rogue baron in order to win their freedom. If they fail...they face death.

In Deathlands, the unimaginable is a way of life.

An unholy alliance lights a deadly
new fire in the Golden Triangle...

CONDITION HOSTILE

Two radical Islamic fundamental groups have joined forces
with a Chinese narcobaron to form an unholy trinity
and seize control of the drug trade in Southeast Asia.
Stony Man's anti-terror squad hunts down the enemy in
the concrete jungles of urban America, while Mack Bolan
and Phoenix Force wage warfare in the Forbidden
Zone, to raze a massive heroin-producing operation....

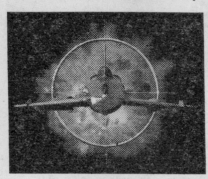

STONY MAN

*Available in
April 2002
at your favorite
retail outlet.*

Or order your copy now by sending your name, address, zip or postal code, along with
a check or money order (please do not send cash) for $5.99 for each book ordered
($6.99 in Canada), plus 75¢ postage and handling ($1.00 in Canada), payable to Gold
Eagle Books, to:

In the U.S.
Gold Eagle Books
3010 Walden Avenue
P.O. Box 9077
Buffalo, NY 14269-9077

In Canada
Gold Eagle Books
P.O. Box 636
Fort Erie, Ontario
L2A 5X3

Please specify book title with your order.
Canadian residents add applicable federal and provincial taxes.

GSM58